SUCCESSORS

Book 1 of
THE WARDEN

FELICIA JEDLICKA

Felicia Jedlicka (FelJed)
Find me on Facebook: www.facebook.com/feljedauthor
Visit my website feljedauthor.wordpress.com

For my birches

SISTER WITCHES
THE DEVIL'S SHADOW
THE DEVIL'S SOUL

DESTINY REJECTED
DESTINY RECLAIMED
DESTINY RAZED
DESTINY RESTORED

DÉJÀ VU

SAVE THE HUMANS

THE NECROMANCER'S CHILD

<u>**THE NEBRASKA APOCALYPSE NOVELS**</u>
CORN COWS AND THE APOCALYPSE
COW TIPPING AFTER THE APOCALYPSE
CORN HUSKING AFTER THE APOCALYPSE

<u>**THE WARDEN SERIES**</u>
SUCCESSORS
RIVALS
LOVERS AND LIARS
BAD BLOOD
TENANTS AND TYRANTS
THE RING BEARER
GODS AND MONSTERS
BEASTS AND BURDENS
MAGIC AND MAYHEM
FORK IN THE ROAD
DETAILS AND DEADLINES
*CURSES AND SACRIFICES**
*WITCHES AND WOLVES**
*SAINTS AND SERPENTS**
*ENEMIES AND ALLIES**

*MARRIED TO DEATH**

SUCCESSORS

FELICIA JEDLICKA

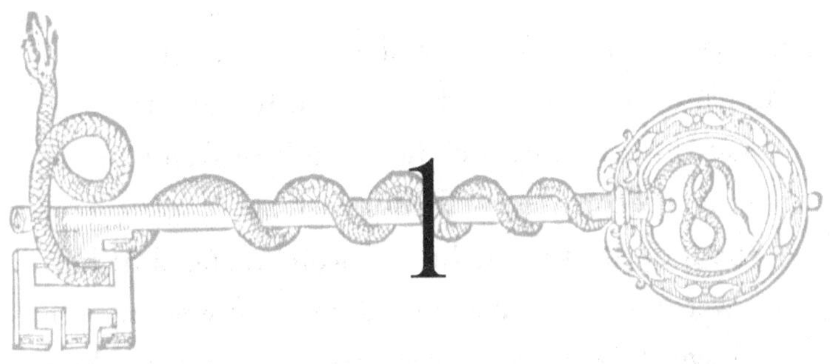

ORI CAUGHT SIGHT OF the woman responsible for her captivity. She had been fantasizing about killing her for two weeks, and not just bullets or poison. She had descended into the dark depths of pliers and sharp, pointy things.

She wasn't normally so vicious. In fact, she had a high regard for life, but being the victim of an underground slave trade operation had weakened her respect for life and bolstered her tolerance for moral flexibility.

Yvette stared back at her from the bar, lazily slapping her riding crop against her leather clad hip. Cori had felt that particular device more than once across her face—among other places. Not that she had learned her lesson. She never was very good at following orders.

She was a "does not work well with others" type of gal. Not that she was mean or anything. Taking out of consideration her current flirtations with homicide, she was actually a rather nice person. She just preferred to work alone.

The harder Cori glared at the blonde dominatrix, the higher her mouth curved. The sick sadistic bitch had been trying to break her so she would be servile and compliant for her sale at the auction. Beaten, drugged, and raped—certainly, but they hadn't broken Cori. If anything, the torture had focused her.

She looked over the line of women ahead of her. They were young and old alike. Scared and weeping, the men dragged them into the center of the bar's dance floor to exhibit their bodies for the mad, hungry bidding.

She couldn't blame them for their pitiable condition. At a different time in her life, she might have been in the same state of shocked stupor, but her heart was already raw. Being kidnapped into slavery was certainly traumatizing and worthy of a steady supply of therapy for the remainder of her life, but at the moment, it was just another card in the crap hand that had laughably been called her life.

Yvette's lackeys returned to the line and grabbed her by the arms. They pulled her forward, drawing her out onto the dance floor. They stopped on their marks and stepped back to give everyone a good view of her. Rather than shy away from the probing eyes of the surrounding men, she gave the entire room a hard glower, being sure to let each and every one of them know she hated their existence.

The minions stepped forward again to take her on a tour around the room, allowing the buyers to inspect her closer. No one had noticed that the cable tie around her wrists was a little too loose. Nor had they suspected she had hidden a pencil in her bra. They also didn't know that she was trained in defensive combat.

Cori ripped her hands out of the cable tie and threw her palm up into the nose of the man on her right. She expected more of a fight, but he dropped like a rock.

Before the other one could contain her, she dove and punched his crotch—a much needed addition to her future therapy. As he crumpled into a pathetic heap of bruised balls, two more men arrived. She punched them each in the throats and kicked them in the face and knee successively.

A hand wrapped around her from behind, lifting her from her path of carnage. She grabbed the pencil shiv and thrust it toward her attacker. She stuck his face, and he released her. She followed his retreat and stabbed his neck. She shoved him to the ground and continued to impale him yellow #2 style.

Several seconds into her adrenaline spike, Cori became aware of the bloody mess she had made of his neck. She backed away from the frothing wound, feeling her stomach turn sour. Fortunately, she hadn't eaten enough to warrant vomiting or she might have lost claim to her badass status.

She stood, clenching her trusty pencil with a bloody fist. She looked around for another asshole to fend off, but she was as much entertainment now as a threat. The men stared back at her in subdued shock. No one was going to bid on her now.

"I'll take her." A man said.

Except him.

Cori frowned and looked at the large man standing at the edge of the dance floor. Even after everything he had just witnessed, the idiot wanted to buy her. What did she have to do to prove she was not a wise investment?

She summoned her courage, narrowed her eyes, and charged at the behemoth in front of her. He was big enough to crack her skull like an egg, but she was already in the fry pan. Might as well grease it up a bit.

She felt a sharp pain in her shoulder and she feared the worst, but she hadn't heard a gunshot. She slowed to inspect the cause of her anguish. No blood. She reached over her shoulder for the hot knifing pain. She gritted her teeth and groaned as she pulled the feather ended cylinder free. She stared down at the pink tufted dart in her hand.

Cori scanned the room for the source of the ammunition and found Yvette leering back at her, a handheld dart gun gripped in her palm. She perked her brow and bowed slightly. The entire scene had no doubt played out to her satisfaction. Another slash under her win column.

Cori seethed and took her first step toward becoming a murderer. The menacing approach failed as her legs gave out and she dropped to the ground. She cursed her damnable luck as the blackness overcame her and swore that if it was the last thing she ever did, she would kill that bitch.

2

THE COLD GROUND SLAPPED against Cori's back. The laughter that followed diminished with the slamming of a door. Through blurred vision, she could just make out a man leaning over her. She threw her lashed fists upward to fend off the would-be rapist and caught his cheek. He yelped and drew away. She jumped to her feet and attempted to kick him, but he dodged the blow. Unbalanced by the lingering effects of the drugs, she fell down again.

"Please, stop! I'm not one of them!" the man complained.

Cori blinked her eyes and took in the young man before her, holding his reddening cheek. His loose sack clothing, bare feet, and terrified anger matched her own. His blue eyes were red from the same repetitive bouts of tears that she had been enduring. His dirty blonde hair was more dirty than blonde. Puce bruises marred his arms, nearly identical in shape to her own.

Cori stood and looked around the moonlit alley for guards, but it was only her and the young man. "What's happening?"

"I don't know. They just dumped us out here." His voice rang with a familiar English accent.

"What are we supposed to do now?" she asked.

"We get out of here." A voice spoke from behind her. Cori whipped around and noticed the outline of a man standing in the shadows.

"Says who, dirtbag?" Cori shifted into a defensive stance. She was hardly as tough as she was pretending to be, but so far, her luck was buffering her bullshit.

The man stepped forward, his silver-tipped cane tapping the cobblestone beside him. The shadows hiding him melted away, revealing his girth. Cori recognized him from the auction, her undeterred buyer. He was over six feet tall and as wide as a linebacker. He had a thick neck and biceps the size of watermelons. He carried a good amount of weight in his midsection, but he wasn't the type of man you could call fat. He wasn't the type of man you could call anything, other than "sir."

Cori's bravado shrank away as he closed the distance between them. He stopped in front of her and stared her down. "Says me," he answered. Just like the deep rumble she expected to hear from a semi-truck, his voice matched his physique.

She shifted back a step and tensed her jaw. "And who the hell are you?"

"Danato Calibria." He glanced behind her. "What's your name, boy?"

"Ethan Xavier Pierce," he answered with unwarranted pride.

Danato's brow dipped slightly, and he looked down at her again. "And you?"

Cori spat in his face. His hand lifted, and she flinched. He wiped the moisture from his cheek and shook his head. "We don't have time for this. We need to get out of this village."

"Where are you taking us?" Ethan asked.

"Someplace with ample food and warm beds," Danato answered.

Cori snorted. "Yeah, I bet they keep the beds real warm for us."

Danato's stern gaze slid back to her, forming into a frown. His narrow, sleep-deprived eyes looked her over with a mixture of sympathies she didn't understand.

She had guessed his age to be early to mid-forties. His graying five o'clock shadow and brown hair were deceiving. She suspected he might be an errand boy for a wealthy benefactor. By the looks of his slouchy clothes and frowzy hair, he certainly wasn't rich.

Despite the sympathy hiding in his eyes, she could tell he had every intention of delivering her—as any good lackey would. Still, she didn't intend to give up. Perhaps her luck would hold out against this brute.

"We need to hurry." Danato took a firm grasp of her wrists. He directed the comment to Ethan, but he gave her a menacing look before tugging her along behind him.

They left the confines of the alley and reached a main road. Despite Danato's cane and noticeable limp, he maintained a faster pace than Ethan, who was lagging. Cori struggled to keep up too, but once she reached the end of her tether, Danato simply yanked her back up to speed again.

To add misery to the already maddeningly cold barefoot journey, it began to snow. The tiny flakes turned to thick puffy blobs that blotted out the color all around them. Danato paused momentarily to observe the sky, then looked back at Ethan. "Keep up, we don't have much time."

"Not much time for what?" Ethan asked, putting a jump in his step, which kept his feet off the road for a millisecond longer.

"Not much time to escape the city before it moves," Danato answered.

"Moves?" Ethan scrunched up his nose and glanced at her. "It will move? How do you mean?" He looked around for something that might substantiate this allegation.

"It just does. I don't want to move with it, so let's go." He waved for Ethan to keep going.

Cori, unconcerned with Danato's schedule, took what would likely be her last opportunity to escape captivity. She kicked him in the back of his bad leg and wrenched her wrists out of his grip. She turned around and ran past Ethan. "Run, you idiot!"

He frowned at her, not even attempting to follow her lead. As she bolted down the road, she could see the alley they had just come from. Two men stood at the entrance, smoking cigarettes and laughing. One of them stepped out into the street. He said something in a foreign language and waved his hands towards his thrusting hips.

She slowed her sprint and looked back at Danato, who was fast approaching her. She scanned the surrounding buildings, but the businesses were closed up for the night. The people long since asleep, oblivious or indifferent to the commerce that took place after dark.

She could run in circles for hours and still only have two options. Them or him.

Danato slowed to a stop several feet away and stared at her. "I shouldn't have taken you. I just thought I could help you." He nodded back to the men behind her. "I thought I was the lesser of two evils, but that isn't my judgment to make." He stepped forward and grabbed her wrists again. He raised them up and snapped the plastic binding with ease. "I didn't put you in this situation, but I am taking advantage of it. I need the boy." Cori looked at Ethan, who was in a state of frenzied shivers. "I don't need you."

Danato turned around and walked away. Cori frowned and stared after him. "Wait. What?"

Cori glanced back at the men, who were taking a deeper interest in the events unfolding before them.

"What am I supposed to do?" She stalked after him, distancing herself from the danger behind her.

"Go. Run. Hide." Danato motioned for Ethan to move as he rejoined him.

"You're just going to leave me here now?" Cori could hear the irony in her words. She wanted nothing more than to get away from this man, but she also felt abandoned.

"This town will shift into Norway or Sweden next. I don't remember the order. You'll be able to get back home from there."

"That doesn't make any sense."

"It doesn't need to."

"Why did you buy me, if you were only going to throw me back to the wolves?"

Danato stopped and turned around. His face held the same mixture of worry and remorse she had seen on him earlier. "Where I am going, you can't return from. I already have the burden of enslaving one person. There is no reason to add a second."

Cori looked back at the men by the alley. They were still waiting to see what the outcome of this event would be. Yvette would be delighted to have a second chance at disciplining her.

She didn't know which was worse: being taken captive again, or purposely leading herself into an unknown form of slavery. The fact that this man was willing to let her go was the only thing supporting her hope that he wasn't a monster. Hopefully, his boss was equally amiable.

"If I come with you, will I be safe?"

A tremor moved through the village, rattling windows and causing dogs to bark. Cori felt the hair on her head lift. She touched it, trying to discern the reason for the sudden case of static electricity.

Danato's jaw clenched as he observed the ground around them. "There's nothing safe about where I would be taking you. If you come with me, then your previous life of normalcy will cease to exist. The slavery I'm offering isn't perverse, but you will be a prisoner just the same."

Another tremor rippled through the village.

"We are out of time." Danato grabbed Ethan's shirt and pulled him along at a near-jogging pace. Cori stood in the road, trying to decide. If she followed him, she was giving up her freedom willfully. If she didn't follow him, she was risking being recaptured, and she already knew what that entailed.

The ground beneath her started to vibrate, forcing her to widen her stance just to stay upright. Windows around the town shattered. The recently fallen snow skidded off the rooftops. Every shift in her movement ignited static electricity.

She wasn't sure what the lesser of two evils was, but she was certain what the worst of three evils was.

"Wait!" Cori screamed and ran after them. Between her frostbitten feet and the violent shaking of the ground, she could hardly maintain a straight path. "Wait!" she yelled again over the ruckus. Ethan glanced back at her and then to Danato, but he didn't dare stop since he was having just as much trouble.

She continued to grapple for purchase, practically skating across the snowy stones. She finally fell, landing painfully on her knees. "Please!" she yelled after them once more.

Even above the racket of squawking wood and scraping rock, she heard Danato's growl of aggravation as he turned back to help her. He reached her and lifted her up with one arm. He half pulled, half carried her alongside him.

She buried her face against him as she heard an explosion behind them. Rock fragments pelted her in the back and legs, but she didn't want to give up her shielding to see what had happened. However, she could tell by Ethan's wide eyes ahead of her that something frightening was developing behind them.

Cori didn't need to be told to move faster, but the pain in her feet was forcing her to limp, which interfered with Danato's already rocking gait. Ultimately, they were slowing each other down. She tried to pull away, hoping they might each do better on their own, but before she could separate, Danato scooped her into his arms. Neglecting to rely on his cane, he ran with her, wincing with every step.

From over his shoulder, Cori could see the uprooted outskirts of the town. A wide barrier of freshly upturned dirt circled the area they had just left. The village within remained intact—minus the repercussions of the tremors.

Danato came to a sudden stop and dropped her from his arms. He doubled over in pain, hissing in agony as he leaned on his cane for support.

Behind them, the rumbling stopped, and the vibrations ceased. Cori looked over the village. It was quiet. Only the distant sound of a few perturbed canines tainted its eerie stillness.

"Why—?" Before she could finish her sentence, the rumble of rock on rock filled the air and the undamaged village epicenter flipped. The hinge-like movement overturned the land, the buildings, and everything contained within.

All that remained after the impossible transformation was vacant ground. The snow was already accumulating on it, hiding any sign that a community had recently been occupying the space.

Cori and Ethan gaped at the shocking event.

"What the hell was that?" Cori asked incredulously.

"Did they all just die?" Ethan asked.

"No, they just got moved with the town," Danato answered.

"How do you even know that?" Cori asked, shivering in the snow.

"I just do. Don't worry, they're used to it," Danato explained.

"Who gets used to *that*?" Cori pointed out to the field before them.

Danato looked at the empty land before turning his attention to her. He frowned and shook his head in disappointment. "You'll get used to the unbelievable soon enough. Let's go."

"I don't know if I can walk any farther," Cori said, looking at the soles of her feet. There were already dark patches of burned skin. "My feet hurt so much. I don't even know how many toes are still functional."

"It's not far," Danato said.

Even as he responded, Ethan took off his shirt and ripped it in half. The weak, worn cloth tore easily between his teeth. He ripped each piece again, leaving him with four long straps of fabric. He tossed two of them to Cori. "Wrap your feet with these."

Cori stared at him a moment, unsure how to respond to the kind gesture. Danato offered the boy a small smile, as if he were proud of his clever chivalry.

She wrapped her toes as thickly as she could, to save them from a horrible death. She could see Danato watching her out of the corner of her eye, but she ignored him. Whatever his agenda was, she would deal with it later. She looked at Ethan, who was wrapping his feet just as carefully.

"Ethan, was it?" she asked. He looked up at her and nodded. "Thanks. Nobody's ever given me the shirt off their back before."

Ethan smiled. He was cute, but the slight sparkle in his eye, as innocent as it was, made her look away. "What's your name?" he asked.

"No reason to get into all that now." She smiled apologetically. "I don't know how long I'll be with you guys." Cori looked at Danato, who was making no effort to hide his gawking.

He took in a deep breath and rose to his full height. "I've already offered you your last chance at freedom." The grit in his tone matched the determination on his face. "The only options left now are slavery or freezing to death."

She looked around, searching for some identifiable features in the landscape. Anything to disprove his allegation.

"It's barren arctic tundra, nearly a hundred miles in every direction." Danato pointed out. Her brow dipped in confusion. "You're in Russia, sweetheart," he clarified.

She shook her head in disbelief. She was feeling the full impact of her decision to follow them. There was no one around to rescue her. No road to guide her home. No shelter to protect her from the cold. Her options were just as he said: slave or popsicle.

S LAVES.

That's what Danato had resorted to.

Without an heir of his own, it was the only remedy for his failing legacy.

Despite his objections to the endeavor, he still found himself lumbering through the snowdrifts of the Kola Peninsula with not one, but two indentured servants.

As conflicted as he was about the situation, the arguments had already been made for and against it. In the end, he still needed a successor, and it wasn't a job that he could simply put out a classified ad for.

It was one thing to ask someone to move to the bitter climate of western Russia and work for virtually no pay or respect. It was a whole other thing to ask someone to give up their former life—including friends, family, and useful technology—just to support the secret agenda of protecting the world from violent supernatural creatures.

Yeah, that wasn't a job bid he expected to get a lot of responses to.

On the other hand, a slave...

The rational part of him believed he might be saving these young people. A different buyer would repeatedly beat and rape the girl, a fate he assumed she had already experienced. The boy could arguably face a worse fate—depending on the proclivities of the buyer. Danato was not a cruel man, and would never harm them in such a way. However, he wasn't lying that they weren't going somewhere safe. After all, he could hardly call a place that houses criminal monsters safe.

He also wasn't lying that he didn't need the girl. He needed a young man to replace him when he was no longer able to perform the functions of his job. Ethan was young. Young enough to adapt to the strange new life he was about to be introduced to. Danato could mold him into a man, the way his father would have if he were still alive.

The girl, on the other hand...

Granted, she wasn't more than five years older than Ethan, but he could see the fire in her eyes. She might have been a headstrong woman before, but after this trauma, her distrust would make her downright problematic.

These were, of course, things he contemplated after he purchased the volatile woman. Had the familiarity of her wavy blonde locks and rosy cheeks not entranced him, he might have prevented this potential debacle.

Danato glanced back at his new *employees* trudging through his tracks with barely bandaged feet. The girl was continuously scanning the horizon for evidence of civilization, but he knew there was nothing to find.

Outside of overachieving hikers and seasonal fisherman on route to the ocean, this area was unpopulated. Ethan was positively vibrating since he had given up his shirt. It was a generous offering, one that Danato suddenly realized he had not matched.

Danato slipped off his wool trench coat and handed it to Ethan. "Here."

Ethan only questioned the offering for a moment before slipping it over his shoulders. He lifted the ample fabric for the girl to join him under, but she just shook her head.

"Don't be daft; it's freezing out here." Ethan tossed the black fabric over her shoulder. Danato could see her stiffen as Ethan tugged the fabric together, consequently pulling her closer to him. "Good?" Ethan asked, and she nodded with glazed over eyes. She most likely would have preferred to keep her distance from the boy, but it was surely difficult to refuse the warmth it provided.

She looked up and locked eyes with Danato. For a moment, he saw what she had been hiding behind her anger. She was terrified. Yvette had brought her to a precipice. If she fell; she would break and possibly never recover. The only question was if Danato was pushing her over or pulling her back.

He wanted so much to say something that would make her feel safe, but she wouldn't trust anything that came from his mouth. Not yet anyway.

"What's all this about?" A gravelly voice asked behind him.

Danato turned and saw his assistant, coming over the next snow drift. At 56 inches, Belus was a tall dwarf. His tomato-red wiry hair and beard gave him the look of a Scottish terrier: cute, but only because he was small.

Despite his lesser size and rank, he was a formidable companion, and Danato dreaded updating him. Belus was not likely to approve of his change to their plan, and Danato wouldn't enjoy having to rationalize it to him.

"Please tell me you forgot how to count?" Belus's hoarse voice always made him sound like he had a cold. Twenty-plus years of smoking had taken its toll on his throat before he got the message that it wasn't good for him. Danato had never taken up the habit, but when Belus finally quit, he found that twenty years of second-hand smoke had left him just as cranky with nicotine withdrawals. That wasn't the best month for either of them.

"And is that a girl?" Belus looked at the huddled mass of fabric behind him and the two inhabitants therein. His disapproving frown relaxed into a blank-faced stare as the girl looked up at him. After a pause, Belus shook away the thoughts that had prompted his stare and turned his attention back to Danato. "What happened?"

"I had some money leftover," Danato explained. "I put it to good use."

"Good use?" Belus narrowed his eyes. "If I recall correctly, you vehemently opposed this idea. Now, instead of abducting one person; you have two."

"It's done. I can't change it now."

"Clearly. Do they have family?" Belus asked.

"The boy is an orphan. In and out of foster homes and juvenile detentions," Danato explained.

"How do you know about that?" Ethan asked.

Danato glanced back, noting the surprise on his face. "Yvette keeps excellent records on her acquisitions. She prefers orphans. The investigations don't last as long."

"The girl's mother is dead," Danato continued. "Her aunt was basically taking care of her, but she died rather recently." The girl glared at him, but didn't deny the details. When he looked back at Belus, he found the dwarf inspecting him for a loose screw in his brain.

"You say that as if you intend to keep her on. We need the boy, but what did you have in mind for her?"

"We'll take her on as an employee. We could use more full-time help. Someone that we can train and don't have to replace in six months." Belus stared back at him. "We're already skirting the boundaries of morality here. I don't see why one more will make our path to hell any smoother." Belus still didn't respond. "If you have a better solution for this situation, please offer it. I'm already at my limit for underhanded deals today."

Belus shook his head and looked around at the vast emptiness. "We could wipe her and let her go," he muttered.

Danato glanced back at the girl. It was true. That was an option. An option he had not offered her. "I think we could use her," he whispered back. "She'll be better off than she was."

Belus examined him again. Whatever he found made his frown deepen. "We'll take her then," he said, dropping the argument entirely. "She'll hate us for it, but at least this way, the boy will have a companion." He nodded to the pair huddling under Danato's coat.

Danato nodded. He was glad Belus agreed. He didn't want to be the only one responsible for dragging two people into their strange and dangerous world against their will.

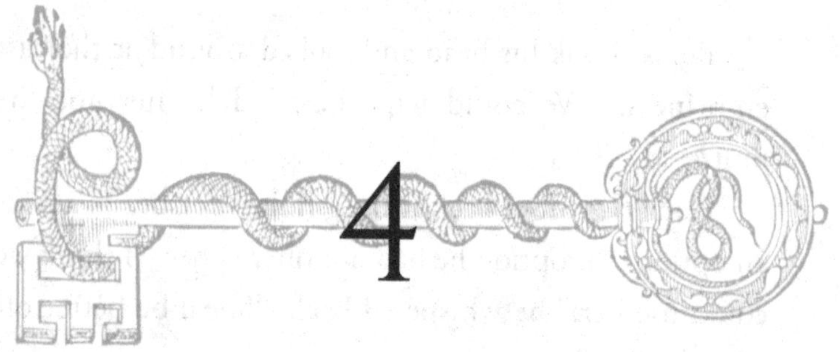

BELUS DROVE THE SLED carriage deeper into the uninhabited tundra, while Danato monitored his purchases inside the coach. The girl sat across from him, giving him caustic looks, while she repetitively twisted a gold ring on her right thumb. Ethan let her take the entire trench coat, so she was now fully swathed in it.

Danato was unruffled by the girl's haughty attitude since he knew it was going to be her sword and shield for a while. However, he wasn't about to lose the appearance of authority, so he stared right back at her. Since both of them were stubborn to the very core, the game of chicken left them staring at each other for most of the trip. Uncomfortable with the ocular warfare, Ethan huddled against his window to watch the scenery. Such as it was, in the tundra, in the dark.

"What is that?" Ethan asked and wiped the fog from his view.

"What?" the girl asked and leaned over to look out her window.

Danato didn't have to look to know what the daunting stone structure looked like. He had seen it many times. Usually close up, though.

"What is it?" Ethan tried to see.

"It's a castle," she told him dubiously, almost asking for verification.

"No, it's a prison," Danato corrected. He rested his head back on the seat and closed his eyes. He hadn't even been away for a full day, but he knew what trouble awaited him on his return. He rarely left the prison, and rarer still did he take his second in command with him. However, for this particular endeavor, he needed someone he could trust. Not to mention, Belus wanted to come along to make sure he did what he needed to do.

Belus was nothing if not dutifully officious.

"We're going to be prisoners here?" the girl asked, as if being a slave was a lesser sentence to her than outright captivity.

"We're all prisoners to this place, one way or another. I am the warden here. I make sure what is held in that prison stays in that prison, and now, so will you two."

The girl frowned in confusion, but resisted asking her questions. She pressed her face to the glass to observe their approach.

Unlike a prison, but similar to a castle, a drawbridge lowered to allow the carriage passage through the thirty-foot stone walls that surrounded the prison. The inner courtyard provided enough room for multiple outbuildings, including residences, storage sheds, stables, and a few more non-vital appropriations. With most of the buildings on either side and to the back of the prison, the area near the gate entrance was just open acreage.

The prison stood at the center of it all. At nearly two blocks long and a block wide, the prison in excess of seven-stories wasn't a minor operation. In contrast to the antiquated rock wall blockading it, the prison had modern poured concrete walls. Each floor offered a narrow window that allowed just enough light in to keep everyone inside from going stir crazy. Except the basement, where the inmates required the exact opposite.

Several armed guards punctuated the rooftop. Their duty to the prison was as much about diverting trespassers as it was about stopping runaways. They were miles from anything resembling civilization and concealed in a valley, but the occasional outdoorsman would find them by accident.

"Why would anyone house criminals out here?" the girl asked.

"I try not to think of them as criminals. I prefer to think of them as mental patients: very violent and ingenious mental patients." He paused in reflection. "They're all just a pain in my ass, really."

She started to ask something else, but the carriage jolted to a stop and several guards rushed over to it. The doors opened on either side. Ethan and the girl jumped back, bumping into each other to get away from the double-sided attack. Danato raised a hand to calm them, as he listened to the guards ramble on simultaneously about fires, electrical outages, and melted walls.

"Damn elementals," he murmured. "Okay, okay, I'll get things coordinated with those idiots upstairs." Danato looked at his two new guests. They looked back at him, concerned, but curious. He supposed that was better than anger. "Take these two to my house," he ordered the guards on his left. "She's expecting company." He beckoned Ethan to exit toward the guards. "Go on. It'll be alright," he assured the nervous boy.

He stepped out, and one of the guards took him by the arm and led him away. The next man stepped in line and reached for the girl, but the fresh memories of her captivity were making her recoil.

Danato could only imagine what they had put her through, but he knew no one here would hurt her. He would make sure of that. He pressed down the guard's insistent reach.

"What's your name, sweetheart?"

She looked at him, then her eyes skirted the floor as if she couldn't remember, but he knew she was just debating if she should tell him. When she looked up at him with her telltale obstinacy, he knew he hadn't earned it yet.

"This man is going to take you to a warm house. There's food there. You can clean up. He's not going to hurt you. Are you Paul?"

"It's Pow-ul," the man corrected. Danato gaped at the man, who was interrupting his attempt to console the poor girl. The man blanched and stammered to correct himself. "No, sir. The girl is safe with me."

Danato didn't disguise his exhausted frustration, but the girl seemed to find some slight amusement in his predicament. As insignificant as it seemed, she moved toward Paul. At the last second, she stopped and peeled his trench coat from her shoulders.

He touched her hand, barely putting a feather's worth of pressure, but it was enough to stop her movement. "Keep it." He resisted the urge to squeeze or caress her hand like his instincts demanded. He just withdrew and nodded again for her to go.

She slipped out and Paul, following his example, didn't touch her as he led her away. She glanced back, but he was already being mobbed by more men begging for orders, and couldn't afford her the reassuring nod that she probably wanted and needed. He maneuvered his clamorous entourage toward the prison and began to repair the damage a day away had left him.

5

THE GUARD DIRECTED CORI into the darkened house behind Ethan. The door slammed shut, and she heard a click. She reached back for the doorknob, but she already knew the answer.

Locked.

She combed the walls in search of a light switch. She flipped the first one she found and turned to see the devastating conclusion to her captivity. The dungeon that would stand as a backdrop to her final days. However, the living room area, illuminated by the soft glow of table lamps just to the left of the door, was hardly the oppressive confinement she had expected.

The strictly defined space had a stacked stone fireplace corralled by a plush tan couch and two brown leather chairs. A few taxidermied animals adorned the mantel, and the wood lamps rested on slate end tables that flanked the couch. In the center of everything was a brown tinted-glass coffee table.

She flipped up the remaining two switches, revealing the rest of the open floor plan. Above her, the vaulted ceilings dramatized the log-cabin style. A wrought iron faux-candle chandelier designated the dining room space ahead of her. Crafted from gnarled wood, the table and chairs beneath it had a glossy red mahogany stain.

Just to the right of that, the kitchen's L-shaped island squared off the L-shaped counters against the wall. The stainless-steel industrial-sized fridge/freezer opposed the end of the island. The apron sink on the long counter offered an easy back-and-forth with the stove on the island. On the far side of the island was a three-stool breakfast bar that overlooked the kitchen.

Cori gaped at the bachelor pad. It looked like a photograph straight from a design magazine. Drawn in by the warmth, she meandered to the fireplace that was already roaring.

She stood in front of the billowing heat and closed her eyes. The orange flames lapped behind her eyelids, temporarily abating the concerns that were rolling around in her mind. Of which there were many.

Behind her, Ethan was banging around in the kitchen, raiding the cupboards and fridge for food. That didn't surprise her; he looked far too skinny to be healthy. She wondered how long he had been in his state of malnourishment. She had already speculated that the scars on his back and down his arms were most likely inflicted prior to his abduction.

Eventually, the smell of food drew her back into reality. She found Ethan just behind her. He kneeled over the coffee table devouring cold chicken, ice cream, and chips with no regard for appropriate palate order. At one point, he even dipped his chicken into the ice cream. She smiled and sat back against one of the chairs to watch him.

He paused with stuffed cheeks and looked at her. "Do you want some?"

Despite being famished, she shook her head. She got the impression he would have held back eating so much if he knew he needed to share. Given his condition, she didn't want to interrupt. She had been on more calorie restrictive diets than the last two weeks. Besides, it was the least she could do to repay his kindness.

After a few minutes, Ethan let out a cavernous burp and sat back against the couch. "I'm so stuffed." He looked back at her and shoved his plate over to her. "There's a chicken leg there I haven't touched."

Satisfied that he was indeed done, she leaned over and took the untouched chicken. It tasted like heaven—cold, chewy, glad-to-be-alive heaven. After she finished the chicken, her hunger spiked, demanding more than the meager drumstick as a meal. "Any ice cream left?"

"Yeah." He shoved over the carton. "You want a new spoon?"

"No, I've had worse than cooties." She gave him a half smile.

Ethan moved to toast his body by the fire. He rotated himself like a pig on a spit. Cori eventually gave in and grabbed the chips off the coffee table, too. She was hungrier than she thought. "I'm surprised he doesn't have a big screen TV sitting above that mantle instead of dead animals," she said between bites.

"He probably couldn't get reception out here," Ethan pointed out.

"And where is here?"

"I think we're in western Russia."

"Siberia?"

"Sort of." Ethan shrugged. "I'm still trying to figure out what happened to that village. That was not an earthquake."

"Yeah." Cori nodded. "That was too weird."

"You don't think it really moved, do you?" he asked.

"I don't know. I have as many questions as you do."

"Maybe we should check the rest of the house." Ethan nodded to the hall leading to the open staircase. "We might get some answers."

She looked back at the other half of the house. Perhaps there was a backdoor. "Yeah, that's a good idea."

They searched the remaining rooms down the hall on the lower floor, but didn't find a backdoor. They found a master bedroom with bland gray walls and simple furnishings, a pristine bathroom, a laundry room, and a study with ample books. None of the rooms contained a television or anything resembling modern electronics.

"Well, he has books," Ethan said, fanning his finger over the books lining the wall in the study. "If we read past the boring descriptions of inanimate objects, it might be like watching a sitcom." He pulled out a dusty, red, leatherback book with yellowing pages and a spine that cracked when he opened it.

Cori rummaged through the study desk for anything that might clue her in to what she had gotten herself into. Or at least something that might help her get out of said predicament.

The only thing of interest on the desk was a red rotary phone. Unfortunately, the antiquated device was missing the finger plate that would allow her to dial. There was just a single button in the center. That was perhaps her answer, though. The key to her buyer's true identity.

He was Batman.

"Check out these titles." Ethan pulled out a few more books. "The Hobgoblin Lineage, Mating Habits of Merfolk, Examining the Werewolf Hierarchy, Understanding Vampiric Digestion." Ethan laughed and shoved all but one of the books back into place. "This place just keeps getting stranger and stranger. What do you make of this guy?"

"I don't make anything of him. I don't plan to get to know him well enough to make anything of him." Cori slumped back in the desk chair.

"Oh, yuck, there are pictures!" Ethan grimaced at the remaining book in his hand. "You have to look at this. It's like porn for fish." He laughed raucously at his discovery and turned another page.

"Aren't you freaked out?" Cori asked, shocked that he could find any humor in this situation.

He looked up at her, still holding his smile. When he saw the stern look on her face, his delight faded. "I was freaking out two days ago when I got a rag full of chloroform shoved in my face. And when I woke up half naked in a dog kennel. And when I was standing in line waiting to be bought like a piece of meat." Ethan clapped his book shut and shoved it into place with the other red leather spines. "Now I'm just locked in a house with you. Not the worst thing I've been through so far this week." He shrugged and left the study.

"And what happens when the worst gets here?" Cori followed him out and up the stairs to the upper floor. "What happens when he comes back and turns out to be a boy-molesting old man?"

Ethan glanced back at her, baring a perked brow. "I'm a little old for perverts."

"Close enough," Cori grumbled.

Ethan peeked his head into the far back room on the second floor. Cori looked in beside him and found a standard spare bedroom, streamlined with a bed, side table, and dresser. There was nothing particularly appealing or memorable about the room.

"He'll probably keep you locked up in a cage and only feed you when you give him a handy," she said before biting at her nails.

Ethan frowned at her. "This isn't about me, is it? You're deflecting."

"What are you talking about?" Cori dropped her hand and faced him from her side of the doorjamb. Their close proximity, revealed that she was about an inch shorter than him. Between cramping shivers and aching feet, he must not have been fully upright before. She lost some of her bravado to face him and shifted out of the door frame.

"Deflecting. Do you know what it means?" he asked.

Her eyes glittered over him, trying to reestablish her image of him as a docile, half-starved boy. "Enlighten me, oh learned one." She crossed her arms, ever so thankful that Danato had let her keep his coat.

"It means you have a lot of pent-up emotion about what you've been through."

Cori couldn't help but think of the last two weeks in captivity. She wondered how long it would take to clean off the stink of Yvette's rotgut lackeys. The encounters hadn't broken her, but only because she had already stonewalled every emotion about them. "Yeah, so." Cori shook her head as if the images were only an etch-a-sketch in her brain.

Just shake it off.

"Since you don't want to just crumple into a ball on the floor and bawl all night long," Ethan continued. "You have to find some way to alleviate that pressure. So, you take the internal high road of anger, and the external low road of projecting your fears onto me. That way, you don't have to admit to yourself that you're terrified of what's going to happen to you here."

Cori stared at him as a nervous heat rose up her spine. She hadn't realized that was what she was doing, but it sounded about right. The fact that Ethan was reading her rawest emotions, like the back of a damn cereal box, only added to her discomfort.

"How the hell do you know all that psychobabble?" She bit her lip to control any tremble that might threaten the firmness in her voice.

"I've been to a lot of shrinks." Ethan quirked a small smile. "A lot."

Cori took in a deep breath and looked down at the floor. "I don't think I can go through it again."

"Hey," Ethan said softly, and reached for her shoulder. She pulled it away, and he gave up the pursuit of physically consoling her. "If it turns out that he brought you here for that, I'll do everything I can to stop it."

Cori snorted and looked up at his frowning face. "Sorry, I..." She shook her head. "I appreciate the chivalry, I really do, but that guy would clobber you."

Ethan shrugged. "Wouldn't be the first time." He brushed past her to check the remaining rooms.

Across from the first bedroom was another bedroom, not unlike the first. Back by the stairs, there were two more rooms, and then the hallway ended with a railed balcony overlooking the living room and kitchen.

The first of the remaining rooms was a bedroom that held the same dresser, side table, and bed, but this one also contained a box. Ethan stepped inside to check the contents. He pulled out several items of clothing; men's clothing.

He looked at her with concern in his eyes. He was undoubtedly a little disturbed by the planning that had been put into his acquisition.

She checked the last room, which was also a bedroom. She saw a box on the bed. She checked the contents. It contained women's clothing.

She looked up as Ethan stepped into the doorway. "I thought he wasn't planning on getting me."

"Why don't we get dressed and ceremoniously burn these rags we're in," Ethan suggested, crashing her train of thought.

She agreed and shut the door to what had presumably been designated as her room. She rummaged through the box and found a set of pajamas and slippers. They looked comfortable and warm. She slipped out of her rags and made a mental note to rip them to shreds before she threw them on the fire.

She opened her door just as Ethan opened his. He looked back at her, wearing the same style top and bottom pajama set she was wearing; only, instead of fluffy clouds like hers, his were plaid. She smiled and shook her head.

"Great minds... Ready to burn our shrouds of scourge?" he asked.

Before she could respond, an explosion shook the entire house. Ethan dove to the floor as if he was avoiding gunfire. She planted her feet and ducked down to ride out the trembling house like a surfer.

The loft-style overlook gave her a clear view of the prison through the second-story windows over the front entrance. She could see flames spewing from the top of the prison. "What now?" Cori approached the balcony railing and peered out at the activity stemming from the prison roof.

As the flames subsided, blue lightning bolts followed, dancing over the prison's exterior walls. Trails of black blemished the building wherever the electricity touched. "What are we in a war zone now?" She pressed against the banister, mesmerized by the scene.

"Hey, come this way." Ethan peeled himself off the floor and moved back into his bedroom. "We can see the other side through my—ahh!" Ethan let out a yelp. Then Cori heard a *thunk*.

She ran to his aid and found him back on the floor behind his bed. Nothing was in the room, but he was visibly disturbed. "What is it?" she looked over the room more diligently.

He pointed at the window with an unsteady finger. "Something's out there. It just flew past."

"A *bird*," she enunciated sarcastically.

"Yeah, that's why I'm on the floor! A bird flew past the window," he shouted. "It was something big!"

She moved to the window by the bed. She kneeled on the mattress and looked outside into the dark. The prison no longer looked like a castle to her. The interspersed lighting at the base made it look more like a Vegas Casino than a legitimate facility.

"I don't see anything, Oh, but the guards are pointing up at the sky. They must have seen whatever you saw." She looked back at him. "What did it look like?"

He peeked over the mattress with wide eyes. "Like that."

She turned back to the window and saw a pair of flapping wings coming at the window. She couldn't make out the features, but she was certain of its size. "That's definitely not a bird." The creature made a quick approach and flattened its wingspan and lower body against the window. She screamed and lobbed herself over the bed to join Ethan on the other side.

"What is that?" Cori whispered to him as she peeked back up to get another look at it.

The creature was almost as tall as her. Its legs were short, with sharp, clawed feet. Its wings extended from the depth of its back and spanned beyond the reach of its upper body, which was unmistakably human...ish. Pale, sickly skin covered the pectoral muscles and biceps of the human torso. The neck, which was barely there, held an oblong head with short tipped ears, a flattened nose, and solid black eyes.

The creature looked through the window at them and opened its mouth. Two tiny rows of teeth lined the jaw. It shrieked, piercing the air with a dreadfully high-pitched sound. They both cringed, protecting their ears. Two teeth in the creature's upper jaw lengthened into sharp, penetrating fangs.

"What the hell is that thing?" Cori yelled over her covered ears and the shriek.

"Vampire!" Ethan answered. The screeching stopped, and the creature flew away from the window.

"What?" She uncovered her ears.

"It's a vampire," Ethan repeated.

"That's not possible."

"More impossible than an entire village up and moving to another country?" Ethan asked. "I know it's insane, but what other name would you give it?" he reasoned.

"Fair enough," she conceded. "It's a vampire. As long as we both agree, that explanation is ridiculous."

"Most insane thing I ever spoke in my life." He nodded.

The window shuddered as the creature crashed into it and flew off. They both screamed and sank down deeper behind the bed.

"We can't just hide here. We need to defend ourselves." Cori stood and grabbed a standing lamp from the corner of the room, and brandished it in front of the window.

Ethan found the matching table lamp and did the same, with slightly less effect. "You don't suppose all those books in the study are documenting real stuff?"

"I don't suppose anything." Cori shook her head, trying not to think about the things that go bump in the night. There were enough monsters in the world already. She didn't need ghouls and goblins too.

Ethan turned to face her. "Maybe this is some kind of top-secret lab. They're probably doing genetic experiments to create hybrids."

She turned to face him. "I don't care what they do here! I am not going to be any part of it. I'm going to get out of here and go home." Her lip quivered, dismantling the fervency of her claim.

Ethan looked her over sympathetically and nodded. "Okay."

"I'm sorry. I just..." Cori trailed off, sensing a change in her peripheral vision. She felt the hairs on the back of her neck raise. Ethan must have had the same feeling, because his face went pale.

They turned their attention back to the window. The creature had perched itself on the ledge outside. Blood dripped from its descended fangs and a decapitated human head dangled from its clutches. As if the vampire's attentive stare wasn't enough, the glazed dead eyes of the head also stared in at them.

Cori's throat convulsed, ready to return her chicken and ice cream.

"Is that real?" Cori whimpered. "Please tell me that's not real."

"This is rubbish. Forget the lamps." Ethan dropped his lamp.

"But…" she objected, her gaze fearfully frozen on the *vampire*.

Ethan yanked the lamp out of her hand. "We are not fighting that; we are running from that." He pushed her out the door and shut it behind them.

She ran downstairs and headed to the front door.

"What are you doing?" Ethan yelled and tried to intercept her escape. "You know it's locked."

"I have to get out of here. I have to try." She grabbed the knob and tried to wrench it open by the sheer will of her hands.

"You can't go outside!" Ethan grabbed her shoulder to pull her back.

She reflexively threw him off, catching his face with the back of her hand. He stepped back, touching his lip. She hadn't drawn blood, but it would be a little puffy.

His face dimmed in anger, but he didn't retaliate. "That *thing* is outside," he explained firmly. "Not to mention we are in a barricaded facility. *And* it's like a thousand degrees below zero out there. Just stop and think about what you are doing."

Cori rubbed her face and nodded. He was right. She was being impulsive—as usual. She needed to think. There was only one person who could help them in this situation.

Batman?

Cori ran back to the office. Ethan followed her in and locked the door behind them. The room only had one small window covered with a thick drape. She peeked behind it to assure their solitude.

She could hear thumping and screeching from upstairs. She listened for the sound of glass breaking, but she didn't hear it.

She grabbed the phone and held the receiver to her ear. She pushed the center button and the other end rang and rang. No one answered, and she cringed, ready to cry.

"Hello." A curt voice finally answered on the other end.

"Hello?" she responded. "Danato?"

Ethan perked up and shifted to sit in one of the chairs facing the desk.

She heard some low voices in the background and then a scuffle, presumably the phone being handed off.

"Hello." Danato's voice huffed through the earpiece. Cori was relieved to hear his voice. She hated the man, but for the time being, he was her only link to understanding this wack-a-doo place. "What's wrong? Are you two okay?"

The irony of his concern dissolved her relief, and she was instantly back to being irritated. "You mean other than the fact that I've been kidnapped and sold for Siberian slave labor?"

She heard him take a breath. "Yes, other than that. Are you hurt?" he clarified.

"No," she admitted.

"Good, why are you calling?" he asked.

"Why am I..." Cori chuckled. "I wanted to order a pizza, but I left my wallet in Norway or Sweden. Could you spot me a twenty?"

"Would you just..." Ethan stood, reached over, and ripped the phone from her hand.

"Hey!" she objected.

"Danato? This is Ethan. There is some kind of vampire outside the house, banging on the windows. ... Well, regardless of what it's called, it looks dangerous. ... What do you mean, don't worry about it?"

Cori reached over and ripped the receiver back from him. "It has a human head in its claws!" she barked into the phone.

"I know." Danato responded. "I'm sorry you had to see that, but if it's any consolation, that man was dead before the creature got to him."

"Oh, yeah, that totally makes me feel better." She shifted the phone to speak to Ethan. "The severed head guy was dead before that thing got to him." Ethan frowned, and she returned to the phone conversation. "So, I guess there is only one question. Who killed him to begin with?" she shouted into the phone.

"Listen, Missy," Danato said firmly. "I want to answer all your questions, but I don't have time right now. Even if I did, you wouldn't believe me. I need you to just stay put for now. The house is locked for your protection. You are safer in that house than anywhere else in this facility."

"Don't call me Missy. It makes me sound like a cheerleader," Cori snapped.

"You certainly are not that," he mumbled, "but until you tell me your name, I have to call you something, so *Missy* it is. Just stay *inside*, don't open any doors or windows, and ignore him at all costs. His species usually only drink blood from unconscious bodies, but they are notoriously good at tormenting people. The more you ignore him, the sooner he'll settle down," Danato assured her.

"And what if he breaks into the house? Should I leave a voice mail or just write a letter with my own blood?" She heard him take another breath. When he didn't speak, she lowered her voice and spoke again. "You're talking about a creature that only exists in folklore and teen movies, like it's a nuisance pet. What is this place? Where have you brought us?"

"They'll be time to explain all that in the days and weeks to come. I don't want to sound like I am abandoning you," he said with marshaled sympathy. "But I have much bigger things to deal with than that thing... much bigger. Please, trust what I say. You are safe in that house; safer than anywhere else in this prison." The phone clicked as he hung up.

She pulled the receiver away and stared at it as if it were directly responsible for Danato's dismissive conclusion.

"What did he say?" Ethan asked.

She hung up the phone and threw her hands up in frustration. "Don't open any windows and doors, and ignore the damn thing until it goes away."

"That's it?" Ethan wasn't enthusiastic about the plan, either.

"Yeah, I wouldn't advise to sleep, though." She left the office, no longer concerned with the banging upstairs. The fear she was feeling was only going to grow if she stayed hidden in the office. Sometimes pretending to be brave was the same as being brave.

"What happens if we sleep?" Ethan called after her.

After an hour of staring at the walls and trying to block out the mocking creature outside, they made up games to play. Games that could only be invented by bored, uneasy, sleep-deprived people.

A simple game of chip football became an elaborate food football/baseball game. The fridge provided several chip dips that kicked off the game. The objective was a full-on field goal attempt from nearly three yards away.

Each play required a new chip. The fouls were cleared by the five-second rule, and "bases loaded" meant you had more chip dip to eat. The final challenge was making the three-yard "kick" without breaking your chip, as per baseball rules, three strikes, and "you're out."

Eventually, the thumping outside stopped, the chips ran out, and two dip-covered faces lay on the coffee table, waiting to awaken with sore necks.

The early morning sun had pinked the sky when the front door unlatched and creaked open. Cori grabbed her confiscated paring knife from the coffee table and jumped up before she was awake. She ran to the door, ready to attack the vampiric intruder.

Through fogged eyes, she saw Danato and found a new purpose for her attack.

"You son of a bitch!" She lunged at him.

Danato seemed unconcerned about her attack until she raised the knife to stab him. Fortunately for him, her groggy state left her off balance, and her attempt to stab him only nicked his coat.

She wobbled to one side and toppled over right in front of him. He reached out his arms and caught her before she could hit the floor. He grabbed the knife from her hand and checked it before tossing it on the dining room table.

Cori stared up at his bloodshot eyes and unshaven face. "What is this place? Where have you brought us?"

"It's just as I said, a prison."

"A prison that holds vampires?"

"Search your nightmares, my dear." He tapped her forehead softly. "Whatever you find in them is locked up behind those walls."

Cori frowned at him. "My nightmares aren't as scary as my real life," she said.

"Don't worry about all that now," he whispered. "It's time for bed." With little more effort than lifting a bag of groceries, Danato scooped her up and took her upstairs.

Irrationally, Cori's mind flashed back to Yvette's lecherous men and their vile indulgences. She turned to look away from him as he carried her up the stairs and into one of the bedrooms.

She felt the bed under her body as he set her down. She let out a sound she intended to be a defiant outburst. Instead, it was more of a whimper. She clenched her eyes tight; hot tears spilled out over her cheeks. "Please don't." Her objection to the approaching assault fell short of vehement and landed on supplicatory. She felt the weight of his body sit on the edge of the bed. She sobbed. "Please, no."

"Open your eyes, sweetheart." His hand brushed her hair off her forehead. It was an innocent touch, but it still made her shudder. "Look at me." His voice could never be soft, but it came close. She opened her eyes. He used the bend in his finger to wipe a few tears away from her cheeks.

"No one is ever going to hurt you like that again." She didn't really believe him, but she nodded. "I think you and I have a rough road ahead, but you can be as much of a pain in the ass as you feel necessary, because I will never raise a hand or fist to you, and I will most certainly not..." He paused as if even the word made him uncomfortable. "...rape you. I won't let anyone else do that, either."

There was something paternal in his declaration. Whether it was within his power to keep that promise, she wasn't sure, but his inability to do so wouldn't have been because of indifference.

He stood to leave, but turned back. "I'll forget about that little knife incident for now."

She nodded, and he left her to get some sleep, which came far easier than she expected.

6

ETHAN AWOKE TO STOMPING footsteps and yelling. He glanced at the flip clock on his bedside table. The numbers read 2:13. It surprised him he had slept so long and so well. The last thing he remembered from earlier that morning was Danato carrying him to his bed. It had been a good number of years since he had needed someone to carry him to his bed. It had been even longer since he had anyone to actually do it.

He hopped out of bed and went downstairs to investigate the hullabaloo. He found his female cohort in the office having a one-sided argument with the phone. Given the scowl on her face, he surmised the phone was winning.

Each time she raised an objection, he could hear a loud, curt response that shut her up. The interruptions fueled her scowl and caused her free hand to fist until the knuckles were white. He crossed his arms and leaned against the doorframe, patiently waiting to hear the result of this heated discussion.

"What?" she spat into the phone. Her eyes shot directly at him. "Why?"

Her clenched fist slammed into the desk, followed by the phone. The plastic receiver smacked on the desk, making him jump. He straightened his stance to mask the flinch. She stood up and punched the wall nearest her. To Ethan's surprise, she actually dented the drywall, exposing a little of the pink insulation behind it. She turned back to him.

"It's for you," she said and stormed toward him. He steeled himself for the same punishment the wall took. She moved past him, smacking his shoulder with hers on the way by. Even though it hurt, he was glad he hadn't offered her a soft shoulder to bully.

He sat on the edge of the desk and picked up the phone. "Hello," he said as he rubbed his shoulder.

"Ethan," Danato confirmed on the other end. He sounded relieved. "Good, a rational voice. Missy is having difficulty with the idea of staying at the house today. I would like you to do your best to keep her from ripping apart my home."

Ethan glanced at the hole in the wall with a grimace. "I'll try."

"I understand you are both frustrated, but please consider this the calm before the storm. Tomorrow I will be ready to introduce you to the prison. I would have done it today, but given last night, I figured you and I could both use a day to recuperate."

"What exactly will I be doing here?" Ethan could hear Danato breathing on the other end, but he said nothing. "Hello?"

Danato cleared his throat. "I don't mean to be reticent, but if I gave you the entire list of duties at once, you might become overwhelmed and simply shut down. Allow me to get you acquainted with the work environment before I assign any duties. Your first priority will be education, and then we will get you in shape for guard rotation, so you can start working with the men."

Ethan looked down at his hands. They didn't display the callouses of a working man, but they had scars. One scar he got from broken glass, during his days as a thieving juvenile delinquent. He got a couple of scars from cigarette burns during a short but memorable stint with a less than loving foster father; his interpretation of aversion therapy.

He even had one scar down his left wrist, remnants of his first and last attempt at suicide. The infliction earned him six months of intensive psychological evaluation and the realization that suicide wasn't for him. Ultimately, his therapist summed up his diagnosis as: "Patient is depressed."

You think?

"I don't have any choice about this, do I?" Ethan asked warily.

"No," Danato answered. The blunt response should have bothered Ethan, but it didn't. At least it was honest.

His life up to this point had not really been his own. Danato was just another person dictating to him about who he should be and what he needed to do. A parole officer or a foster father, at this point, it just really didn't matter.

The difference was Danato had already offered him more respect than his previous judicators had. So, he wouldn't let the trifling label of "slave" upset him.

The conversation ended with details about the house and plans for the next day before they hung up.

Ethan searched for "Missy" and found her in the living room sulking on the sofa. He hung back and watched her. She was furiously biting her nails. He wanted to offer her some sympathy for everything she had been through, but he also couldn't help but think she was directing her anger at the wrong person. If it hadn't been for this man, she would still be in captivity, or worse.

He wasn't sure what the future held here, but the cage that was holding him now was warm, stocked with food, and so far hadn't come with an extra helping of backhands. As far as he was concerned, things were looking up.

"What did he say?" she asked without removing her fingers from her teeth.

"He said I'll be heading into the prison tomorrow and I should consider today to be recuperative."

"What about me? When do I get out of this hellhole?"

He glanced at the comfortable surroundings. "Do you really want to go inside that prison?"

She stilled and looked up through the windows of the vaulted ceilings. "What else do you think is in there?" she murmured.

"I don't know, but apparently tomorrow I'm going to find out."

She looked back at him. Curiosity tinged the scowl that had barely left her face since they met. "How can you be so calm? We're trapped here. You get that, right?"

"Yeah, I caught on to that. You do recall begging him to take you with him, right?"

She stood up to face him. "That was hardly a decision to be made. Those goons were right down the street. Not to mention the village was being swallowed up by the freaking earth."

"I know, but you have to admit your future prospects were pretty downtrodden with or without his help." She opened her mouth to object, but he interrupted her. "You do see that he's saved us, don't you?"

Her face blanked, and she shook her head. "Out of the frying pan and into the fire." She perked a brow. "Doesn't it bother you to never see your family and friends again?"

"Criminal orphans don't usually have a lot of friends," he said, "at least not the type that would be long missed." Ethan moved into the kitchen to scrounge for breakfast—or lunch.

"So, you're saying you would rather be here than free?" She followed him into the kitchen and leaned on the sink while he prepared a bowl of cereal.

He shook his head. "I think what I'm saying is, the last five years have been shit, and I'm willing to give anything else a try, so I don't have to end up dealing drugs or using them."

The scowl on her face finally ebbed away. "That bad?" she asked.

He stared down at his breakfast for a moment. "Bad enough." He took a bite of the cereal. The reconstituted milk left something to be desired, but given their location, he understood the sacrifice. "Want some?" Ethan said over his mouthful. He pointed to the cartoon box on the counter. She looked at it and shook her head. "Come on, I know you're hungry. They can't have fed you that much."

He pulled a bowl out of the cupboard and handed it to her. She took it and begrudgingly poured a bowl of cereal. For a few minutes, they chomped in silence.

Without the innocuous droning of a television or radio, the house was quiet. Too quiet. He was used to listening to sports games or hearing the background noise of passing cars and people. This place was going to take some getting used to.

He slurped the last of his milk out of the bowl and resisted pouring another bowl. He watched the girl do the same, albeit less gracefully. He smiled as she wiped her chin clean.

"What?" she questioned his attention.

"I take it you have someone or someplace you would like to get back to?" he asked.

She set her bowl in the sink before answering. "Not specifically. I'm kind of on my own. My family is... gone."

"Friends?"

"A few. Not close. I never did get the hang of that. I had a guy friend for a while, but then I slept with him. Fastest way to break a friendship, I tell you what." Ethan chuckled at her joke and a microscopic smile crept onto her face. "What about you? Why no friends?"

"I went through a really long phase of punching all my friends."

"Oh," she laughed. "I stand corrected. That is probably the fastest way to break a friendship."

"Yeah, it really is." Ethan leaned back against the fridge. "I did have one person I considered a friend. He was technically my parole officer."

"Well, that's someone, at least," she said.

He scoffed. "He was actually the one who introduced me to the 'employment agency' we just came from. I'm pretty sure he received a small bribe for it." Her face melted into pity for him. He preferred her scowl.

"You know, just because you didn't have a good childhood, doesn't mean you couldn't make something of yourself as an adult," she insisted. "You don't owe this guy anything. Certainly not the rest of your life."

Ethan nodded and noticed that she was cradling her right hand in her left. She must have been feeling the ramifications of boxing with a wall. "You should ice your hand."

"It's fine," she answered with a knee jerk response.

Rather than accept her answer, he opened the freezer and pulled out a bag of frozen peas that would do the trick. He found a towel hanging on the stove handle and moved to aid her swelling hand.

"What are you doing?" She stood upright, ready to bolt.

"It's an ice pack for your hand," he explained, revealing the picture of peas on it.

"I can see that, but I said I'm fine."

"You're not fine. Your fingers are swelling like sausages. Take it from experience. You want to ice your hand." He grabbed her hand and drug it forward.

"I don't want the ice!" She ripped her hand away and smacked it into the cabinetry behind her. She yelped and bent over to cradle her hand.

"Are you okay?"

"No, I'm not okay."

"Come on, let me help." He touched her back, trying to comfort her.

"No!" She threw her arm back, slamming her elbow into his chin.

He growled and stepped back, cradling his chin. "Would you stop hitting me!"

She stared at him, eyes wide and teeth bared. "Then stop touching me!"

"I am not going to hurt you! I'm trying to help!"

"I don't want your help! I don't want anything from you! Just leave me alone!" She stomped off. A moment later, he heard her door slam.

He sighed and pressed the peas to his own sore chin. "Can't imagine why she doesn't have any friends," he mumbled.

7

WHEN DANATO CAME HOME that evening, he recruited Missy to help him prepare dinner. After several snide remarks, she agreed to the task, but only because he insisted it would be faster if she helped him. Her appetite was likely the tipping point in the debate.

She looked a good deal cleaner and rested than she had the night before, but a shower and bed had done nothing to improve her spirits. The only difference in her temperament was that she had traded her open defiance for sullen avoidance. He wanted to do or say something to evoke her civility and bridge the gap between them, but even the innocent movements of his kitchen tasks made her flinch.

"Missy," he chastised when his reach to turn down the stove temperature nearly caused her to spill a pot of hot water on herself. "You have to get hold of yourself. Your jumpiness is going to get one of us scalded."

"Just... back off."

He sighed and leaned his hands on the counter next to the stove. "Do you want to talk about it?"

She scoffed. "I'd rather talk to that vampire thing than you."

He sighed and tapped his fingers on the counter. "What would you say if I told you I could erase your memory of everything that happened to you?"

"Erase; like amnesia?"

"Yes, but you would never remember. Every painful memory would just go away."

"All of it?"

"I would need you to remember the kidnapping and coming with me, so you have a frame of reference. It would just be as if you blocked out the entire experience." He watched her contemplate the idea. "Would you want that?"

Her face dimmed, and her telltale stubborn frown returned. "Is that what you want me to do? So I'm easier to handle?"

Danato shook his head. Removing her trauma would certainly make his life easier, but forcing her to forget was not wise. There were downsides to memory gaps—especially if her emotional scarring remained. "I'm trying to make this transition easier for you."

"I don't want it to be easier. I don't belong here."

"I meant your transition back to trusting men again."

Her eyes widened slightly, and she took a step back. "I think I would rather know what the world is really like. Monsters and all."

He nodded and moved back to the sink. "Well, the offer is available if you ever change your mind."

Come dinnertime, the three of them sat down to tuna noodle casserole and a tossed salad. Danato watched as his two recruits avoided eye contact with each other. The few times their eyes met, it spawned a glare or eye roll from the other. He had hoped that their day together would have given them a chance to bond, but it appeared to have done the opposite.

"Is something wrong?" Danato finally asked.

"Nope," they said in unison.

"Good, I would hate to have to split you two up. The only rooms left are in the prison." Neither one balked at his threat. "Missy, I won't be ready for you to begin working in the prison yet. I'd like you to concentrate on keeping up with things around here. There isn't much. Dusting, vacuuming, and a little something for supper tomorrow night would be appreciated."

"I'm a house slave?" she asked, appalled.

"The prison is a very detail-oriented place. Certain things are done certain ways, for very important reasons. Neither my staff nor myself can afford mistakes or outright disobedience. Your attitude," he nodded to her swollen hand, "and distrust needs to be under control before I send you in. If things go well here, I will gladly get you involved in other duties."

"I will never understand why you keep playing like this is employment," she said, plopping another helping of casserole on her plate.

"It is employment."

"What's my salary?" she asked.

"I can pay you, but the money would be worthless, since you would just give it back to me to pay for your food, clothing—"

"What if I want something you haven't offered me?" She leaned over the table, challenging him with the tilt of her head.

"I can get you almost anything you need, within reason. We do have a budget like any other prison."

"Who pays for that budget?" she asked.

"Mostly private benefactors. We do have a few under-the-table military operations."

"I want a television," she declared, as if she already had that request in mind.

He looked at Ethan, who was nodding in agreement. They must have been bored out of their minds being in the house all day without spoon-fed entertainment. "I'm so used to being without one, I forgot what it must be like here without it for the first time."

"So, can we get one?" Ethan's brow raised in anticipation.

"Unfortunately, that is not allowed. Neither are radios."

"Says who?" Missy narrowed her eyes as if cocking the gun to her next argument.

"Says about eight dead guards in 1953. Certain electronics can be used to heighten telepathic channeling... so to speak."

They both looked at him, not realizing the explanation was finished. He didn't bother going into it more since it only would have brought about questions he wasn't willing to answer yet. Or ever.

"Maybe I *don't* want to get out of this house, to work in the prison." Missy offered a grimace to Ethan.

"Eventually you'll get sick of being here," Danato assured her before turning to Ethan. "We will be up early tomorrow. I suggest you get plenty of sleep." He wiped his chin and cleared his dishes before heading to his bedroom for the night. Even as he shut his door, he heard them moving to do the same.

8

SHORTLY AFTER SUNRISE, DANATO awakened Cori. The fright of a still strange man over her bed sent her heart into overdrive. She must have screamed or whimpered because he hushed her gently and brushed her hair away from her face.

He asked her to help him with breakfast. She was halfway between sleep and fear, so she agreed to the demand that he cleverly disguised as a request. She crawled out of her warm bed to do his bidding. Feeling no need to dress for the occasion, she went downstairs in her pajamas. She arrived in the kitchen with a full yawn, expressing her objection to the early hour. She stood at the end of the island and awaited directions from Danato, who was already heating his griddle.

"Do those clothes not fit?" Danato asked, looking over at her sleepwear.

"What?"

"Wasn't there a box full of clothes in that room?"

She scoffed. "Yeah, but it's like 5 a.m. and if you think I'm up for the day, you are so wrong."

"Oh, well, as long as some stuff gets cleaned up, we should be fine. This isn't the type of place you want to let get messy."

"Really?" She raised an eyebrow and took on toast duty when there were no other instructions given.

After a breakfast of toast, eggs, and fruit, the men prepared for their day of gainful employment. She cleared dishes as they put on their coats by the door. She caught Ethan watching her. "What?" she asked, picking up all three glasses with one hand.

"I..." He cleared his throat. "Thank you for breakfast." His recognition, albeit gracious, sounded forced, like he didn't really want to say it.

"He made it. I just made the toast." She shrugged and took her glassware to the sink.

"I didn't have any toast," he said to her back. "So, I guess what I should have said was 'burn in hell you heinous bitch.'"

She made a slow pivot back to him. Her mouth had dropped open in awe of his audacity. He glowered back at her.

"Ethan, that was unnecessary," Danato scolded him.

"Unnecessary, but accurate," he mumbled.

"Oh, screw you, I hope you get eaten in there!" she shouted.

"Both of you knock it off!" Danato hollered. "You're angry at your situation, and taking it out on each other."

"No, I'm pretty sure she's a bitch," Ethan contested.

"Out, Ethan." Danato shoved a coat at him and pushed him out the door. He looked back at Cori. "How old are you again?" he said, coming into the kitchen.

She rolled her eyes and turned away from him. His hand cut across her face as he grabbed her shoulders. Before she was even aware of any pressure, she was dizzy from spinning back to face him. "What? Twenty-three." She raised her shoulders to shrug him away, but he had already released her.

"Really? Because not only did you sink to a grade-school level of immaturity, you brought him down there with you."

"He started it!" She laughed as she said it because it didn't seem to help her case, even though it was true.

"He was trying to thank you. To reestablish some courtesy in your communication, and you dismissed him instead of acknowledging him."

"I don't want to reestablish the communication. I shouldn't have established it to begin with. I shouldn't be here!"

Danato raised his chin, looking down his nose at her. "Do you know why I let you come here?" he asked.

"Let?" Cori nearly choked on her own saliva. She opened her mouth to barrage him with the many errors in that statement, but he continued.

"Yes, *let*. Don't think for one second that just anyone can pass over that drawbridge." She rolled her eyes back and turned back to the sink. "Look at me!" She jumped, feeling the impact of his voice through her spine. His gruff voice still commanded more respect than she could deny. She slipped a fork out of the sink and turned back to him. She crossed her arms effectively hiding the flatware, as well as giving her a comforting barrier between them.

"This place is the most highly guarded secret in the world, and you have just become one of the privileged few to safeguard it. I brought you here because you are strong, quick-witted—"

"You don't even know me," Cori defended. "I'm just somebody who got shoved in a car... blindfolded, duct taped, raped, and sold to a stranger!" Cori ground out the words.

Danato paused, taking in her words before speaking. "Yes, all of those things happened to you, and you are still standing. You are bucking my authority—which is something of a novelty for me. And you are still..." Danato grabbed her wrist and dragged it away from the crook of her elbow. He forced the hidden fork from her hand and held it up to her. "...fighting." He tossed the fork in the sink behind her and she waited to see what her punishment would be.

"We have a long road ahead, but just do me a favor and remember that Ethan isn't to blame for you being here. Keep your anger and bitterness directed at me until you accept the responsibility of this place." Danato stepped away from her and headed to the door.

"I don't think that will be a problem," Cori murmured.

"Listen, Missy," Danato paused at the door and looked back at her. "I'm going to remind you once more about keeping the house tidy. I hope you hear me. If not... well, you just have a nice day. We'll be back in time for supper. I'll leave that up to you, if you can manage it."

"Clean the house, fix supper; I think I can handle that, master." She raised her folded arms and blinked her eyes for effect, even though years without a television probably left him clueless about the origin of her joke.

He left without another word. As soon as the door latched shut, she went upstairs to sleep, leaving a third layer of dirty dishes in the sink.

E THAN AND DANATO MADE their way down a thin stone path to the entrance of the prison. The entrance was one small door against the towering concrete slabs that made up the outer walls of the prison. Though the short distance only took them a couple of minutes, Ethan was reminded that they were, in fact, in an arctic tundra.

Though he hadn't really thought about trying to escape from this place, he realized running away wasn't an option. He would have a red face and frostbitten fingers just from this one-minute commute.

Inside the entrance there was a niche with a series of lockers to place their coats. Beyond that, the main foyer was just a big empty room with a white waxed floor. Though it was spacious enough to hold an elephant or two, its only purpose seemed to be directing one in four different directions. Straight from the lockers up a short set of steps was a hall with a green label sign that read *Main Offices*. The other options were two hallways that branched the same direction away from the foyer. Each had signs hanging from the tall ceilings. One hallway led to the *Docks*, and the other led to the *Cafeteria* and *Gym*. Left of the hallways in the main room were a set of elevators and a door that read *Stairs*.

Ethan wasn't sure what he had expected: dark concrete, wet from dripping pipes, fluorescent lights flickering from above, and the faint sound of screaming creeping in from beyond thick metal doors. Instead, it was well lit and clean, sterile even.

He looked over at Danato, who was patiently waiting for him to observe his surroundings. "We'll head to my office first." Danato took the lead to the short staircase. Despite the man's limp, he hefted himself up the stairs with ease.

Ethan followed him while lagging back a little. He wasn't sure if it was intentional or instinctual, but they were walking down a long hallway with no discernible exits. They passed by several open doors, but they led to darkened vacant office spaces.

At some point, no closer to the end of the hallway than they were from the beginning of it, Danato turned into a room. The door to the room was wood, with a clear window in it that bore bold black letters: WARDEN. Unlike the other offices, this also had a plexi-glass window looking into the hallway.

That was apparently the only perk about the room, because it smelled of old coffee and stale cigars. It was furnished with a heavy metal desk, three chairs—a swivel one for the desk and two vinyl cushioned ones facing it.

There were also two rusty file cabinets—one short, one tall—and a water cooler that looked like it hadn't been drunk from in years. Even the chairs appeared to be rejects from a business foreclosure.

"Is this it?" Ethan didn't mean to sound pretentious, but it *was* a disappointment.

"Yes, this is where I sign endless papers that have nothing to do with what we do here." Danato sat down at his desk and pulled out a pencil and paper from the middle drawer.

"What do you do here?" Ethan asked.

"This facility holds nearly 300 chronic and/or intrinsic offenders," Danato started with no prefacing. "These... inmates are here because they are either dangerous or onerous on human resources. They are not all at fault for what they do. For some, the behavior is innate. It cannot be changed or rehabilitated. Do you understand that?"

He shrugged and nodded, not sure whether to answer for his comprehension of Danato's lecture or the English language in general. He sat down in one of the chairs facing the desk and leaned in so he would at least look studious.

"We do not rehabilitate prisoners, because they cannot change their behaviors," Danato clarified a little further. "If there was even the slightest chance they could be, they wouldn't be here, understood?"

Ethan nodded.

"I'm going to take you on a tour today, to familiarize you with the basic layout of the prison. I certainly don't expect you to remember everything today, but keep in mind, when I tell you to walk a certain way, talk a certain way, it is important. In this place, details can mean the difference between life and death."

"What will I be doing here?" he asked.

"First and foremost, you will be put on a diet regimen and an exercise program. Your primary duties for the time being will be researching and studying the inmates. Those files behind you hold detailed descriptions of each inmate. You must be able to identify all the inmates, know their strengths, and know their weaknesses. As well as feeding schedules, medications, etcetera. On top of that, I have an entire library of books on the specific genres of inmates that you may encounter here."

"How long will that take?"

"It took me nearly two years, but I wasn't pressed to do it any faster," Danato said.

"What happens after that?"

"You'll work as a guard. I'll bump you to different levels of the prison as you become comfortable with each group. The floors are divided into categories of offenders. We are on the main floor, which contains offices, supplies, the docks, cafeteria, kitchen, and the gym." Danato drew a haphazard building diagram and designated the main floor. "Below us is the basement and sub-basement. The sub-basement contains the incinerators, the furnaces, the electrical work, and the basement contains the *photophobes*, as we call them."

A question was just beginning to form on Ethan's lips, but Danato placed up a finger to stop him. "The level above us," he continued, "houses the animals, along with the infirmary, which provides the complex and varying sustenance needs for each animal, as well as medical care for the animals and the staff." Ethan's rutted brow did nothing to slow Danato's description. "Above that are the part-timers, then the transmorphs, followed by the seducers, then the sorcerers, and finally the elementals." Danato scribbled each label on his diagram with unintelligible script. "We have roof access by stairs. I always have a number of guards watching our perimeter, just in case."

Ethan waited for him to elaborate on the "just in case" part of his sentence, but he offered no further explanation. As it was, the vague information conjured more questions than he could choose between.

"Understand?" Danato asked, shoving the scribbled diagram to him for reference.

Not in the least.

Ethan gave an absent-minded nod, despite his confusion. "This prison..." He let the sentence hang in the air while he tried to phrase the end just right. "It doesn't hold any humans, does it?" He waved to the paper.

"No." Danato offered nothing more, but he continued to watch him, probably to gauge his reaction.

He wasn't sure if it was the abundance of information being thrown at him, the weight of responsibility being placed on him, or the overall upheaval of his definition of normal, but he was feeling sick to his stomach. The man sitting across from him hadn't just purchased him for slave labor. He had recruited him to learn, grow, and serve as an asset to his staff.

Even though refusal was clearly not an option, he wanted to tell Danato he had made a huge mistake. His only talent, besides being a punching bag and stealing, was running away from responsibility. He had always assumed he would end up in a prison, but as an inmate, not a guard. How could Danato have chosen him?

There was a tap on the window of the door. He turned back to see the short man with the red hair and beard who had driven the stagecoach for them. Danato waved him in. "We didn't get a chance for introductions the other day," Danato said. "Belus, this is Ethan. Ethan, Belus. Belus is my right-hand man. He keeps me informed of what's going on in the prison at all times. Without him, I'd be lost."

Ethan stood to greet him. Belus could have stood eye to eye with most ten-year-olds, but Ethan loomed over him by a foot. Which put Danato over a foot and a half taller than him. Ethan wondered if that created any problems. If anything, it made the partnership interesting.

Belus put out his hand, and Ethan shook it. The dwarf had small hands, just as he expected, but they were coarse and strong. "Good to meet you, boy." He turned to

Danato. "I hope your first order of business is to beef him up."

Ethan pulled his hand away. He wasn't sure how to take the almost insult.

"Yes, it is," Danato said as if he had already written and highlighted it on his to-do list, right along with buying milk.

Danato stood from his desk chair and moved around to the door. "Today I'm going to show Ethan around. I'm expecting a call from my other purchase. We're calling her Missy for now. She's reluctant to offer any personal information." Belus gave a grunt and rolled his eyes. "If you're still here when she calls, would you explain to her that she's going to either have to start doing as I ask, or deal with the issues that arise from her insubordination on her own?"

"Yup, will do; not much of a housekeeper?" Belus asked as he took up Danato's chair behind the desk.

"Not yet," Danato said with a conspiratorial grin before ushering Ethan out the door.

10

T HE BASEMENT REMINDED ETHAN of a dog kennel. If that dog kennel were in the dungeon of a castle. Out of the elevator, they had the option of the first long corridor perpendicular to them, or they could have gone left, which would have offered access to several more aisles of cells.

The passages were lit with migraine-inducing yellow fluorescents. The sounds of the inmates reacting to their presence soon drown out the incessant hum they gave off. The pitched screams reminded Ethan of the creature outside his window that first night.

"This is the basement," Danato yelled over the noise. "It holds our photophobes." Danato air quoted the word. "Our night dwellers and light-sensitive inmates are down here."

Danato moved forward into the first passageway, and Ethan followed directly behind him as instructed. The centerline between the adjacent cells held a narrow trench to drain off excess *fluids*. Despite the precaution, the area smelled clean, perhaps a little musty, but not overpoweringly so.

The creatures pushing their arms through the bars of their confinements all looked pale, but not one looked like the other. Some were hairy, some were bald, some had fangs and claws, and some looked almost human.

"Night dwellers?" Ethan drew in closer to Danato's back so he could hear him.

Danato glanced back, apparently interpreting his proximity as distress. "Just stay in the middle between the cells and you'll be fine. They will try to scare you. Don't jump back, or you'll be too close to the other side."

As they moved further down the corridor, they went through a glass-windowed door. On the other side, the air was noticeably warmer, and moister. As they passed by a new set of cells, Ethan saw the flying creature they had hid from on their first night.

"You keep vampires down here?" Ethan hollered over the new racket this section offered.

"Yes, but vampire isn't a specific term for us. There are many types of vampires. They come in different forms, some humanoid, others animal-based. All 'vampire' means to us is that the creature sustains itself by drinking mammalian blood. Not all vampiric creatures are photosensitive, and not all photosensitive creatures are vampiric. The vampires that you're familiar with are actually seducers. They aren't photophobes and they aren't vampiric."

"So, not all of these things kill people."

Danato stopped and turned around. His face was grave. "With very few exceptions, all the inmates in this prison have killed humans; that's why they are here. Killing humans to receive sustenance has been deemed illegal. Vampires will drink the blood of humans, others will eat their bones, and some just eat everything. There is no room for the romantic fantasies of Dracula in this place. These creatures are contained for a reason. They have become human predators."

Ethan felt his anxiety-furnished stomachache shift into his throat. Danato took no notice and moved further down the hall. As he continued after him, he witnessed every variation of humanoid and animal and the mixes between.

At the end of the corridor, they stopped to transition into the next section. Ethan noticed something glinting on the floor near his foot. He bent down and picked up the bobble that looked like a diamond. He rolled it around on his palm, trying to determine if it was real. He noticed a hair hanging off it. He clasped the stone and tried to rip the thread away, but it was as strong as a fishing line.

"Ethan, no!" Danato yelled at him.

Before he understood the man's intensity, the thread snapped forward, pulling the diamond and consequently his hand with it. He lost balance and fell forward into faceless claws that were grappling through the bars of a nearby cell.

His face stung with pain as sharp boney hooks dug into his cheeks. A mouth of fangs appeared next to him, futilely pressing against the bars. Something wet tickled his face—a tongue.

He heard a crunch. He feared for his own bones, but it was the creature that wailed in anguish. The grip on him released, and he scurried back to the center line on his hands and knees.

Ethan looked back and saw Danato's hand clamped onto the creature's wrists. The monster within the cage moaned until he released it. It shuffled away with as much haste as Ethan just had.

Danato's gaze scoured him with unspoken rebukes. Ethan opened his mouth to apologize for his stupidity, but laughter trickled out of the darkened cell behind him. He jumped up to protect himself from another attack, but the creature didn't even come to the bars.

"You should have bought a smarter boy, Danato." A haunting male voice spoke from the shadows.

"He'll learn," Danato answered, still reprimanding Ethan with his firm gaze.

"Who is that?" Ethan asked.

"An exception," Danato grumbled. "Let's go."

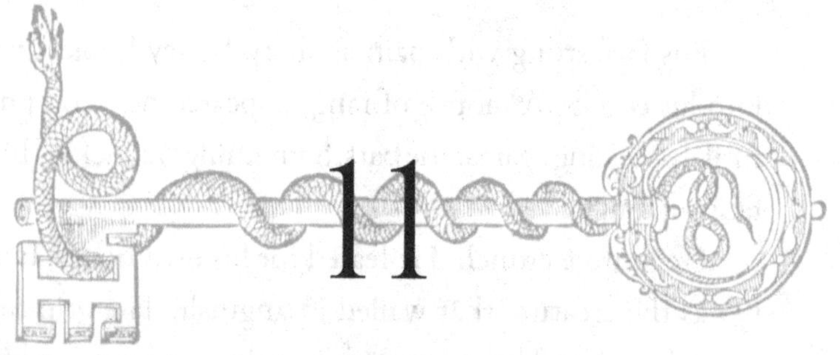

11

S EVERAL HOURS AFTER GOING back to bed, Cori's eyelids forced themselves open. Somewhere in her dream, she had heard a loud bang, but now that she was awake, she wasn't sure it was a dream. Another bang and a crash jerked her from her warm mattress.

She paused, cautiously listening for Danato's thunderous voice. Somewhere downstairs, a glass shattered. She jumped from the bed. The flip clock read 11:32. It was too early for Danato to be back. She stepped out of her room. Edging along the wall, she moved to the loft overlook.

Downstairs, broken dishes and dented pots littered the floor in and around the kitchen. The fridge door and the cupboards were open, their contents a disheveled mess. She couldn't see the invader, but she could hear scraping sounds coming from behind the island beyond her view.

She grabbed a set of decorative antlers off the hallway wall and tiptoed down the stairs to the kitchen. The ruckus continued out of sight behind the island. Armed with her hunting paraphernalia, she jumped into the kitchen with an "ah-hah" approach.

Unfortunately, the half dozen small green gremlin-like creatures that hissed back at her through food-filled mouths seemed unthreatened by her presence.

Her first response was to let out a solemn yelp, followed shortly after by an irritated groan. She abandoned her attack, holstered her antlers, and headed to the study to find the house's only legitimate technology.

This time, the phone rang only once. A cheerful man answered on the other end, introducing himself as Belus. "How can I be of service, miss?"

"I need to speak to Danato," she said.

"I'm afraid he is away from his desk for the rest of the day. Can I help you with anything?" Belus spoke in a breezy, secretarial tone, but it didn't hide his hoarse baritone.

"Yes, you can tell him that there are gremlins in this house."

"I think you mean goblins; there are only a few physical differences. Also, if they were in fact gremlins, they would be tearing out your eyeballs as we speak. They aren't, are they?" he added as an afterthought, with a touch more concern.

"No, just tearing apart the kitchen."

"Yes, they are fond of processed foods," Belus said.

After a brief silence, she continued. "What should I do?"

"Well, until the food is entirely gone, they won't leave. They are attracted to food and warmth, but mostly food."

"Don't you keep them contained?" she scolded.

Belus laughed hysterically on the other end for nearly a minute before he composed himself enough to speak again. "No, the goblins are uncontainable, but it doesn't matter because, like I said, they are attracted to food and warmth. We just keep an area warm with foods they like, and they tend to stay out of our way."

"Clearly not, since they have invaded this house," she sneered. She got the impression that this guy was dicking around and had no intention of doing anything but provide her with a sounding board for her problems.

"The house is usually reasonably secure. You didn't set any baked goods out on your windowsill, did you? They have an excellent olfactory sense."

"You mean they just smell the food in the house and come running?"

"No, they mind themselves when people are in the house. They hate people, really. It's just when the house is quiet and leftover food has not been properly disposed of in the garbage disposal. If the dishes were left unattended for too long, they would be attracted to that."

"Son of a bitch!"

"I beg your pardon?" Belus said, affronted.

"He knew this would happen. That bastard knew they would come in here. He should have told me."

"Danato didn't tell you to do the dishes? That seems unlike him." Belus's tone indicated sarcasm, but he was playing it off innocently enough.

"No, but he didn't tell me why."

"He didn't tell you why to clean the dishes? For the same reason you do any other household chores, my dear: cleanliness. The only difference is, here there are consequences much bigger than roaches."

She rolled her eyes and lowered her voice to a growl. "He should have explained."

Belus lost his secretarial voice, revealing the depth of his gravelly vocals. "Danato is the warden of the most dangerous prison on the earth, filled with the most dangerous entities on earth. He can hardly be expected to explain everything he asks you to do. Someday, it may be a matter of life or death. You should learn to trust him. He is a good man, despite his burly ogre appearance."

She didn't know who this Belus was, but she could already tell she wouldn't get along with him any better than Danato. "Fine," she drawled, "he's a swell guy. I shall endeavor to be a better slave in the future. Just tell me how to get rid of the goblins."

"Well, you could try to catch them." Belus started another bout of laughter.

"Stop that!"

Belus coughed to regain control of his comical outburst. "Or you could remove the food from the house. Sometimes they follow, depending on how cold it is outside."

"The door is locked," Cori said.

"Are you sure?" The tone of condescension in his voice annoyed her. "I have a feeling, not today."

Cori realized she had never even checked it. "What if they don't go out?" she asked.

"Then you will have to wait until they decide to leave on their own. Just remember, though, they don't like humans at all."

"Will they attack me?"

"Not viciously, but they will throw a lot of stuff at you. Whatever they can get hold of; they aren't especially strong, but they are quick—very quick."

Cori hung up the phone and prepared for her mentally and physically challenging day. She returned to the kitchen with her antlers cocked and her neck freshly cracked. She looked over the six Little Debbie addicts with the fortitude of Dirty Harry. "Okay, you little green twerps, it's time to—" Her clever pre-attack speech was interrupted by something wet slapping up against her cheek. Cacophonic chittering spread contagiously throughout the room as she wiped away the greenish-brown glob.

Concerned by its appearance, she sniffed it, to be sure. She was positive. It was, in fact, goblin poop. "Oh, you have got to be kidding me!"

12

AFTER THEY FINISHED VIEWING the basement, he and Danato moved up to the animal level via a lift on the east end of the building. Ethan noticed the elevator didn't offer a main floor button like the west side, but he didn't ask why.

They arrived on the second floor, and Ethan was relieved to see that there were other human beings inside the prison. A couple of men, dressed in militant black, passed them as they exited the carriage. They each offered Danato a respectful nod, just short of a salute.

He was also relieved to see and feel the warm sunlight streaming through the high windows of the level.

"Let's check out the infirmary. You can get your cheek looked at while we're there." Danato said and guided them toward a glass enclosed section off to the right, labeled *Infirmary.*

According to Danato, the infirmary held a central position on the floor, with entrances on both the east and west ends. The animal cages were located parallel to it, skirting the outside walls in environmentally controlled sections.

Ethan followed Danato through a small entryway, followed by another hall of windows. On either side were rooms with hospital beds. Some were basic cots divided by curtains, and others were fully loaded *gonna-be-there-for-a-while* beds.

At the end of the hall was a c-shaped reception desk. Two women leaned against the counter, talking. They were both well into their forties and neither had an exceptional figure, but he was thankful to see someone of the opposite sex that wasn't on the verge of a dissociative disorder.

The woman saw Danato and jumped to attention. "Yes, sir. How can we help you?" The older of the two said before she caught sight of Ethan's cheeks. Her eyes widened, and she waved at her partner. "Ah, Marcy, get the ointment."

The nurse bypassed Danato and grabbed his hand. "You poor dear. Is this your first day on?" She dragged him forward into an exam room just off the hub. "It's a rough ride the first go around, I tell you what." She continued to babble as she gathered supplies. "Don't you worry, next time it will be easier."

"Next time?" Ethan asked.

"Ethan is going to be full time," Danato answered his question from the doorway.

The nurse froze and looked over at him. She gave him a small smile that looked like pity. "Just you wait." She returned to her chipper mood. "You are going to see things that will make you renew your faith in God."

"And hate him," Danato mumbled at the door.

"I didn't hear that," the nurse said in a singsong voice.

"Excuse me, warden," a tiny voice spoke from the hall, and Danato shifted to let the nurse Marcy into the room.

"Ah, here we go," the lead nurse said as she plucked the ointment from Marcy's fingers. "Those grimy little buggers are ripe with infection causing bacteria. You be sure to come see us anytime you get a scrape down in the *darks*. Okay?"

"Okay." Ethan smirked and leaned forward for his treatment. He hadn't had this much doting in a long time. He was almost glad about his stupid mistake now.

13

Cori ducked on the other side of the island, dodging Twinkie and Ding Dong grenades. So far, her attempts to infiltrate the kitchen had failed, but she still had hope that she could penetrate the northern defenses and make off with the remnants of the chip inventory.

She stayed low, crawling between the island and the dining room table. She peered around the corner by the fridge. It was all clear, but she could already see the shrapnel of downed potato chips. It may have been too late for the salty snacks cupboard.

Determined not to be beaten by the foreign invaders, she scooted further in to flank the front line. Just as she suspected, the powdered-sugar-festooned buggers were busy defending their southern position.

She moved forward, ducking low, and avoiding the plastic crinkle wrappers that littered her path. Two feet away in the pantry cabinet, she gathered the lone surviving bag of tortilla chips and a fiesta trail mix no one was going to eat, because it was ridiculously hot.

She searched for the others, but they were gone. Chocolate chip cookies. Gone. Cheesy crackers. Gone. Those little doughnuts covered in that coconut crap. Gone!

Overcome by digestive grief, she stepped wrong and planted her foot right on a cupcake package. The crunching plastic might as well have been a call to arms for her wayward enemies.

They turned to face her. Six little triangular green faces, each angrier than the next. They hissed, chittered, and screeched before leaping up and over the counters. All but one scattered, taking so little of their abominable smell with them.

The remaining critter sat on the counter by the stove, hissing at her. Denying her claim to the kitchen and the food it contained.

"You want this, you little bastard?" She flaunted the chips at him. "Come get it!" She moved sideways and tossed the two bags out the open front door.

The goblin screamed in displeasure, but didn't move from his perch. Cori dusted off her hands and moved back into her newly established territory.

"Don't like that?" She popped open the fridge and found its contents similarly diminished. She pulled out the jelly. "I bet you didn't even know what was in here." She opened the jar, courtesy of her opposable thumb, and waved the jelly around. The creature leaned forward and sniffed the air.

"You want that? Go get it." She tossed it out the front door. She came back to the kitchen and searched the cupboards. "Wait till I find the peanut butter. That is going to blow your mind."

She found the peanut butter safely ensconced in a critter proof jar. She pulled it out and turned to exhibit it, but she had to duck to avoid another object being thrown at her. It hit the wood cabinet above her with a solid *thwack* and stuck.

Cori looked up at the potential headache and found an eight-inch chef's knife embedded in the wood, inches from her skull. She looked back at the goblin hopping up and down gleefully on the island. An entire wood block of knives was only inches from his clawed fingertips.

She screeched and ducked again, avoiding the continued onslaught of his cutlery ammunition. After narrowly escaping the loss of an ear, she surrendered the front line and retreated to safer ground.

He had won the battle, but not the war.

14

EVEN BEFORE THE FIRST official section, the hot humid air bathed them with the smell of a cattle yard. As they continued on, sporadic brays, cackles, and shrills echoed through the high ceilings.

"This is our animal sanctuary," Danato said loudly over the animal outcries. "These creatures are either animal mixes or humanoid-to-animal mixes. Either way, the only way to maintain them is through zoological standards. We take as much care feeding and tending to these creatures as a zookeeper would a cage full of lions, maybe more."

Ethan had thought the creatures in the basement were strange, but the animals here looked like lab experiments gone wrong. From folklore to mythology, this place was definitely the sum total of Dr. Moreau's wet dreams, and then some.

After they moved through a dizzying arrangement of metal and glass enclosures, they slipped through an airlock. On the other side, the air became notably more humid. The deafening hum of water pumps replaced the jungle hullabaloo. The manure smell was a fragrant memory compared to the dead fish smell that lingered in this section. Ethan raised his hand to his nose, defending against the upheaval of his breakfast.

"These are obviously our water-bound serpents and sprites," Danato said. "There are a few mermaids and mermen in this area. They won't come out while I'm here. They are tricksters, though, so don't make any assumptions when you're in here. I would much prefer to have them on the fourth floor, but we don't want to move the water system. Anyway, mermaids are a generalized term for us as well. The type you are familiar with are seductive sprites, while the type I am familiar with... well, let's just go back to the part where I said all the inmates here are human killers."

They walked between cylinder aquariums that reached ten feet tall and up to fifteen feet in diameter. He saw several mermaids, or sprites, as Danato had called them. They pushed against the glass, blowing him kisses and rubbing their hands over their scaly feminine bodies. He kept his head low, but he couldn't help but peek over at the fisherman's fantasy.

It wasn't until he bumped into the back of Danato that he realized they had reached the next airlock. Danato glanced back at him. Ethan had expected the big man to lecture him about paying attention, but Danato just gave him a knowing smile. "Look, but don't touch."

Ethan cleared his throat and bit back a smile as he felt heat rise into his cheeks.

Through the next air lock, there was no particular smell. The air was drier, and the temperature was noticeably warmer. There weren't any cages either. The room was an indoor forest. Gigantic potted trees, much like one might expect to see at a mall, lined the walls. "What is this, a conservatory?" he asked.

"Aviary."

"For what?" he asked, probing the air for any manner of flying creature.

"Come on. She's more afraid of us than we are of her." Danato moved on, and Ethan kept right in line with him.

After passing the west entrance to the infirmary, they finished the remaining loop of enclosures and ended up back where they started at the east elevators.

With the whole of mythology in their wake, they got back on the lift and headed up to the next floor.

15

ORI SCREAMED AND FLUNG the vicious creature from her shoulders. He landed in the fireplace, which was sadly not lit. She ignored the searing pain in her back and picked up the broom from the floor in front of her.

She raised the straw bristles high and continued to smack the annoying goblin that was swinging on the dining room chandelier. "Get off! Get off! Get off!" she chanted through gritted teeth.

The dexterous little brat was quick, but she got one good whack that launched him into the living room where he collided with a lamp.

She turned her broom to face any other attackers, but there were none in sight. She felt something warm on her leg and looked down. The smallest of the slime-balls wasn't much of a fighter, but he was the sneakiest. He looked up at her, sneering, or perhaps grinning, as he freely peed on her leg.

Cori raised her head and screamed into the rafters. "I hate this place!"

16

THE ELEVATOR DOORS OPENED with a muted "ponk" rather than the usual melodious "ping." Ethan moved to exit, but Danato put out his arm to stop him. "This is our part-time level. We don't need to tour through the whole level. Even with full attendance, we barely use a third of it. For the most part, it's all lycanthropes. They maintain themselves well enough on their own except a few days out of the month, which, if registered with us, they are obliged to check-in for."

Danato pushed the button for the next floor, and they went up again. *Ponk.* This time, Ethan waited. The large man chewed his cheek as he looked out onto the floor before them. He opened his mouth to speak, but stopped.

"Do you want to skip this one, too?" Ethan asked just as the doors began to close.

Danato shoved his arm in the way, and the doors receded again. "No." He cleared his throat. "These are our transmorphs, as we call them. You may be more familiar with the term shape-shifters. We only house about a dozen right now. Again, the remainder of the floor is virtually empty. Someday we may have the ability to track down more of them, but as you might imagine, they are difficult to identify and even more difficult to acquire. Alive, anyway."

Danato paused, chewing his cheek again. "We don't have a lot to fear from them, while they are in containment, but they can change into anyone they have seen, in person or in a photograph. As long as you know that they can do that, there really shouldn't be any threat." Danato stepped out of the elevator, but abruptly turned back. "That's not to say that they aren't dangerous. They are very talented manipulators."

"I get it."

"No, I just need you to understand that I have been here many, many years, and every time I come in here, they are different. No matter what you see, it is not the truth. It's always a lie."

"Okay," Ethan said.

They went into the hallway of barred cells. There was nothing to see. Humanoids standing, sitting, leaning against the bars. If Ethan had seen this level first, he would have assumed this was a normal prison.

No one had strange faces or animal parts. None of them hissed or clawed to get to him. In truth, it was boring compared to the previous levels. They walked through with no events.

Danato growled as they headed through to the next uninhabited section. "That was too easy."

"What?" Ethan asked as he looked over the empty cages.

"They know I've warned you. They are trying to underplay my concerns, so that you will drop your guard. I hate transmorphs; they *are* dangerous, but not in an obvious way. I hate that."

"Do they eat people too?"

"No, actually. They don't eat humans, but they will kill humans so they can take over their life, and some of them have the additional ability to encase the body of their victim. They become a rubber mask on the original being. Those are worse than others, because they are harder to identify. They have the ability to read the thoughts of their host, which allows for more realistic interaction."

"Wow."

"Yeah, there's a *big* file on them."

They trekked down to the west elevators and headed up to the next floor, which, Danato reminded him, was the seducers level. Judging by the twist in his mouth, Ethan assumed Danato was about to bite straight through his cheek in regard to the danger posed by these inmates.

They arrived at the level, and Danato led the way into the first section of cells. Ethan followed, observing the beauty that each enclosure contained. The aptly named seducers were behind thick glass or heavy metal bars. Hardened criminals they weren't. If the mermaid was a fisherman's cabin-fever fantasy, this place was the sane man's fantasy. Nothing short of the playboy mansion could compete against it.

"If you discount the destructive nature of the next two floors of inmates," Danato said softly, as if he didn't want the prisoners to hear him, "this floor is likely the most dangerous group you will ever meet. These are the seducers, mostly women, as you can see, all beautiful, all sexy, and all very dangerous."

Ethan offered some kind of response. It might have started out as 'mmm-hmm,' but it seemed to stop at the 'mmm.'

"Are you listening?" Danato elbowed him.

"Yes," he said. Whether it was true had yet to be determined.

"Oh, that reminds me, some of them are in soundproof glass. If for any reason the glass becomes compromised, plug your ears and run like hell."

"That doesn't sound reassuring."

"It wasn't meant to."

As they walked through the first section, a feminine giggle caught Ethan's ear. He glanced over at a cell with a woman in it. She wore a kimono and her hair wasn't hair, but rather long barbs like a porcupine. They came nearly two feet off her head.

He smiled at her, amused by her outrageous hair. He was about to laugh when Danato's hand clamped tightly around his mouth. "That's Harionna. We don't laugh at her, *ever*." Danato released his face, and they walked on.

Harionna giggled behind them, but Ethan had lost the tickle in his funny bone.

17

IT WAS JUST AFTER four when Ethan and Danato finished touring the upper levels. The details of the caging, restraints, and schedules for the seducers, sorcerers, and the elementals were boring beyond tolerance, but each detainee was as dangerous as the last and Danato wasn't remiss in reminding him of that with each and every prisoner.

He tried to make mental notes in his head, but after the hours, each detail blurred into the next. He wanted to explain to his self-appointed teacher that he was a terrible student and couldn't remember an important phone number, let alone the specifics of the different inmates, but Danato was oblivious to his brain fog.

They made their way back down to the main foyer to bundle up against the cold arctic temperatures outside. Ethan was famished; his cafeteria lunch was now only a memory to his stomach. He was looking forward to a home-cooked meal. He hoped beyond hope that Missy had already prepared the meal and that he only needed to sit down at the table and serve up his plate.

As they approached the front door, his stomach lurched in sickening hunger as he saw what had to be the house's entire food supply spilled onto the front porch. He glanced at Danato, but he didn't seem affected by this discovery. His stride, however, did increase to a limping gallop.

Ethan didn't bother speeding up. He lagged behind in case Danato wished to rebuke Missy in private. When no such bellows followed Danato's entrance, he went in.

The scene was no less than devastating: shattered dishes, ripped curtains, mashed food. Every cabinet door was ajar, its contents scattered across the floor. Yellow foam spilled from the eviscerated couch in the living room. Soot from the fireplace dusted all the furniture. Even the wall hangings were off kilter or outright missing.

"What the hell happened in here?" Ethan asked almost peevishly, but then he spotted Missy. She was crouched against a living room chair, nearly catatonic. Scratches and bruises covered her face and arms. "Bloody hell, are you okay?" he asked, significantly more sympathetic.

In addition to her disheveled hair and clothes, Missy was covered in all manner of food and... "What's that smell?" He wrinkled his nose at the foul odor permeating the air.

"It's shit," she said, staring out from glassy eyes. Her voice sounded hoarse. She didn't appear to be angry or sickened by the situation, just exhausted. "They threw shit at me. They peed on me, and I think one even—" She gagged.

"Ethan," Danato said in a quiet voice as he stood over her. "Why don't you run Missy a bath: warm and sudsy. There is a bottle of disinfectant below the sink for her wounds and another liquid in an orange bottle for the bath water. Just a tablespoon of that in the water will get rid of the smell."

"Sure." He headed to the bathroom and started the water, running it until it got nice and hot. He added the orange bottled liquid, which smelled pungently like orange rind.

When he returned to the living room, Danato was sitting on the arm of the couch, looking over Missy carefully. He seemed to be evaluating how to handle her. "You got them out, I take it?" Danato asked.

"No," Missy said, still catatonic.

"No?" Danato whipped around, rechecking the room.

Ethan jumped at Danato's sudden alarm and repositioned himself to see behind the island. He didn't know what he was looking for, but judging by how Missy looked, he didn't think he would miss it.

"The others finally left," she continued, "but he stayed. Little bastard nearly took my head off with a cleaver."

"Where is he now?" Danato stood.

"In the fridge." She pointed vaguely.

"He's hiding in the fridge?" Danato questioned.

"No, I locked him in there."

Danato shook his head vigorously. "No, that's not possible. You can't catch goblins. They are too fast to be caught, too clever to trap, and too resourceful to imprison."

She finally made eye contact with him. She looked at him with a flat expression. She shrugged her shoulders. "He's in the fridge," she said, offering no new information to explain the apparent impossibility.

Danato headed to the kitchen, and Ethan followed. All the while, Danato still shook his head in disbelief. He opened the fridge without concern to its contents. Inside the plundered fridge sat a small, gangly green creature.

In one hand, the goblin had a tiny LED flashlight, and in the other a prism. The creature flashed the light on and off, hypnotized by the tiny rainbows inside the glass object. Danato looked back at Ethan before turning his wide eyes to Missy. "What did he... How did you... " he rambled.

"He likes the rainbows," was all she had to say about the situation.

Danato gently closed the door to the fridge and returned to Missy. He looked her over and chuckled. His headshake had a different disbelief powering it. He leaned down to pick her up.

"Don't touch me. I'm covered in poop," she warned. Danato scooped her up without pause and propped her on her feet. He pulled her chin to look at him. "Thank you." He hugged her.

Ethan couldn't imagine how a trashed house had prompted this grateful response, but he kept his questions to himself.

"Oh, now you're going to stink," she moaned.

"I've been covered in worse," Danato said as he released her.

"What's worse than this?"

Danato smiled. "You may have just made a few men's jobs easier, including mine." He nodded to the fridge when she didn't seem to grasp his meaning.

"It's just a glass paperweight from your desk." She shrugged. "Why did you do this to me? You left me here knowing that they would come."

"I knew you wouldn't follow my instructions."

"I have three knobs on my head from random things being thrown at me." She felt her head so she could point out her specific injuries.

"I empathize. I assure you. I really do, but if you can't wash a dish when I ask, how do I know you won't leave a door open, or leave something laying too close to a prison cell? This was a test and a lesson."

"Getting pissed on is a lesson?" Her voice cut out as she tried to raise her volume.

"No, the lesson was for me. It taught me I can't trust you yet." Danato walked away. Missy glared after him. She seemed to notice Ethan's presence for the first time and shared her scowl with him.

"What did I do?" he asked. Her face softened. "Oh crap, the water." He ran into the bathroom to prevent an overflow. He swirled the water with his fingers. "Is this too hot?" he hollered out to her.

When she reached over to check the water, he jumped, not aware she had followed him. "No, it's perfect. Thank you," she said softly.

He nodded and scooted around her to the door. He pulled the door shut to give her privacy. Just as he did, she yelped. He pushed back in. "What? What's wrong?"

"My back, my shirt is stuck."

She turned around, and he saw the large bloodstain that had clotted her shirt to her wound. Soundless tears streamed down her face in her reflection. He could tell she had met her stress limit for the day. "Yeah, you've got a big gash back here. Hang on, let me moisten it. The shirt will come off easier." He dampened a washcloth with cold water from the sink and wet the shirt down. Slowly, he peeled the shirt from her back.

He concentrated so much of his effort on making it painless; he was hardly aware when he finished pulling the shirt over her head that she wasn't wearing a bra. She was still in her pajamas from the morning. She shielded her breasts under her crossed arms, but not before he glimpsed her reflection in the mirror.

All at once, he could feel the soft skin of her back against his fingertips. He dabbed the wound a little longer as an excuse to keep touching her. His hormones left him more inebriated than any liquor could. The only thing that kept him from pressing his lips up against the back of her neck, aside from common decency, was the fact that she still smelled like goblin crap.

"Is it bad?" she asked, ignorant of the exotic fantasies going through his mind.

"No, well, yes. We should definitely get the disinfectant on this one once you're clean." He dared to trail his hand down her back as he reached down to pick up her shirt where she dropped it. "I need to get out of here. That smell is noxious," he said to reestablish an asexual banter. "Just hand your pants out the door. I'll get them in the wash right away." He frowned at the shirt in his hand. "Or throw them away."

He stepped out the door, leaving it slightly open. She handed her pants out just as he asked and shut the door. After getting her clothes in the washer, he waited in her bedroom with the disinfectant.

Not entirely sure how casual sitting on the bed would look compared to lying on it, he skipped the bed altogether and sat on the floor, leaning against it. Nearly an hour later, he had drifted off with his head back, mouth open, and snoring. Not the image he wanted to pose for her.

He woke when he felt water dripping on his arm. She was standing over him with her usual malevolent demeanor back. "What are you doing?"

He searched around with his hands and found the disinfectant. He held it up, but she still looked at him, clearly annoyed. "Fine, forget it. Reach around your own back."

He tossed the bottle on her bed and left. Expecting to hear nothing from her the rest of the night, he dove straight into a mystery novel to take his mind off her, but by chapter two there was a knock at his door. "Come in."

She peeked in and saw him reading on his bed. "Are you busy?"

"No." He put the book down.

"Can you put this stuff on my back?" Though she sounded genuinely apologetic, he raised his chin, debating whether he should cast her off. She rolled her eyes. "Please."

He sighed and waved her in. She was still in her towel. She sat on the edge of the bed and gave him the bottle. She loosened her towel to reveal more of the wound, as well as the soft skin that had been so alluring to him earlier.

He dabbed the disinfectant on gruffly at first, but he saw her back stiffen and jaw clench, so he changed to a more gentle application. As her muscles relaxed, he felt the warmth for her he had felt before.

He hadn't had many opportunities to be this close to a woman. His body was ever vigilant to remind him of it, too. He forced himself to stop before he created a situation that he couldn't come back from without agony. "There, all done." He handed the bottle back to her.

"Thank you." She turned to face him, and her eyes narrowed on his cheek. "What did you do?" She nodded to his fresh scratches.

"Oh," he touched the wound. "Ah...vampire...or whatever Danato calls them. It's just a scratch."

"Well..." She swallowed hard. "I'm glad you didn't get eaten."

Ethan smiled at her. "Thanks."

She turned away and shifted her towel to tighten it. The adjustment left the towel parted at her thigh. He immediately noticed the soft, damp, muscular leg on his bed, just inches from his hand. He wanted nothing more than to touch it, to squeeze it, to trail his fingers up toward the warmth between—

"Stop it."

His eyes shot up to hers. She had seen him ogle her leg. She didn't look angry, just disappointed, and almost sad. He felt his cheeks burn with shame.

He scrambled for a lie. "I... wasn't..."

She moved off the bed and stomped to the door.

"Missy, wait," he scrambled to stop her before they once again lost the civil ground they had achieved.

"Leave me alone," she conditioned as she left his room and headed to her bedroom.

"Can I at least apologize?" He jammed his foot in the door before she could slam it in his face.

"Move!" she yelled at him.

"Missy?" Danato's voice traveled upstairs. "Are you okay?" They both glanced toward the balcony and then at each other. Ethan dragged his foot out of her doorway and crossed his arms, waiting to hear her answer.

"Missy?" Danato called more urgently.

"I'm okay," she called down to him. He waited for her to close the door on him, but she didn't. "I'm not going to be that girl for you," she said.

"What?"

"I can't be that girl for anyone anymore. Let's not pretend that this little arrangement is somehow a romantic love story in the making."

Ethan nodded, feeling the sting of rejection. "I am not asking you to be anything, or do anything. I can respect your boundaries, but..."

"But what?" she narrowed her eyes.

He braced his hands on the door frame. "You have got to cut me some slack. I am not like those bastards. I'm not going to hurt you."

Missy shifted back a little. Ethan frowned at the contradictory response to his appeal, but he understood it. She was so fearful of the wrong interaction that every interaction felt dangerous.

He waited for her to acknowledge his statement, but she didn't speak. Her gaze danced at his feet, avoiding his face. If she hadn't been holding the door and her towel, he thought she might be furiously biting at her nails.

"Ethan," Danato called up again. "Come help me clean this mess up."

Missy finally looked up at him, seemingly relieved by the interruption. He held her gaze a moment before shifting away from the door. "Coming," he called back down to Danato.

For now, he needed to give up on trying to convince her he was a good guy. Simply saying it wasn't enough. In time, she would see it for herself. Until then, he would just have to be patient.

D ANATO LOOKED UP WHEN he saw Belus come into his office. His usual aloof demeanor seemed to have an agenda. He looked over at Ethan, who was reading one of the many files he needed to memorize. He had been on the task for two weeks now, and was making a rather good dent in the material. Despite his aversion to studying, he seemed to be good at it.

"Hey, kid." Belus waited for Ethan to look up at him. "Go for a walk." He nodded his head to the door.

Ethan looked affronted by the request. He looked at Danato, and he gave him a permissive nod. Ethan placed his folder in the file cabinet and left the office. Danato imagined he wouldn't go far. At best, he might go to the cafeteria and wait for someone to tell him otherwise.

Ethan was a wise choice in many ways, but the traits that made him a good and compliant student were also his shortcomings. Danato wasn't sure how, but somehow he had to get Missy's audacity to rub off on Ethan, and Ethan's compliance to rub off on her. If he could have combined them, he would have had the perfect successor.

After Ethan was gone, Belus sat down. "It's time to talk about this."

"Talk about what?" Danato asked, feigning ignorance. He knew exactly what Belus wanted to talk about. He was actually surprised he had waited this long to bring it up. His restraint probably had more to do with letting Danato's temper settle than any regard for his privacy.

"You know what." Belus was his second in command, but sometimes it felt the other way around. Had Belus been a few inches taller, that might have been the case. Not that he would ever allow that as an excuse for his runner-up position.

"Everything is going fine, Belus. There is nothing to discuss. Ethan has taken to the idea of working here rather well. I think he is happy to be out of the foster system. The duties are giving him perspective."

"Yes." Belus crossed his arms. "You've chosen well. I look forward to seeing him develop. Of course, we both know it's not Ethan that I'm concerned about."

Danato sat back to face off with Belus, like high noon on the western frontier. All that was missing was the gentle breeze to push a random tumbleweed between them. "What do you want me to say, Belus? It's done."

"Yes, and now it can't be undone. Not without violating a lot of rules, but again, that's not why I'm here, either. I'm sure she'll work out if you can get her to accept her new situation."

"Then why are you here?"

"Do you really think I didn't notice?"

"What?" Danato said, honestly dumbstruck by Belus's question.

Belus threw his hands up and stood. He turned away for a moment. Most people would have taken that for anger, but Danato knew it was far more complex than that. Everything between them was complicated, whether it was or not.

Belus turned back to him. Whatever emotion he was feeling was gone from his face. He was in control again. "She's a spitting image of *her*."

There was no malice in his tone, but Danato rose from his chair, anyway. Belus didn't flinch. There were not many men that could stand tall in the face of Danato's girth, but Belus was at the top of that short list. "And?" he offered Belus the option to continue, but it wasn't a pleasant invitation.

Belus stepped forward with a long sigh and placed his hands on the edge of the desk. He gripped it hard and looked up at Danato. He looked like he was about to tell him he had just run over his dog: a mixture of grief, shame, and determination. "I need to know what you intend to do with her."

Danato could feel the blood rush to his face. His whole body felt feverish. If he had the ability to turn into a big burly green comic book monster, he would have at that moment. Instead, he just turned into a red-faced man shaking with the adrenaline of his anger. "What are you suggesting?" he said without the composure he had intended.

"I'm not suggesting anything, Danato." Belus raised his volume a little, if only to match the intensity of the conversation. "I'm asking you."

"You think I brought her here..." Danato felt his upper lip twitch. "...for me?" Belus looked away, confirming the accusation. "She's... just a girl."

"She's hardly a child."

"She is to me! Christ Belus! How could you think I would do that?"

"I wasn't assuming anything with regard to you personally, but it's been four years. You haven't exactly dealt with things."

"Oh, don't bring that up," Danato said, sitting down again. He was as much embarrassed as he was angry now. His second in command had all but accused him of using Missy as a mail-order bride. Aside from the fact that he was old enough to be her father, that was exactly how he treated her. Like a father.

"I was concerned you might have considered her as a replacement." Danato looked at him blankly. He wasn't entirely sure Belus meant what he thought he meant. "I just wanted to make sure you weren't trying to get her back."

Danato stared in amazed shock at Belus. Too many emotions were crashing together. Just as all mixed colors eventually turn to gray, his mixed emotions turned to dumbstruck and rendered him speechless. He wasn't even sure that what Belus was suggesting was possible, but even if it were, he would never have done it.

"I'm sorry if I've insulted you. I just needed to make sure you weren't heading down a dangerous path."

Danato nodded. He understood now why Belus was concerned. He was only trying to protect the girl, and him, in his overbearing way. "I don't know why I brought her here. I can't deny the similarities, but I assure you, I meant no harm to her. I just know I couldn't have left her there."

Belus nodded sympathetically. "How is she doing with the transition?"

Danato rolled his eyes at that. "She's a hot-headed, stubborn, pain in the ass."

"Huh." Belus rutted his brow in consternation. "I've never known anyone like that." He chuckled before Danato could offer him a glare. "Good luck with that," Belus said as he headed out again.

19

REMARKABLY, IT ONLY TOOK Cori a few weeks of good behavior to get out of the house and start training for her duties inside the prison. She was more than happy to be rid of the constant duties of cleaning up after her male roommates. However, two months in, she realized she had just graduated to being the maid for bigger and smellier animals.

She shoved her janitor's cart out of the elevator and onto level 2—or level 1, depending on if you called the main floor level 1 or level M, which apparently no one in the prison, including Danato, could decide on. Fully garbed for her day in a pale yellow jumpsuit, she completed her outfit with safety goggles and gloves.

She had the recurring task of cleaning the facilities, cages, and tanks of the sixty-plus creatures that inhabited the animal floor. They did nothing but eat, sleep, and poop. They all did each as messily as possible, too. The ones that barely slept ate more, and therefore pooped more. The ones that barely pooped made up for it by throwing their food all over their cage. The ones that did almost nothing but sleep seemed to go through violent attacks in their slumber, which mashed the food and poop onto every surface of the floor, walls, and even ceiling of the cell.

No doubt about it, she had gone from bad to worse. Her only consolation was that she was plotting her escape. She had already learned that semi-trucks arrived at the facility almost daily to deliver food and supplies. It was only a matter of time until she could coordinate her schedule with a delivery time, and conceal herself on the outbound truck.

She wasn't really worried about either, since to her knowledge, no one in the prison cared where she was as long as she cleaned up the animal dung. Since most of the guards were men, she could succumb to her baser female talents and manipulate one into helping her, if need be. It wasn't her preferred angle, but at this point, she was desperate enough to try anything.

After she finished cleaning her designated cell for the day, which took her nearly four hours, she loaded up her cleaning supplies. She put a big orange sticker on the front of the cage to let the transporters know the animal could be returned. Not that the *de-crap-a-fied* cage wasn't completely obvious, but it was all part of protocol.

Cori removed her goggles, gloves, and jumpsuit. She bundled them together and shoved them into a laundry chute on the wall. Each section had a similar depository for contaminated or dirty materials.

The prison laundry service was highly effective, since everything that dropped through the chutes went directly into the incinerator. After all, the remaining ash of the deposited material was no longer contaminated, nor relevantly dirty.

Although wasteful and expensive, it prevented any and all cross-contamination between cells which, depending on the prison cell, could cost far more in lives than in money. She had surmised that it might also have something to do with the fact that Griffin crap smelled as bad as isonitriles—which were patented as nonlethal weapons. There wasn't a laundry detergent on the planet that could get that smell out.

She pushed her squeaky cart past the aquarium section on her way to the west elevators. She noticed a glimmer of gold in one of the tanks. It was a ring. More importantly, it was *her* ring. It was a cheap thumb ring she used to wear with a series of rings on her hands. She had long since lost the other nine, but her thumb ring she had lost only a few weeks ago. She had taken it off to clean one of the cells and never found it again.

"Shit." She smashed her face against the tank to see what manner of evil lived inside. She couldn't see all the way to the back, but it appeared empty. "Damn it."

She leaned against the tank and surveyed the floor for the other staff. She wondered what the protocol was for this. The rules didn't allow her to retrieve the ring by herself, but her greater concern was pissing off Danato because she misplaced it in the first place. So, the real question was, could she get it out without him finding out about either indiscretion?

Due to the high concentration of magical elements, the facility had very few modern security features. There were no cameras anywhere in the prison. There were alarm systems rigged to the airlocks, cells and, as Danato had put it, a few borrowed spells to keep certain inmates in their place. That meant no one had to see her correct her mistake, but more importantly, she didn't have to be lectured about it.

She saw a hook attached to a long stick on the wall between the tanks. She retrieved it and climbed to the top of the ladder on the tank. She looked over the cool blue water. The water was blurry, but she could see all the way to the bottom.

Empty.

She dipped the stick in. After a few tries, she managed to tip the ring up and hook it. She towed it in and grabbed it. With the ring safely in hand, she checked the tank once again.

Empty.

She set her hook on the ladder and slipped the ring into place on her right thumb. A flicker in her peripheral disrupted her moment of admiration.

There was a movement in the tank. The tiles lining the bottom of the aquarium shifted. Before she could understand what was happening, the eyes of a chameleon creature fluttered open, followed by a razor-toothed mouth. It shot up through the water at her.

The chameleon's male torso emerged from the water. There was barely time to gasp before he had her. He grabbed her shoulders and pulled her into the tank. His fish body kicked away from the surface, dragging her deeper.

She struggled and pulled one arm free. His mouth opened, revealing shark-like rows of teeth. She pushed on his neck to keep the teeth as far away as possible, but she knew he could just wait out her air supply. She was about to die.

Killed by a flippin' mermaid. What a lame death.

As she struggled to push him away, she felt the creases of gills on the side of his neck. She shoved her fingers into them. He shrieked at this torture. Encouraged, she pulled her legs up around his neck and placed a vice grip hold on the gills, then yanked at them as if she intended to pull his head clean off. The creature screeched and bit her leg. Tiny sharp teeth dug into her like a miniature bear trap. She ignored the pain. Her desperation for air was outweighing the pain.

He pushed up off the floor of the aquarium and shot out of the water. She rocketed out right along with him. They landed on the floor out of the tank and broke apart. His slick body slid across the floor while she took the brunt of the impact on her back. Despite her urgent need for air, her lungs negotiated with her brain before letting her take in a full breath.

The alarms sounded from the sudden change in water volume. Help was on the way, in the form of heavily armed guards dressed all in black. Danato, her enraged owner and boss, would certainly join her saviors.

The merman shrieked angrily at her. He wasn't ready to give up. He was now more or less a paraplegic on the floor. He flopped forward, getting surprising speed with only his upper body. He lunged for her and tried to get at least one more bite before the guards interrupted his meal. She scrambled back, missing his grasp by only inches. She jumped up and grabbed the hook off the ladder just as he made it close enough for another swipe at her. She swung it at his head, hoping to knock him out, or at least daze him.

"No!" Danato's voice bellowed over the alarms, but his objection came a second too late. She hit the creature's head. The hook stuck with a sickening splotch. His skull wasn't firm like a human skull, and her hook buried deep into his occipital lobe. He fell flat against the floor, dragging the stick away from her as he did.

She had killed the merman.

She stared down at the scene, trying to rewind the last few seconds. She felt herself sweat with panic and she felt disconnected from her body. She looked up at Danato.

He stared back at her. A mixture of disappointments filtered through the rage on his face. The half dozen guards that were lined up behind him looked at the body. A few of them exchanged looks before lowering their unnecessary weapons.

She opened her mouth to speak, something in the way of a profuse and abject apology. Before she could get her words out, a piercing screech forced everyone to cover their ears.

"Contain her," Danato yelled over the ear-splitting sound. He pointed to the adjacent tank. Long, black, wet hair matted to the cheeks of a mermaid as she hoisted herself from her tank with the strength of her arms. Visible through her parted hair, she directed a loathsome fury at Cori.

The mermaid landed with a smack on the floor below the tank. The impact did nothing to slow her down. Her wet body glided easily across the floor as she clawed her way closer. Cori backed away, not wanting to defend herself again.

Two darts lodged in the mermaid's neck. She seemed unaffected, but after a few more feet, she slowed down. She lowered her torso to the ground, still emanating a muted version of her pitched shriek, even after her eyes closed.

The alarms stopped and the scene unraveled into awkward silence. Cori felt eyes on her. Danato stared her down, preparing for his own attack. Two men gathered the mermaid, while the other four waited to hear her explanation. What stupidity had caused this scene of murder to occur?

In a moment of irrational thought, she considered making a run for it. She needed to escape, before Danato arrested her for murder. He was going to lock her up with the rest of these reject nightmares.

"Come with me!" Danato's voice boomed. It always boomed. The man couldn't ask her to pass the salt without taxing her eardrums. Today was no exception, but today his voice had the added effect of making her legs shake.

Danato moved away from her toward the west elevators where he had come from. She didn't follow. Her legs had turned to jelly and the only thing keeping her breakfast down was the hard knot in her throat.

He turned back slowly and examined her immobile body. There wasn't room for any more anger on his face, but something changed to make him that much scarier.

She ran.

She couldn't understand it. Her legs only moments before were useless, but now she was running at full speed to the east elevators.

She hadn't run from the merman that attacked her; she hadn't run from the mermaid that was going to attack her, but she ran from him. She could face all the horrific monsters of this prison day in and day out, but she couldn't face him.

She hit the elevator with wings to spare on her shoes. She looked back, but he wasn't following. She considered hitting the button for the main floor, but the sluggish, antiquated elevator wouldn't beat anyone going down a flight of stairs, cane or otherwise, so she went up.

20

ORI DIDN'T HAVE PERMISSION to go into the elemental section, but she could get access to the roof stairs without going into the area. The elevator doors opened to reveal a brick wall. Against the brick wall was a solid metal door that required a code to access.

She knew little about the elementals, but she knew not to go through that door. She swung around the corner of the elevator and went into the stairwell to take the last flight to the roof.

When the door opened, she felt the stinging icy wind, but she didn't care. She ran out onto the roof. The brick rim surrounding the edge reminded her again of a castle. However, the multitude of heating vents, air ducts, and fans lining the roof had the opposite effect. Several guards walked the perimeter of the roof. More than one noted her sudden appearance and ignored her. Cigarettes and rifles in hand, they continued to survey the grounds below.

She found two tall air returns and crouched down into a ball to protect herself from the cold. She was crying already, but even if she hadn't, the brisk wind would have forced her eyes to water. She tucked her head into her knees and sobbed.

She felt ashamed on too many levels to count. She even felt ashamed at how ashamed she felt. She could have asked for help with the ring. She could have run when the merman released her. She could have taken her punishment instead of running onto the roof to cower.

She could hear voices and footsteps coming toward her. She covered her ears. She didn't want to hear his voice. She didn't want another lecture.

She was always the one who failed. His impractical expectations made it impossible for her to be the person he seemed to think she was. It only reminded her of how much she didn't belong here.

The footsteps scuffed to a stop beside her. The body looming over her blocked part of the arctic gale. She pinched her eyes shut and waited for the booming voice to crush her into a pathetic, wailing child. As it was, she didn't have far to go.

"Missy." The voice wasn't booming. It wasn't Danato.

She looked up, blinking away the bright sun to identify her seeker. "Ethan?"

She had hardly seen him in the last few months. He spent nearly every bit of his day shadowing Danato and every evening he worked late in the prison, studying the many documents he had to learn before he could start his guard duties.

His shoulders seemed broader; his face and body had filled in. He was no longer a gaunt, starved boy. He was a young man with budding muscles and a great deal more poise than he had the first week here.

"Where is he?" She peeked around the corner of the air duct.

"Danato?" he asked, looking around himself.

"Yes."

"Back in his office. He said you'd had a bad day and I should take you home." He crossed his arms, rubbing the cold out of them.

She shook her head. "This is a trick to get me off the roof, isn't it?"

Ethan moved between the air ducts and crouched down against the opposite duct. "Trick you? If he wanted you off this roof, he would come up and drag you off himself."

"Why did he send you then?"

"He didn't tell me anything more than to come get you. Why, what happened today?"

She cringed and shook her head.

He reached over and smacked the side of her leg. She noticed he was making an effort to keep all of his contact with her, brief and unmistakably chummy. "Hey, talk, what is it?"

"I killed one of the inmates." Her voice cracked, and she buried her head in her knees to hide her tears.

"What? How did you... Why?"

She looked back at him. He looked confused, but sympathetic. "I didn't even... he lunged... I hit him. I didn't know his skull was made of papier-fucking-mache!"

Ethan's lips disappeared as he bit them back. He looked down as he tried to warm his hands between his legs. "If it was self-defense—" he started.

"I got my stupid ring out of the tank. I didn't think anything was in there. He'll yell at me for being stupid, arrogant, and foolhardy. I just can't take it anymore."

"He might just be mad that you didn't trust him enough to come to him for help. All that anger is just his way of showing his concern for you."

"Bullshit, he doesn't care about me," she grumbled.

"Yes, he does." Ethan scoffed. "That's why you're not in some rich man's harem right now. That's why you have a bed, instead of a cot. That's why he yells at you when you put yourself in harm's way. What bothers you more? That he's going to yell at you, or that you've disappointed him?"

"Oh, shut up with the psychology stuff."

"Face it, Missy; our dysfunctional little trio has the makings of a distorted family psychosis. He's the father figure we can never entirely be good enough for. You and I have the sibling rivalry that borders on abusive. And this..." He swirled his finger at her. "This is regression, if I ever saw it."

"Seriously, how many shrinks have you seen?"

His mouth twisted in a resistant smile. "Too many. Look, I know he's tough to take some days, but he must have sent me up here for a reason. Maybe he could see you weren't in any condition to deal with him. Or maybe he just didn't want to come out onto this freezing cold roof. Crap!" He stood and jumped up and down, rubbing his arms and covering his reddened ears. "Let's go, I'm taking you home."

He put out his hand for her to take, but she just stared at him. He waved both hands for her to join. When she still didn't stand, he kneeled back down in front of her. "Hot cocoa with marshmallows." He stuck out a finger on his shaking hand to count off his offers. "A blazing fireplace, a soft warm blanket." He chuckled. "I will even rub your feet." He looked her over, then thrust his five splayed fingers in her face. "I won't let him yell at you." She saw his chin thrust as he made the statement. "I promise."

Whether he could keep that promise was moot, but judging by the resolution in his voice, he intended to try. She raised her hand, and he stood.

He gripped her hand firmly and pulled her up. He shook his head at her as he tucked his fingers under his arms. "Next time, just hide in the stairwell. You know he hates stairs." He walked on, and she followed behind him.

21

Aᶠᵗᵉʳ **FTER WARMING BY THE** fire for a while, Cori slipped into Danato's favorite chair and sipped on the hot chocolate Ethan had made for her. He stayed by the fireplace and watched the flames. His floppy blond locks glowed in the firelight.

"I recall an offering of a foot massage," she mumbled into her cup.

He looked over at her, seemingly surprised she was still there. "I was just saying that to get you off the roof."

She pulled her socks off and thrust her feet at him, wiggling her toes.

He grimaced, but slid over to lean against the chair. He took one foot under his arm. As an afterthought, she grabbed a fist full of his hair, making him grunt. "No tickling."

"No tickling." He conceded and began rubbing her feet. She released her grip, allowing the soft locks to fall from her fingers. She combed her fingers back through his hair to settle the ruts she had created. And then again, just because she wanted to.

His hands were softer than she had expected, but they were warm. He kneaded his fingers into the pads on her foot skillfully. She rested her head back and enjoyed the massage. She jumped when he used his knuckles, but it wasn't painful, just intense.

"Do you want to talk about it?" he asked without looking back at her.

"Not really." She took in a deep breath. "I've never killed anyone before."

"You still haven't. You just dispatched a nuisance rodent."

"That doesn't help. I don't even like using mouse traps. Besides, I don't think Danato will see it that way." She felt his hands move up to her ankle, but she could hardly object, since it felt so good.

"Don't worry about Danato. I can handle him." She chuckled. "What?"

"You really aren't afraid of him, are you?" He didn't answer. "Are you happy here?" He shrugged and touched his cheek. He turned to look at her.

"I suppose that would make me weak in your eyes."

She blinked at him. "No, of course not. Happy is whatever you need and want all rolled up into a ball. This is definitely not something that either one of us could have planned for, but maybe for you it's okay?"

"But not for you?" His hands moved up her leg, grazing her calf gently, unmistakably sensually. "Maybe someday you'll change your mind about this place."

Cori stared into his begging eyes. His veiled question was more about him than about the prison. A question she thought she had already answered. He was a sweet young man, and someday his cute face would be handsome, but until then she could only see a boy. "This place is interesting, and I'd be lying if I said that it wasn't a little alluring, but I don't think I could ever call it home. Maybe if there weren't so many bad memories connected to it."

"It seems like such a waste. Throwing away what might be a happy life, just because the parts leading up to it sucked."

"Yeah, I suppose you're right. Maybe I just need a little more time to get used to everything and everyone." She gave him a small smile. She knew she shouldn't encourage something she couldn't deliver on, but his logic was sound. She might not have hated the prison and Danato so much if she hadn't been through the ringer with Yvette prior to her arrival. Perhaps her camaraderie with Ethan could bloom into more if she didn't have the memory of lascivious men in her rearview mirror. Unfortunately, that wasn't the case. "Ethan, I'm not sure if—" Cori started to dismantle the hope that she had just created, but Ethan interrupted her.

"Are you getting hungry? I should start supper." Before she could continue, he stood and moved into the kitchen.

"Hey, what about the other foot?"

He looked over at her from behind the island. A small mischievous smile crept onto his face. "Rain check. It's not like we're going anywhere."

She nodded. "Not yet anyway," she mumbled.

Ethan prepared dinner, and a half hour later, they sat down to an early meal. In an effort to change up his limited menu of grilled cheese, he made Monte Cristos. Cori hadn't really been hungry, but after sitting by the fire and smelling the food being prepared, she was more than ready when he finally called her over.

She scarfed down half her sandwich before he finished pouring the milk. He smiled at her from across the table. "Good, I take it?"

"Sorry," she said over a stuffed mouth.

"Don't apologize. I'm shit in the kitchen. If you don't get food poisoning, it's a good day."

She swallowed down her mouthful with a sip of her milk. "I'm sorry I screwed up your day."

"You didn't." He looked at his still untouched sandwich. "I kind of missed you." He chuckled. "That sounds stupid, but everyone here is supposed to be here, ya know?" He looked up at her. "Not like us, right?"

"Right." She held his gaze for a moment, not sure what else to say. He was so genuinely sweet. She couldn't understand how someone who claimed to have such a hard life could be so gentle. "How's the studying going?"

"I'm about ready to pitch those damn files into the hearth, but it is definitely interesting stuff."

"Interesting or scary as hell."

He shrugged and took a bite of his sandwich. "You have to admit." He spoke over his food. "This place is pretty damn awesome."

Cori shook her head. "Not for me. I'm getting my introduction to this place from the ass end. And I do mean ass. I've never seen so much poop in my life."

Ethan laughed heartily and she couldn't help joining in. It was the first time she had laughed in a long time. As their chuckles died down, they were left smiling across the table at each other. Ethan reached across the polished wood and touched her hand. "Missy, I know that you—"

Danato's abrupt entrance shattered the moment. Ethan pulled back his hand and straightened in his chair. Cori conversely shrank into hers.

Danato hung his coat and stomped past the table. "In my office, now," he barked without looking back at her. Down the hall, the office door slammed, and she felt every muscle in her body contract, begging her to ball into a fetal position.

"I hate him so much," she whispered, putting down her sandwich. Food, in general, was off the menu for the evening.

Ethan pushed out his chair. "I'll go talk to him."

"He's just going to yell at you, too."

"Good." He stood and wiped his mouth with a napkin, although he hadn't even taken a bite. "Maybe his voice will go hoarse and he won't have anything left for you." He winked and walked away.

Watching him head to the office, she wondered how many times he had faced men like Danato. How many had blustered and blew their authority in his face? Yet he was still willing to endure the wrath that was meant for her.

After she heard the office door open and shut, she moved to the stairs so she could hear their conversation. The walls were well insulated, but she assumed Danato's volume wouldn't be muffled by it.

"What the hell are you doing? You know I wanted to talk to her." Just as she suspected, Danato's voice was clear.

"I'm not letting you talk to her until you calm down." Ethan's voice was harder to hear, but since he was just inside the door, she got the gist of everything.

"This has nothing to do with you."

"I am the only rational person in this. You are angry—"

"You're damn right I'm angry!"

"—and *she* is terrified." Ethan paused. He must have gotten some reaction to that statement. "She feels guilty about what she's done. She knows she screwed up. She just doesn't want to get fed to the lions on top of it."

"I'm not going to pretend it didn't happen. She had no business being near that tank."

"Her ring was in the tank. The merman was chameleoned on the bottom. He baited her. She unfortunately fell for it."

"She should have come to me!"

"Yes, because you are such an understanding man. I'm sure you wouldn't have yelled at her for misplacing her ring in the first place."

She heard a dull thump. "This isn't a damn zoo! I have obligations to this prison. My men are at risk every time she screws up. I have to make her understand."

"I get that, but you also have obligations to this household."

There was another pause. "What are you talking about?"

"We aren't your pets, Danato." Cori heard the first hint of anger seep into Ethan's words. "You didn't stick us in cells in that prison. You put us in your home. We sleep under the same roof. We eat at the same table. You intended to make us a part of this place. If you want this to work, you have to decide between being our master or our mentor. You can't crush someone with your boot heel and still expect them to look up to you afterward."

There was a long silence.

"Send her in."

"I promised her I wouldn't let you yell at her."

"I..." his voice bellowed, but he lowered it. "...will try."

Ethan slipped out of the office and came down the hall. He saw her on the stairs and stopped at the base. He put one foot on the second step and leaned on the railing. "Time to bite the bullet."

She nodded and scooted off the landing to a standing position. She clunked down the stairs like a stalling child. She stopped across from him. She wanted to say something, something to note his gallantry. "I missed you too."

A smile crept onto his face, along with a little blush on his cheeks.

Cori rounded the stairs and entered the lion's den. Danato sat at his desk, looking through logbooks and papers with thick-rimmed glasses on the tip of his nose. She sat down in one of the chairs. "Close the door," he grunted. She stood and closed the door she had intentionally left open. "Sit down," he said before she had a chance to do so again.

He fumbled with his paperwork. He wouldn't meet her gaze. She got the distinct impression this was the only way he could keep his temper in check. "I had to make a decision today; a hard decision and technically one against the rules of the prison. Ask me what decision I made."

"What decision—"

"I made the decision to kill the mate of the merman you killed. Ask me why I did that."

"Why—"

"Because that mermaid would have stopped at nothing to avenge her mate's death. You wouldn't be able to step foot on that floor and possibly the prison without risking your life. I executed one of our prisoners to protect you."

His eyes flashed to her, and for a moment, his hands stopped moving. "I had to protect you because you killed her mate." He looked away and continued to rearrange his papers. "You killed her mate because he attacked you. He attacked you because you allowed yourself to get too close to the tank." His voice rose, and he clamped his hands together to keep them still. His knuckles turned white from the pressure. "You got too close to the tank because you wanted to get your piece of crap metal ring back!"

She cried, hearing the story from his perspective. There was nothing to say to defend herself. She was impulsive, reckless, and selfish.

"Let me see it," he said.

She looked up at him, not sure what he wanted.

"The ring. Let me see it."

She removed it from her thumb and handed it to him. He examined it for only a second before bending it flat between his large fingers and tossing it in the trash.

"There, now you have nothing to lose, nothing to go after, and nothing to risk your life for."

Her tears instantly stopped. Her body no longer felt the tight knot of guilt, and she was no longer concerned with his opinion of her. She met his gaze across the desk and his controlled anger shifted for a moment into confusion. He must have seen the change in her face. "Get out of here," he ordered.

She stood and opened the door.

"Why was it so important to get back?" Danato asked before she could close the door.

"It was my only belonging left from my life before slavery and captivity." She glanced at the trashcan. "Now, thanks to you, I have *nothing*." She slammed the door shut and went straight to bed.

22

C ORI TRUDGED INTO THE main prison, no less optimistic about her life in servitude than the day before. She wanted to find the silver lining in this place that Ethan did, but she just couldn't imagine spending the rest of her life in this unwelcoming place. The repetitive work was annoying, to say the least, but that wasn't what made her hate it so much.

She hated being alone.

Ethan was the only one she had anything in common with—and even that was limited to mutually forced captivity. He was a good guy; sweet and brave. She was glad that she had him as a sounding board to keep her sane. Unfortunately, she wasn't sure she wanted to get too attached to him, and she especially didn't want him to get attached to her.

Danato, on the other hand, was just a blustering, overbearing thug who pretended to be sincere in his concern for her, all the while taking every opportunity to intimidate her into doing his bidding. She wasn't sure how someone as kind-natured as Ethan could find camaraderie with such a man. She was apparently too weak-willed to tolerate him, or not weak-willed enough. The jury was still out on that evaluation.

Belus was the only other person she had interacted with in the facility, and he had thus far given her no impression whatsoever. If she had to gauge his personality from her brief encounters with him, she would assume that he disliked her. He all but avoided speaking to her, and even pointedly refused to look at her when she ventured to speak to him.

There were a number of reasons to be unhappy with her current situation, but the one that stuck out strongly in her mind was that she didn't like anyone. She was being forced to work in a job that she hated, under the scrutiny of an employer she hated and coworkers who hated her. And to top the cake, she could never go home, and she didn't have anyone to complain to about it.

After collecting her supply cart, Cori rolled it into the foyer and jammed her finger into the elevator call button. She heard Danato and Belus coming down the hall from his office. As their conversation drifted closer to her, she quietly begged the slow contraption to arrive promptly. To her surprise, it did.

She jumped in and pushed her cart to the back. She pressed the "door close" button to ensure that they would have to take the other elevator and not join her. She mistakenly pushed the number two and corrected by pushing number one.

The elevator gave a distressing squawk and began its precarious ascent. She hoped it wouldn't suddenly detach from its pulley and crash into the basement. Although that might have been an easy way to alleviate her current problems, she wasn't a big fan of dying.

The doors slid open on the animal floor and she started to back her cart out. She noticed two men waiting to get in. The prison usually contained two dozen guards at any one time—watching the grounds, inventorying prisoners, and doing maintenance—but she rarely saw them. Perhaps it was because most of them opted to use the stairs, or maybe it was because her duties rarely took her off the animal level. At any rate, it was nice to know that she wasn't the only one stuck in the prison.

She excused herself and her oversized plastic cart, but the guards stepped inside without waiting for her to exit. She perked her brow at the obvious elevator etiquette faux pas, but she only offered them an apologetic smile for being slow and cumbersome.

She gave her cart a tug to get it moving again, but the doors closed behind her. "Ah..." She glanced at the panel where one guard was pressing the "door close" button, the same one she had used moments before to escape Danato. "I needed that floor," she murmured.

"Oh, I'm sorry." He smiled and glanced at his partner behind her. She looked back at him and he gave her the same overly friendly smile. "To tell you the truth, I did it on purpose." He grimaced. "You see, my friend and I have seen you around, and we just wanted to introduce ourselves." He stepped forward, and she stepped back, for as little good as it did since his friend was ready to block her already stunted escape route.

Cori felt white-hot fear sink into her body. Paralyzing fear that made her instantly sick to her stomach. It was a familiar dread she had not long left behind.

She looked at the lascivious smiles aimed at her. They were meant to be suave, or provocative, or some other bullshit word to describe a man's I-want-to-fuck-you face. It was a wonder to her that men even bothered with the formality of sweet-talking women before they raped them. Foreplay perhaps; just a little time to get hard, so they had the proper motivation to rip a woman's clothing, security, and faith into shreds while she screamed and begged them to stop.

"Is that so?" she whispered, even though the part of her brain that was listening to them had shut down. That's all she had to do: just shut down. That's how she survived it before, and that's how she would survive it again. Make believe she wasn't even there, because in the end, she really wasn't.

"No need to cry, little flower." The guard touched her wet cheek. She trembled uncontrollably at his touch. "We aren't going to hurt you. We just want to get better acquainted with you."

"You want to get better acquainted with my body, you condescending prick!" Cori snapped. She knew she shouldn't say it. It would have been better if she hadn't. They might have at least been gentle if she hadn't pissed them off.

"Well, that's not very nice, little flower."

"I'm not the flower; I'm the thorns." Cori threw her palm up to break his nose, just as she had done during her auction, but he dodged it and punched her in the stomach. Aside from not being able to breathe, his fist had hit her rib. She doubled over, coughing. From the angle she was in, she could clearly see him unbuckle his pants. His friend pulled her back against his chest in a full nelson.

She should have picked her legs up and racked him. She should have used her body weight to slip out of the full nelson, roll over the cart, and press the emergency stop button, all while shoving the cart into them and screaming for help. That's what she should have done, but even as it all played out in her head, she knew she would still get raped. Maybe not today, and maybe not tomorrow, but in a facility with nearly forty male employees—and her apparently being the youngest of only a dozen female employees—she was going to have to suffer the consequences of this place, eventually. This was just the first of many *incidents* to come. No need to get bloody and bruised over something as trivial as losing her will to live.

The elevator doors opened sooner than anyone expected, without the usual proceeding *ponk*. Cori hadn't even felt the carriage come to a lobbing stop. The men abruptly released her, zipped up, and pretended that life was dandy again and not just an excuse for them to lord over people weaker than them.

For a moment, Cori had a glimmer of hope that today might not be the day, but then she saw the familiar uniform, black on black. Her shoulders sunk, and she looked at the floor. Now she had a third to be passed off to when the first two were done. She was pretty sure it wasn't a record for her, but it would be the first time she was fully lucid for the event. Who knew she would one day be thankful for injected sedatives?

"Well, what do we have here?" the man asked with a familiar American twang; Texan, if she wasn't mistaken. He stepped aboard and tapped the button for his floor. He looked her over, but she refused to look at him. She just lowered her head and watched her tears fall directly to the floor of the elevator.

"Nothing you need to be concerned about, Tex," the guard said as the doors shut again. "Just a friendly conversation with the lady."

"Friendly, huh? When I speak to the ladies, I don't make them cry."

"She's had a tough day; she was just sharing her woes. Isn't that right?" The guard tried to tip her chin, demanding a nod, but Cori just ripped her face away. She wouldn't obey, no matter what the underlying threat was. She might have given up her body, but *never* her mind.

The Texan chuckled and turned around to face the door. "You boys are new here, aren't you? Fresh out of a five to ten, I bet." They didn't answer. "You probably think this place is going to be a nice vacation from your previous confinement. I'd venture to guess by the looks of this scene, you haven't even met the warden yet, have you?" They still didn't answer, but Cori could tell by the way the guard in front of her was clenching his fists he wasn't happy. "You boys should really meet him. I hope, for your sake, that this is the first time you've tried to have a *conversation* with this little gal."

The elevator *ponked* again. The doors opened onto Belus and Danato in the main foyer, seemingly still waiting for an available lift. "It's about damn time," Danato griped before his eyes widened at the situation inside the elevator. Belus peeked in at the sight as well.

Cori froze, looking at Danato as he tried to discern her condition physically and emotionally. She wasn't sure if she should run out and hide behind him, or just wait and report this gross sexual harassment on paper so it could be stamped, cataloged, and forgotten about.

"Warden, sir, just the man I was looking for," the Texan chimed and stepped out to speak with him. With one arm lagging back, he blocked the doors from closing on her again. "You haven't met our new recruits. With all your attentions being split, they haven't had a chance to meet you." The men shifted their stance to look out at

Danato. "They did, however, get a chance to meet your young lady in training."

"Did they?" Danato's shock ebbed away, slowly being replaced by dark intent. "Sweetheart, would you roll that cart out here along with yourself?"

Cori felt her body shake even harder with the anticipation of being away from her aggressors. She shoved the cart out of the elevator and parked it haphazardly before looking at Danato for further instruction. Had he told her to do a handstand, she probably would have done it, so long as he kept her away from those men.

He reached out his hand and gestured with one finger. "Come here," he whispered so quietly she wasn't even sure he actually spoke it. She moved to him, but kept some distance between them. She didn't want to be near anyone at the moment. He seemed to understand her reservations and didn't actually touch her when he leaned into her ear to speak.

"Did they hurt you?" he asked.

"No, not yet," she whispered back.

"They are new. They don't know who I am yet. An oversight I am about to correct. I meant what I said to you before. No one, including my men, will hurt you like that again. If you trust nothing else I say, trust that."

Cori looked up at him. His eyes were sincere as he often seemed to be, but he also looked devastated, as if he had failed her by not preventing this encounter.

He moved his hand ever so slowly to her face and stroked her cheek with the back of his fingers. She allowed it, since he seemed to need to offer the affection as further reassurance.

"I'll take care of them. You can take the rest of the day off."

He lowered his hand and marched into the elevator. Cori turned just as the Texan guard lowered his arm and the doors shut on all four of them. Before the elevator was out of range on the floors above, Cori could hear screams of agony.

She grimaced and looked down at Belus, who seemed completely unfazed by the event. For several seconds, she didn't move, frozen by indecision. "Will he kill them?" she asked the dwarf.

He shook his head. "No. I imagine he will break nearly every bone in their hands, making them virtually useless for anything other than delivering meals."

"Are you serious?" Cori asked. She hadn't truly believed that Danato would be capable of protecting her from his men, but judging by the sounds that had come from the elevator; he was more than capable of keeping them under control.

Belus finally looked up at her. Since he rarely acknowledged her existence, it felt strange to have his full attention. It was as if he was looking at her for the first time. "Don't worry. They won't touch you again, and as soon as word of this gets around to the others, you'll be able to walk through the halls in a bikini without so much as a catcall."

"He would cripple his own men just to protect me? Why?"

Belus furrowed his brow. "I think the reasoning stands for itself. Danato's not the type of guy to let men hurt women, but I think he feels particularly predisposed to defend you."

"Because of my previous captivity," Cori added gingerly.

Belus frowned. "Something like that," he murmured and stared back at the elevator for a moment. He turned and motioned to the cart behind her. "You want me to put that away for you?"

The offer surprised Cori, but she had a feeling he was only doing it so he could dismiss himself or her from the awkward silence.

"Um, no, that's okay." She turned to grab the cart. "I should..." she started to say more to him as she wheeled the cart around, but he was already disappearing through the door to the stairwell. She sighed and pushed her cart back to the supply closet.

Yup, definitely alone.

23

C ORI STARTED THE NEXT day in just as sour a mood as she ended the day before. She was grateful to be saved by Danato and she was relieved he meant to make good on his promise to protect her, but it didn't really change anything. She was still an indentured servant, with no salary, no benefits, and no vacations—ever.

The only thing that had changed was that she didn't view Danato's sincerity as pretense. However, he was still an overbearing thug who was punishing her for inadvertently—and indirectly—killing the merman and mermaid from the other day. Evidently, almost being raped did not amend the ruling on killing an inmate.

Her duty roster unsympathetically dictated she clean the two now empty tanks on the animal level. It was to be her duty as well as her penance to clean them, since it would take her all day to clean both of them.

After garbing up in her pale yellow jumpsuit and gathering her supplies from the main level, she pushed her cart onto the west elevator. With the roster in mind, she pushed the button labeled 2 in the elevator. It sat just above the number 1 and the letter M on the panel.

She left the main floor with the great determination that comes with forced labor. When the elevator doors opened with the abridged *ponk*, she backed the cart out on its squeaky wheels. She stopped a few feet in.

She noticed the silence. There was no cacophony of chittering and yipping. No smell of manure. The air wasn't humid.

She had pushed the wrong button again.

Elevator second floor.

She was actually on the third floor.

She felt the hairs on the back of her neck stand up. She looked side to side and saw unfamiliar cages. Very large unfamiliar cages, and they were empty.

"Hello," a man spoke behind her.

She whipped around to see him. Standing behind her several feet away, she found a thirty-something-year-old man around six feet tall. His longish, wavy chestnut hair offset his narrowed jaw. He wasn't particularly brawny in his build, but his V-neck white t-shirt highlighted the strength in his torso. A fine layer of hair, almost fur-like, covered his chest and arms. His jeans were baggy and covered in something bright red.

She wasn't sure what he meant by "hello," but his smile was too broad to be just friendly and she wasn't about to make the same mistake twice.

She raised her spray bottle cleaner at him. "This is acid. It'll burn you."

He examined the bottle. "Looks like glass cleaner."

"I'm trained in self-defense. I could hurt you." She planted her feet.

"I doubt that," he said smugly, losing most of his smile.

"I've killed before," she said, trying to sound maniacal.

"I don't doubt *that*, but no, you can't hurt me." His Scottish accent became more pronounced as his bravado increased.

"I'm stronger than I look," she said.

"So am I. Not nearly as strong in this form, but still... far stronger than you." He took a step closer to her, and she squirted her Windex at him. The blue stream fell laughably short. He took a few more quick steps, and she squirted his shirt. He examined it. "It stinks. I don't like it."

He took the last two steps he needed to pull the bottle from her hand. He read the faded label and laughed at her. He tossed the bottle back on her cart and his eyes took her in from feet to face. His reddish-brown eyes locked onto her, and winked a set of black lashes that had no right to be worn by a man.

Keeping her eyes on him, she searched her cart for something to defend herself with. He saw the movement, but he bit back his smile. "Oh, please no, not the Ajax." He laughed at his joke just as she found the object of her search.

She pulled the screwdriver from her cart and stabbed it into his chest as hard as she could. She kept her aim low to avoid his heart. The last thing she needed was to kill another of Danato's inmates.

She buried the metal rod a couple of inches into him, evoking a yowl of pain from the man. He stumbled back, dropping the bottle of cleaner. He stared down at the handle protruding from his chest and scoffed. "Oh, you little minx."

She grabbed the walkie-talkie off the cart—that Danato had given her that morning, in case she ran into any trouble—and ran to the elevator. She dove back into the lift and pushed the button for the main floor. Regardless of her finger-bruising pressure on the "door close" button, the doors closed painfully slowly.

"Danato, Danato!" she yelled into the walkie-talkie, pressing and repressing the button to make sure it had in fact been pressed.

"Missy, what is it?" His voice came over the antiquated equipment distinctly.

"I got the wrong floor. There was a man or something out of his cage. He came at me, threatened me. I stabbed him with a screwdriver and ran," Cori ranted, huddling on the floor of the elevator.

"Which floor?" Danato asked.

"Two," she said.

"The animals?"

"No, elevator two. You guys really need to change the rosters!"

"Elevator two? A man? Tall, dark complexion, with hairy arms?"

"Yes, yes!"

Danato sighed. "Oh, Missy."

"Don't, 'Oh Missy' me. I'm supposed to call if I need help. Well, I'm calling. Help me!"

"Yes, good; I'm glad you called." He calmed his voice that much more, no doubt hoping to calm her as well. "You did the right thing. Listen to me very carefully." Danato paused. "Go back to the elevator second floor and give the man you stabbed the walkie-talkie."

"What? He threatened me!"

She heard Danato clear his throat. "He... what exactly did he say?"

Cori opened her mouth to retell the offensive story. "He said... hello." She beat the walkie-talkie against her head. "He did come at me, though."

"I see. Did he try to grab you, or was he just approaching?"

"He... was... just... coming toward me. I didn't like it," Cori added, hoping to rationalize her reaction.

"I know, sweetheart. It's okay, just go back and give him the walkie-talkie. *Don't* stab him again."

She growled, "Going." She crawled back to the controls and slammed her hand on the number two button. She stood up and waited for the doors to open. When they did, she saw the man standing with his back to her next to her cart.

She approached him slowly. "Hello."

He looked back and put his hands up. "Whoa, easy girl."

She danced around him a bit, not sure how to approach him. "I'm supposed to give you the radio." He smiled and put out his hand. She gave it to him and jumped back.

"Danato?" the man asked into the device.

"Vince, are you alright?" Danato asked over the line.

"Yeah, she got me between the ribs, but she didn't puncture my lung." Vince looked down at the screwdriver still poking out of his chest.

Cori crossed her arms and observed the conversation from a safe distance.

"She got the drop on you?" Danato asked, with levity in his voice.

"Lucky shot," he defended. "But she is definitely good. She's cute too." Vince winked at her, which prompted her to shift her position back another few feet and uncross her arms.

"Do you want me to send for the doctor?" Danato asked.

"No." Vince tugged the screwdriver out and tossed it onto her cart. "A stitch will do it."

"Good. Behave yourself, would you?"

"Don't I always?" Vince smirked at Cori.

Danato clicked off, and Vince tossed the walkie-talkie back to her. She caught it and rushed back to her cart. Without delay, she shoved it toward the elevator, more than ready to return to her regularly scheduled torment.

"Aren't you going to stay and help me get stitched up?" Vince called after her.

"No, I have work to do." She put a little more speed in her step.

"He won't mind. I'm one of his best inmates."

"If you're an inmate, why aren't you in a cage?" She waved to the cages on either side.

"I'll tell you, but you have to stay and patch me up. My ride doesn't leave until tonight; I'm really bored."

She kept rolling her cart.

"I'll answer any questions you want about this place."

She stopped. "Anything?"

"Anything I know, which is a lot."

She turned back. His wide smile returned.

"Ouch." Cori poked the needle through Vince's skin roughly. "Not so rough, I'm still a man right now." Vince lay sprawled on the bed in his cell, which looked more like a dorm room. He had pictures hung and small furnishings. The door was ajar and there was no sign of a guard to monitor him.

She kneeled on the floor beside him, playing nursemaid, albeit not very well. She was having trouble getting her needle through the wound. Plus, she had no idea what she was doing. She couldn't even darn a sock. "What are you usually?" She glanced up furtively from her stitching.

"I'm usually a man, but for a few days a month, I'm the not-so-better half of my werewolf self."

"Is that what the big cages are for?" she asked, tying a knot in her stitch.

"We all get two cages, one small for when we are human, and one big one for when we are full werewolves."

She smiled as she cut the excess thread. "So, I got the drop on a werewolf. Not so tough, then."

"Careful," Vince warned with a smile. "Werewolves have notoriously large egos. I will prove myself if provoked."

"What would you prove?" she scoffed, tossing her suture needle back in the small first-aid kit she took from her cart.

"That I can win."

"Win at what?" she asked.

"Anything, everything. Strength, speed, agility."

She looked him over, seeing a potential ally in her plan to escape her captivity. "How strong are you?" she asked enticingly as she traced her finger from the stab wound up his chest through a patch of soft, dark hair.

He glanced down at her finger. "Strong enough to resist an amateur seducer." She pulled her hands away and fidgeted before finding a spot in her lap for them. "Besides, you don't have to seduce me to get your answers. Just tell me what you want to know."

"How do I get out of here?" she asked without a prologue.

Vince chuckled. "I can tell you anything but that."

"Then we're done here." She closed the lid on her first-aid kit and stood. He grabbed her hand and pulled her to sit on the edge of his bed.

"I'll tell you, just not yet."

"When?" she asked.

"Not soon, but I will tell you how to leave here."

She wasn't satisfied with that, but since he was a friend of Danato's, she couldn't expect an outright betrayal from him. "What *can* you tell me?" she asked.

"My name." He arched an eyebrow.

"I already heard Danato say it."

"And...?" he prompted.

"Nice to meet you, Vince." She stood up again, but he didn't release her hand.

"And?" he said.

"What?"

He smiled, licking one of his canines. "And what is your name?"

"Everyone calls me Missy."

"That's not your name, though." Vince caressed her wrist with his finger. She glanced down at the intimacy, but fought the instinct to rip her hand away. As innocent as the flirtation was, it made her feel claustrophobic. As if sensing her discomfort, his hand slipped away.

She crossed her arms, tucking her hands tightly to her body. "That's what they call me." She shrugged.

His eyes flickered over her as he brewed his thought. After a pause, he sat up and pulled his t-shirt back on. "Let's go for a walk," he said, offering her the lead out of the cell.

"Where?" she asked suspiciously.

"To find your name." He placed his hand on her back and gently pressed her forward, out the door. He continued to usher her into the elevator and pushed the letter B.

When the doors opened on the basement level, she tucked herself against the back wall. "I'm not supposed to be here."

"It's okay." With very little effort, he pulled her hand from its tucked position and laced his fingers between hers. "Nothing down here can hurt me." He winked and headed out with her in tow.

"I was more concerned about me," she sniped. She dragged against him, intending to make a stand against his presumptuous plots, but her braced stance only left her stumbling after him. She could see that he wasn't being egotistical about his strength, but factual.

For the first time, she saw the infamous pale sickly creatures that lived in the basement cells. After Ethan's incident with them on his tour, Danato refused to bring her down to see them.

The double-sided hissing and snarling creatures left her whipping her head back and forth to see who the greatest threat was. "I've never been down here." She tried to pull her hand from his, but his grip showed no sign of flexing. She may as well have been in handcuffs. "It's not safe," she whined.

"You're with me," he said flatly, as if that should have made all the difference.

"Danato will be mad." She yanked his arm as hard as she could.

"I can handle Danato." He stopped and turned around. "Will you stop dragging your feet?" He pulled her forward, forcing her to bump right into him chest to chest. "You know it won't do any good." He towered over her, his reddish-brown eyes smiling even when his lips weren't.

"I don't want you to think I'm consenting to this," she fumed.

"I think it's implied. Now, pick up your feet or I'll carry you."

She started walking normally, but remained behind him. When they entered the next section, she saw more creatures expose their slobbering fangs. Several started rattling and humping their cell doors. More fearful of them than her guide, she closed the gap between their bodies.

Near the end of the section, he halted, and she bumped into him. "Okay, we're here."

"Where?" Cori saw no distinction between this cage and the twenty others they had just passed.

"Cleos? Are you awake?"

"Yes," said a voice from the darkened cell.

"I have something for you." Vince pulled her hand toward the cell.

"What? No!" She fought back. She hit him with her free fist and bit the hand that had her bound. He grabbed a fistful of her hair for leverage and pulled her mouth off him. "Let me go!!"

He kept her head tethered and pulled her against him. "Don't bite. Werewolves don't like that," he scolded firmly. "Well, sometimes," he amended before presenting her hand to the inmate.

"I don't like being fed to vampires," she whimpered.

"He's not a vampire. He's a photophobe."

A cold, clammy hand covered hers. She shrieked, but she couldn't stop the sacrifice. "Please, stop!" she begged. The pain she expected to follow never came. The creepy hand was just resting on hers. "What is he doing?" she panted.

"He's a reader. Dangerous, but always honest; partly why he's dangerous." Vince smiled at his joke, but then lost it suddenly. "But seriously, never do this without me."

"I don't want to do it *with* you," she griped.

"She's interesting, but what do you want to know?" Cleos asked. His face was still invisible in the darkness of his cell. All she could see were his pale hands and thick almond nails that bordered on feminine.

"Her name," Vince answered. "The real one, her birth name."

"Corinthia Ellen Reiger; most would call her Cori." The reader pulled his hand away.

She was uncomfortable with the ease with which the reader had discovered her name. However, she was more uncomfortable that her neck was still jack-knifed in Vince's grip. "Let go of me," she said calmly.

"That's a pretty grown-up name. Much better than Missy."

"Seriously, I'm getting a cramp in my neck."

"Oh, sorry." He released her.

"Call me whatever you want. Just get the hell away from me." She turned and ran before regaining her balance. Her confused equilibrium shifted her off the midline, but she couldn't stop it. She wobbled and fell against one of the cell doors.

Clawed fingers reached out, ripping at her hair, and drawing her dangerously close to hungry fangs. She screamed, and the creature moved its viselike grip to her throat.

Vince arrived and slammed his fist into the frail vampiric arm. The bones snapped, and the creature wailed in pain. He helped her up and put an arm around her as he rushed her back to the elevator.

Once she was safely in the lift, she pulled away from him. He turned to her and looked her over. He lifted her chin to check her neck, but she ripped out of his grip.

"Get off me!"

He sighed. "Are you okay?"

"No! I almost got eaten by a vampire!"

"No, never would have happened."

"Because I was with *you*?" she mocked. "None of that would have happened if I wasn't with *you* to begin with."

He huffed and leaned on the wall with her, his shoulder touching hers. "None of that would have happened, if you would have just given me your name," he pouted—if werewolves could pout. "Cori," he added.

She couldn't help but look at him. It was the first time she had heard her own name spoken to her in months. He smiled at her, his eyes twinkling with unrestrained flirtation.

She looked forward to the doors and tried not to encourage his behavior. "You shouldn't have brought me down here."

"I admit that wasn't the best choice for our first date."

"Date?" she scoffed and chuckled at his audacity. Who did he think he was? He was hot, no doubt, but heavy-handed was an understatement. Not to mention that ego.

He touched her arm, interrupting her internal evaluation of him. He trailed his finger down to her fisted palm and gently plucked at her fingers, begging for her to release her grip. She rolled her eyes and shook her head, refusing his childish endeavor.

Ever amused by her dissidence, he continued to tickle her clenched fingers. A smile crept onto her face, completely defying the long list of negatives she had just reminded herself of.

Surrendering to the game, she loosened her fingers, and he pushed into her palm. His long fingers sinuated through hers.

Satisfied with his minor conquest, he gave her hand a gentle squeeze and leaned back on the wall with her. As pubescent as the contact was, she felt her stomach flip.

25

V INCE LED THE WAY to Danato's office with her firmly in tow. He barged in, not bothering to knock. Danato looked up from his paperwork as they entered. Ethan sat with his feet on the short file cabinet, reading one of the books in Danato's substantial library. He did a double take at them, baffled at seeing them together.

"What did she do now?" Danato's shoulders slumped in anticipation.

"Hey!" Cori scowled back at him.

"No, no, I'm fine." Vince waved away his concerns. "I have someone to introduce to you." He announced with a grin as he swung their conjoined hands playfully.

Ethan's eyes shifted to their entwined fingers, and he leered at Vince. She wondered if it would make him feel better to know that her hand wasn't so much being held as it was being detained until further notice.

"We already know her," Danato said dryly, not willing to play along.

"Do you know her name, though?" Vince taunted.

"She hasn't told us." Danato glanced at her, revealing some of his disappointment with that particular fact.

"Her name is... oh, blast, what's the full version? I forgot it already. Cortney, Corrin."

"Corinthia!" she finally said herself.

"Yes, that's it, but we just call her Cori, though, right?"

"Apparently, since you can't remember it," she muttered bitterly.

"I remembered it," he whispered. "I just wanted you to say it yourself."

"You told this fleabag your name?" Ethan snapped.

"Hey, sport, no need to share insult." Vince tightened his grip and tugged her back, as if claiming her. He examined Ethan, gauging if he was a threat to his alpha-male status, but he must have found him to be harmless because he offered a contented smile before relaxing again.

"I'm not talking to you. I guess I'm talking to *Cori*." Ethan slammed his book shut and stood. "You just tell this guy your name in one day, even though I've... we've known you for months?"

"I didn't tell him," she defended. "The reader told him."

"Reader!" Danato stood so fast his chair slammed into the wall behind him.

"No, no, not her." Vince chuckled and pulled her back again, but this time for protection. "Downstairs. Cleos."

Danato came around his desk. He pushed Vince out of the way with one hand and drew her forward with the other. He looked over her neck, twisting her head this way and that. "There are marks here." Danato pushed her head to one side and pointed out the cuts to Vince.

"Only scratches. She lost her balance."

"Vince…" Danato's chest puffed.

"Danato, it's me." He gestured to himself. "I can protect her. You know that," Vince calmed him.

The two men faced off, silently bickering for the right to mount their white horses on her behalf. Meanwhile, her hand was stuck in one vice grip, and her face in another. She was beyond feeling claustrophobic and into the territory of feeling manhandled.

"Will both of you just LET ME GO!" she yelled, and they instantly released her. They both looked at the floor, and Danato took an additional step away from her.

"Cori—" Vince started.

"Don't!" She frowned at him. "Just leave me alone. I have work to do." She glanced at Danato, but he said nothing one way or another.

She didn't give any of them a chance to respond. She walked out, slammed the door behind her, and started her day over again.

She collected her cleaning supplies from the part-time level and went to the animal level to start her work on the first tank. Her trip to the basement had cost her a good chunk of time. She estimated that she wouldn't finish the work until well after supper. However, that wasn't what bothered her about the day's excursion.

The release of her name felt like a violation to her. She didn't care that everyone knew her name, but it was yet another example of something that was just hers, taken away from her.

As she scrubbed the interior of the tank, she noticed Vince outside the tank rummaging in her cart. "Hey!" He turned around and smiled at her. He gloved up and climbed into the adjacent tank with a brush and bottle of cleaner in hand. Through the soapy glass of her tank and the fogged glass of his, she watched him clean.

The gesture shocked her, but she had no intention of refusing it. She went back to cleaning and quickly developed a rhythm with her suds. As she watched his progress, she noticed he was making fast work of his tank as well. If she wasn't mistaken, he was competing to finish cleaning his tank before her.

They didn't speak the entire time they were working, but when they both climbed out of the finished tanks, shortly after five, she thanked him.

"I'm sorry if I embarrassed you today." Vince tossed his gloves back onto her cart. "I thought I was being playful. Turns out I'm just a jerk."

"I'm not embarrassed by my name. I just thought I wouldn't be here long enough to share it. You know?" She pulled her gloves off with a snap.

"You got a better life out there, do you?" he asked, nodding his head to the proverbial *out there.*

"Maybe not, but it would be nice to make sure."

He nodded again. "You'll come back to visit me sometime, won't you? When you aren't busy."

"That bored, huh?"

He smiled as he backed away from her. "That intrigued." He turned around and headed back to his level without another word.

26

T HAT NIGHT AT DINNER, Ethan was less than friendly. She tried to explain the events that transpired to release her name, but he eventually left the table with the excuse of studying. Danato had been fairly quiet through the meal and she eventually couldn't take it.

"Okay, let's have it. Where's my lecture about hanging out with werewolves?"

Danato looked up at her from his third helping of mashed potatoes. "What?" he asked. "Vince? Oh, he's okay. If the floor is closed, you can't hang out with him, and if he goes on leave, you can't go with him, but if you develop a friendship, I have no objections." He poked his fork into his potatoes, but it froze at his mouth.

"I might object to any further relationship based on the burden of werewolf-associated issues." He opened his mouth for the bite, but stopped again. "On the other hand, you're young and I know you must be lonely, so, if a bond would develop, I could hardly object."

She rattled her head, trying to make his words make sense. "Did you just give me permission to date a werewolf?"

Danato smiled warmly and took her hand. He pressed his lips to it for a sincere kiss. "I'm pleased my consent would play any part in your choice, but I have no intention of picking your suitors."

"What about Ethan? Didn't you have something in mind when you brought me here along with him?"

Danato frowned and cleared his throat. "I don't know what I had in mind with you, but I certainly had no designs for your future when I did it." He looked toward the balcony. "As much as I would like for Ethan to have a prospect for a wife, I know that love isn't always as simple as proximity. If Ethan wants your love, he will have to earn it." He looked back at her. "Just as any man would. He knows that. He would just prefer you wait for him while he does."

She nodded. "So, no lecture? No yelling?"

"No." He released her hand and pulled a small box from his pocket. He set it on the edge of the table next to her and pushed himself away from the table. "Goodnight..." He stood. "...Cori."

She looked up at him. It was the first time he had used her name since he had heard it. Despite her objections to the revelation, she did like hearing it. "Goodnight, Danato." She offered him a small smile, and he headed to his bedroom.

She looked down at the box and opened it. Inside, she found her gold thumb ring. Danato had reshaped and polished the metal. It showed the fractures where it had been bent, but it was still hers.

27

O N THE MAIN FLOOR, down the east hallway and to the right, Danato led Ethan into a cavernous room. The room, and its lack of contents, took up the bulk of the main floor. They designated it as the gym, but it lacked the modern equipment Ethan associated with gyms. There was only a small section devoted to some over-used exercise equipment. A set of free weights, floor mats, and various punching bags made up the bulk of its repertoire.

The remainder of the so-called gym was empty. The white glossy floors were the same as the rest of the prison, but marked with red and yellow tape. At the far end of the room was a huge metal door, not unlike the type on an airplane hangar.

"This is the gym?" he asked, circling his attention back to Danato.

He hadn't come in much past the front door. He just leaned against the wall, observing Ethan. "It's time to add weight lifting in with your calisthenics."

Ethan waved his hand back to the space behind him. "Kind of big, isn't it? Or do you have gymnastics tournaments in here too?"

A slight tinge of a smile crossed Danato's face, but it was gone before he spoke. "Something like that."

"What's in there?" Ethan asked, moving toward the hangar door. Even as his feet moved closer, the grandiose nature of the door made him slow to a stop. He looked back at Danato for the answer.

"*The trainer,*" he answered.

Ethan waited for more information but, as usual, the less said, the better, in Danato's opinion. "Right." He nodded, as if he wasn't confused. "So are we talking 'King Kong' or like a 'Godzilla'?"

Danato's brow creased. "I'm not sure either is accurate. You'll need to build your muscles before you start using the trainer. You'll work your muscles daily and cardio-agility twice a day between your studying."

"Isn't that a bit much?" Ethan asked. "Don't I need some recovery time?"

"I have a special beverage that speeds up muscle repair."

"Steroids?" Ethan asked, concerned.

"No, but it will speed things up. I'll have it ready for you in my office each morning. I plan to release the trainer in a few months." He nodded at the hangar. "You'll need to be ready."

Ethan looked back at the door. With no further encouragement or threat, he picked up the first dumbbell he could lift and started curling.

28

 ORI STEPPED ONTO THE transmorphs level with
a little more enthusiasm than she did the other
levels. So much so that she was actually dancing. She
had a tune in her head that she had been humming all
day.

As she sang it out loud, a few other voices similar
to her own joined in. She glided across the floor with a
few hop-steps and turns. Every cell down the line had a
copy of her inside of it. The *a cappella* pop song echoed
in stereo down the line. Her doppelgangers mimicked
her exuberant dancing in every cell.

She was sure that Danato wouldn't approve of her
encouraging the devious manipulators, but she decided
as long as they were images of herself; she would always
know they couldn't trick her. After all, she knew herself
better than anyone.

Aside from this day being the day she got to
perform with the transmorphs, it was also the first
day she had permission to bring in some of the cargo
from the delivery trucks. Finally, she would have an
opportunity to view how she might escape this prison.

After storing her supplies, she received a call from the dock to come down and help unload. She nearly ran to the main level and arrived just as the back of the truck was being opened.

She observed the number of people that were there, and the number of outgoing boxes, which were only a few. Mostly paperwork and a few empty boxes that kept suspicion down, in case the drivers had to answer questions about their purpose in this barely habitable section of Russia.

No one instructed her, so she grabbed a two-wheeler and headed into the trailer to grab something—anything. The cargo space was deep and dark. Dark enough to hide someone from sight.

She smiled at that thought as she shoved her cart under a box and pried it up. Something shifted in her periphery, but when she looked, she couldn't see anything. She looked to the far back of the truck, into the darkness where she had just decided someone might be able to hide. The hairs on the back of her neck tickled.

As her eyes adjusted, she could see the faint outline of something. Something that wasn't a box. It moved, making her jump. She backed away slowly. "There's something in here!" she yelled out to the crew. One man glanced in and shrugged; the others didn't bother looking.

"Hello, Cori." She gasped and whipped her head back to the voice behind her. Vince was inches from her. She recoiled from his sudden proximity and nearly fell back.

He placed a hand on her back to support her and she grabbed his arms for balance. "You're not happy to see me?" he asked, with disappointment in his eyes.

"See you, yes." She pushed herself away. "But breathing you is a bit unnecessary." She rolled out of his supporting hand. Her heart raced from being startled, but she also felt nervous.

She retrieved her two-wheeler, and he followed her out of the truck. He was wearing a long black trench coat, which made him look mysterious and handsome. However, since he was already a werewolf, it seemed overkill to her.

"Do you mind?" She glanced over her shoulder at him. "I have work to do." Outside of the truck, he veered off toward the door as if he had no intention of continuing their conversation. She paused and looked after him. She was a little disappointed that he hadn't persisted in bugging her. She wasn't sure how she felt about him, but she didn't like that his interest had waned since the first time they met.

He caught her looking after him and she looked away, but that was apparently enough to draw his attention back to her. He turned around, but didn't come over to her. "I'll be sequestered at midnight tonight. You won't be able to see me for several days, and I'm unfortunately scheduled to leave directly after. You'll be without me for several more weeks."

She rolled her eyes. "I'll try to fit you in." He disappeared out into the hallway. When she was sure no one was looking, she checked the big caged clock on the wall.

Just after dinner, she cleaned up the dishes at record speed while still trying to look as if she wasn't in a hurry. With every plate she scrubbed, she wondered why she wanted to go see him. With every bowl, she demanded that she not let her past dictate her future relationships. The forks reminded her that Vince could potentially help her escape, and the knives reminded her that his help would come with a price she wasn't sure she could offer him. Danato peeked over his newspaper from his chair in the living room as she scrubbed the dried food off the table with insistent vigor. She sensed he wasn't fooled for a minute. He knew Vince had arrived, and he also knew that she had cooked a quick dinner. He smiled at her as he adjusted the hideous thick frames of his reading glasses. "Need some help?"

She paused, but shook her head. "No, I think that's everything." She tossed the rag into the sink from her position by the table.

Danato looked over at the landing position. "Looks good."

"I should get back to the prison." She undid her ponytail as she went for her coat. "I didn't finish my area before the truck came in," she lied.

"Of course, don't work too hard," Danato said, ducking back into his newspaper.

"Hey Cori, would you rub my neck?" Ethan popped up from the couch just as she reached for the door. "I think I pulled something lifting today."

She doubted whether Ethan had actually pulled something. More likely, he just wanted to make it known that he had lifted weights. She anxiously danced at the door, trying to think of a viable reason not to. "Come on, you owe me. I can't ask Danato. He'll break my neck with those hands."

Danato grunted from behind his newspaper.

She glanced at the clock. "Okay, but just a bit. I don't want to lose sleep over janitorial work."

"Just wait until tomorrow," Ethan suggested as she came over to him. "Danato doesn't care what day things get cleaned on."

Ethan and Cori both looked at him for opposing answers. He peeked over the paper, cleared his throat, and went right back into it, appeasing neither of them with an answer.

Ethan stretched out on the couch and she sat down beside him. She gruffly massaged his neck. "Ouch, can you try not to think about strangling someone while you do it?" She relaxed her grip and massaged more gently. His shoulders and neck relaxed in her hands. Soon enough, he was practically asleep on the couch. She left him be and moved to the door. "Thanks, Cori," Ethan mumbled into the pillows. "You're the best."

She frowned, knowing that she wasn't the best. For some reason, Ethan was blind to all her selfish faults. She glanced at Danato, and he gave her a sympathetic smile. She put on her coat and slipped out the door.

29

CORI SKIPPED THE ELEVATOR and ran all the way to the third level. She slowed her pace just before she reached his cell, so she didn't look like she was flushed from running. As she reached Vince's human cell, she saw the door was closed. She looked at the locked door and then the caged clock on the wall. 10:30.

Vince came to the bars and smiled warmly, reaching for her hand.

She concluded his playful behavior had gone to the side of the jerk again. "You were just teasing me." Her brow crumpled, and she set her jaw.

"I normally get sequestered for 24 hours before being moved to the big cage, and the same for the aftermath. The 24 hours will officially start at midnight."

"Then why is it locked already?" she asked.

"Because I knew you would come to see me tonight, like I asked."

Her eyes watered slightly. She was right; he was just playing some sort of game with her. "Fine, I won't bother showing next time." She walked away.

"Cori!" Vince called after her with distress in his voice. "Don't make me wait three weeks to explain. Cori!" His voice cracked like a teenager in puberty, only instead of a high-pitched squeak, it was a deep rumble that bled through his vocal cords.

It was perhaps only the strangeness of the sound that stopped her, but her curiosity prevented her from moving again. Midway between his cell and the section break, she argued with herself. She wasn't about to let this man play her like a high school girl at a frat party. She wanted to know why he didn't want to see her, though.

"Cori." Vince's voice was soft now, no sign of the monster within him. "I can smell you from here. I can smell your emotion like any fool could see them. Please come back, so I can make you understand. I'm trying to protect you, not hurt you."

She shook her head, more to remind herself that she could, but she turned around and walked back to face him. Vince held out his hand again. "I won't bite. Not yet."

She moved closer, but just out of his reach. He smiled and put down his hands. "You don't know enough about me to be afraid of me. Not the way you should." He was smiling, but he was serious. She rolled her eyes. Everything in this prison was dangerous.

"Listen, you get that I'm a werewolf. What you don't get is that 24 hours before and after being a werewolf, I am a violent, lecherous man. However, it's a gradient. I knew this afternoon I could get you here this evening. I knew this evening, I could get you to that bed." He nodded back to his bed. "What I didn't know is if that was what you really wanted or what I wanted from you."

"You think I'm that easy?" she snarled at the implication.

"No, but I am that good. I can smell your emotions. It's very easy to manipulate people when you know how they are feeling. I didn't want to manipulate you into thinking that you liked me when you haven't made your mind up about that yet. I do find it encouraging that you were disappointed to see this door locked," he said, tracing his finger over the keyhole.

She looked at her feet, but all at once pulled her chin up high and took a deep breath. "What now?" She wanted to keep control of this. It was her choice to be here, no matter what he thought of his skills. She could leave, but she didn't want to.

Vince checked the clock on the wall behind them. "I have over an hour to talk to you, hold your hand, and run my fingers through your hair."

"What happens after that?" she asked.

"The guards put you back on the line." He motioned to the yellow line on the floor that marked his reaching distance.

"No, I mean, what would you do to me?" She looked away. "If they didn't put me back on the line?"

He took in a deep, hissing breath. She thought she heard a tremble in his exhale. "Maybe just pull your hair, hold your wrists a little too tight, and get to as much of you through these bars as I could. Hopefully, I'm not making that sound erotic, because I'd likely take your arm off trying to get to you. I could kill you just as easily as a man as I could a werewolf."

"Could you kill me now?" she asked.

"I have control of myself now. It just gets harder after midnight."

"I think I'm starting to feel that fear I'm supposed to be feeling." She shuffled her hands around, trying to find the right spot for them. The pockets of her jeans were too shallow and the belt loops were ripped. She fisted her hands and clenched her jaw. "Would you..." She shook even before she could get the words out. Only her anger and determination let her vocal cords form the words. "...rape me?" Surprisingly, the word didn't make her cry. It shook her to the core, but it didn't shatter her.

When she looked back at Vince, he wasn't offering an answer. "Danato came to see me this afternoon. He wanted me to understand the situation surrounding your previous captivity. That's partially why this door is locked."

"Danato said he didn't have a problem with me seeing you."

"He doesn't, but it doesn't mean he isn't going to have a chat with the boyfriend to set some ground rules." Vince kicked his feet into the base of the door. "To answer your question, Cori, the midnight cut-off point is where I can no longer trust my actions." He paused before adding, "You don't have to stay, Cori. You don't ever have to see me again if you want."

She stepped forward and took his hand. He tensed at her movement, but didn't move away. She took a deep breath and laughed at her own nervousness. Part of her wanted to run screaming, but another part of her felt like if she did, then she would always be running. "I want to be here. If I don't want to be here, I will go."

He smiled and nodded. "Okay."

He held her hand, touched her face, and conversed with her about his life outside of being a werewolf. Just before midnight, they gave in and kissed awkwardly through the bars. At first, she was glad the bars were there, but after she relaxed and pushed away her bad memories, she wanted the bars gone. Those metal bars were the only thing keeping their desires at bay.

As he said, the guards came out and pushed her back to the line. She wanted to stay longer, but he asked her to go. He said her being there would only aggravate his hormone imbalances and make him more violent.

Back at the house, Ethan was awake and studying in the living room. She gave him a half smile as she hung up her coat.

"Everything go alright?" he asked.

"Fine." She wasn't interested in conversation, but he was staring her down as if she needed to report her activities to him. "You weren't waiting up for me, were you?"

He didn't take his eyes off her, just lifted the stack of books from his lap. "I've been looking ahead in my books. I wanted to know a bit more about werewolves."

She averted her eyes, feigning interest in adjusting the way her coat was hanging. "Really? How's that going for you?"

"I wonder if I shouldn't update your knowledge of them. Just in case you need to know about them. Do you need to know about werewolves?" His eyes were double-dog daring her to say yes.

She knew he was jealous of Vince. She also knew that she was the only woman remotely close to his age in the entire prison, which left him with no prospects for dating. Despite her sympathy for his situation, she couldn't force herself to feel differently. Ethan just wasn't the one for her.

She shook her head. "No, I think I get the gist. Tread lightly near a full moon. Don't tread at all on a full moon. That pretty much covers it."

He slammed his book shut so hard it made her jump. "I'm sure that will at least keep you alive. I won't bore you with the details." He gathered his things and headed upstairs. He paused on the first landing as if he was rethinking his exit, but after a moment, he ascended again without delay.

30

DANATO SAT IN THE living room with Ethan some three weeks later. His large frame took up nearly the whole couch as he enjoyed the last of last month's newspapers. The newspapers were only delivered once a month in bulk. Though the news was perpetually one month behind the rest of the world, he still liked to stay up-to-date on the current events. He always tried to keep one newspaper for each day as if he were receiving them from his own personal paper boy, but every month he finished a few days early. He couldn't resist letting a potential follow-up story lay unread.

He squinted and held the paper at arm's length, despite his glasses being only a few steps away in the study. As he turned the pages of his paper, he caught Ethan staring at the door rather than at his books.

Ethan had taken Danato's chair for his studying. Danato had suspected it was also because it faced the door. Ethan had been checking the clock all night. He had also been changing positions sporadically, apparently uncomfortable no matter what he tried.

Danato watched him change from sitting straight up to slouched down. He tried putting his feet on the coffee table, but the action was promptly met with a glare. After that, he switched to sit lopsidedly with his feet over the arm of the chair.

Ethan eventually sighed and slammed his book shut. Danato looked at the book to see which culprit volume deserved the mistreatment.

"I can't do this," Ethan groaned. "I'm so sick of studying and weight lifting and studying. If I read another line about the lineage of hobgoblins to tree gnomes, I'll rip my damn eyes out."

"I told you that was a boring volume," Danato said, returning to his own reading.

"How is any of this going to prepare me for in there?" Ethan shook the book as if it was possible to strangle it.

"Knowledge is always power, and strength protects you when your knowledge falls short. Trust me, that book will save your life someday."

"I don't want to do it anymore. I don't want to be here anymore. I hate this place!" Ethan flung his arms out to indicate either the house or the prison in general.

Danato folded his newspaper neatly and placed it beside him. He had expected Ethan to have trouble with Cori's new relationship, but he hadn't anticipated him to be so uneasy. Perhaps he had become more attached to her than he realized.

"I know you don't want me to repeat the obligation you have here; so, let's move on to what has changed in your life to make this place so much more frustrating than a few weeks ago."

"Ten volumes later, is what has changed, and about three thousand reps," Ethan snarled.

"No, it isn't that at all." He knew Ethan wouldn't admit what he was really feeling. "You don't like it when she isn't here."

Ethan paused. "She should be here. I'm not allowed to go gallivanting around the prison at night."

"That isn't entirely true. I've never made any specific objections to leaving the house at night, but given that you don't have any reason to go there, I might be reluctant to approve."

"You're right. I have no business going to the prison, because we have no female werewolves in the program, so I have no one to date."

Danato furrowed his brow. "The day I voluntarily let a fem-wolf in this prison is the day I get committed." He shook his head, seeing the disinterest in Ethan's eyes. "Never mind, the point is... what was my point?"

"That I don't have anyone except her, and now she has someone else." Ethan threw his book on the coffee table. "Thanks for the pep talk. I really needed that spoken out loud." Ethan stormed off toward the stairs.

"Ethan!" Danato bellowed, forcing the boy to stop and look back at him. "I can't make her love you... and neither can you. You'll have your chance again. You know that. But in the meantime, you need to start handling your crush with a little more dignity."

Ethan nodded and headed upstairs.

Danato rolled his eyes and shook his head. Who knew that his biggest problem with his recruits would be the drama of young love.

31

ORI ARRIVED AT VINCE'S human cage. Like her last visit with him, they had limited time. He was to be sequestered at midnight. However, unlike her last visit, the guards had left the door unlocked. Instead, she found him inside with his hands and legs shackled. He must not have trusted himself enough to go without some degree of restraint.

She hovered at the door to his cell and knocked on the metal framework. He looked up from his reading, which wasn't much more than a car magazine. He smiled. "You came back?"

"Yeah," she said, feeling as awkward as a teenager on her first date. "Didn't you want me to come back?" Though they had already kissed, the time between their encounter had left her time to doubt his interest in her and question her own desires for him. As close as they may have been that night, three weeks had put large barriers between them.

"Of course I wanted you to come back. I just wasn't sure if you had come to your senses or not." He smirked. "Would you like to sit?"

She looked at the long bed cot.

"I can stand," he offered, seeing and probably *smelling* her apprehension.

He stood, rattling his shackles as he did. He motioned for her to sit as he backed himself to the wall. She wet her lips and sat down. She was still nervous, and she didn't know why. So many thoughts were going through her head. She could hardly stand it.

Was she ready to be with a man again? Was he honest with her? Could she even enjoy herself with the memories of so many violent encounters running through her head? Wouldn't it just be easier to leave? Could she leave this place without his help, if the opportunity arose?

"Cori?"

"What?" She stumbled out of her own thoughts and realized Vince had been speaking to her. "I'm sorry."

"You..." He sighed and shook his head. "I don't know what to say. Your emotions are so frazzled right now. I can feel that. I don't know if I can say anything to relax you."

"You can tell me why I'm here," she said.

His brow lifted in surprise. "You're here because you think I'm hot." His eyes glittered with amusement.

She found it funny too, but not enough to keep the smile she was offering. "You have a whole other life outside of this place, don't you?"

The humor on his face faded as well. "I don't know about *whole*, but I do have a job, an apartment." Vince slid down to the floor.

"Family and friends?" she asked.

"Family is mostly gone. I think I have some cousins still running around in Scotland, but they aren't part of this program, so I don't hear from them much."

"Friends?"

"Some coworkers I have drinks with once in a while, but I try not to get too close to people, in case they start to figure out that I'm always taking time off around the full moon."

"Female friends?" she tried to ask casually.

He raised his chin in an "ah-ha" way. "I see. You think that I have a girlfriend in this other life and I'm just interested in you for my trips here?"

"Do you?" she asked again, noting that he had not challenged the accusation.

"I've dated. A few relationships worth distracting myself with, but no, I am emotionally and physically available." She couldn't help but look at his body when he said physically. "Apparently, I really am a jerk. I'm arrogant, competitive, and controlling."

"I have some of those same qualities."

"You're competitive, I've seen that. Controlling? Well, you're a woman, I'm not sure that's an optional quality. Arrogant... I don't think so." He shook his head.

"No?"

"No, because if you were arrogant, you wouldn't be questioning my motives; you would assume that I'm completely enamored with you for reasons of obvious beauty and intellect."

Vince crawled across the floor to her legs. He lay his head on her lap and gripped her calves. Her breathing increased and her face flushed. But that was all he did for the moment. He massaged her calves down to the ankles.

She reached to touch his head, but she couldn't help but think it would be like petting him, so she stopped. She sat back and enjoyed the calf massage, which made her think of Ethan, but she pushed away the memory of his hands and focused on Vince's.

They didn't talk much, but shortly before the guards were due to join them, he pulled her off the bed cot and into his lap. His shackles left him struggling to embrace her, but she wrapped her arms around him just fine.

He kissed her hungrily. His hand slipped up her shirt, tethered just shy of his goal. His other hand gripped her thigh, pulling her against him. She could tell the restraints frustrated him, but she relaxed in his cumbersome embrace, knowing that she still had control of the interaction.

She wrapped her arms around him tightly and pushed herself against him. She felt him bite her neck playfully, and she pulled away. He smiled to let her know he was still being frisky. He nibbled down her shirt until he reached the swell that was evident even through the cloth of her bra and shirt. He glanced up at her before tracing his tongue over the cloth. Her breath caught, and she thought she might rip her shirt off to give him full access.

The clang of keys down the hallway disrupted their privacy. Vince kissed her again, before the guards could take her away. They announced time was up and she peeled herself away from Vince. He caught her wrist after she was up. She looked back at him. His eyes had glazed and his expression looked austere. She pulled her hand, but he wouldn't release.

She looked at the two guards, who were already coming to her aid. They tried to force his hand open. She noted how strong his grip was on her, and yet he wasn't actually crushing her wrist.

Vince's eyes had turned lustful, and she felt genuinely concerned when the guards couldn't force his hand open. She could see why they separated them at midnight. One guard spoke loudly to Vince as if he was an old man hard of hearing. He said his name multiple times before Vince drew his eyes away from her. "Open your hand!" the guard said firmly. Vince looked at his hand as if it was a foreign object. He released, and she put some distance between them.

His features softened a bit, and he lost his lustful gaze. "Midnight?" he asked the guards as they helped him off the floor to his bed.

"Yes, Vince," one said, still speaking loudly but with a more parental tone. "Time to rest. Cori will wait outside."

"Cori." Vince peeked over their shoulders at her.

Once he was situated, they pushed her out the door and locked it. They warned her once again not to go near him, but she didn't need the reminder. He mumbled her name drunkenly inside the cage. She stayed a little longer to talk with him, but when every sentence from his mouth became pornographic, she decided it was time to go to bed.

32

THE NEXT DAY, ETHAN didn't go to the gym or to the office to study. He roamed around the prison, trying to better acquaint himself with some of the things he had been reading about. One inmate in particular had caught his fancy when he had read about her.

Danato had told him he couldn't force Cori to love him, but that wasn't necessarily true. There was a way to tilt her heart in his direction.

Ethan knew what he was considering was wrong, but he wasn't prepared to spend the remainder of his life alone. Nor was he willing to just let Cori commit herself to a man she had no future with. At least with him, they would have a long life together.

He stepped out onto the seducer's level a little reluctantly. He knew whom to avoid eye contact with, and whom to keep away from entirely. The others were still dangerous, but relatively benign in their cages.

The only prisoner in a posh cell was the only one safe enough to look at and talk to. "Mezula?" he asked when he reached her cell.

The cell contained a hand-painted bureau, a glass vanity, a mahogany sleigh bed, and a beautiful woman. She was human. She sat on the bed, uncrossing and crossing her long legs like scissors. It made the slightest noise when her panty hose scraped.

Her long silky orangey-red hair constantly fell over her left eye, even after she drew it behind her ear. She wore a black dress with a high leg slit. "Can I help you?" she asked casually, as though he had entered her office in need of services. She didn't lift her head to look at him, even though from his point of view all she was doing was looking at her own feet.

"I'm Ethan," he said.

"I know; the replacement. What do you require from me?"

He wasn't certain what she meant by him being the replacement, but no doubt she had heard he was in training to be a guard. "Did you know I was coming?" he asked, curious as to the extent of her psychic strength.

"No, but the only time anyone comes to see me is if they need something."

"Does that bother you?" He had noted a slight bitterness in her voice.

She looked up at him, brow rutted in surprise. "That is an odd question. It shows concern for me. Are you sure you should be offering that much concern to a convict?"

He paced before her cell as if he was strolling in the park and not in the belly of a concrete prison. "From what I've read on you, or your kind, you don't really have an angry or vindictive nature. You are here because of a specific circumstance."

"Very good. I suppose you want to know what that specific circumstance is."

"Not especially," he said. He had his own agenda today.

"You're brave then, or just stupid. I guess time will tell." She stood and linked her arms in the barred door. "To answer your question: no, it doesn't bother me when people ask me for favors. It makes me feel useful. Not to mention, I usually acquire lovely things when I am helpful to men." She motioned to the items in her cell.

He frowned at the furniture. "Why would Danato approve this?"

"I have my uses... and so does he."

Ethan decided not to let her ambiguity sidetrack him. "I understand that you do love spells."

"I have on an occasion awoken the heart, but I do all manner of *spells*. Love is just my specialty."

"Can you make someone fall in love with someone else, even if they don't currently love them?"

She paused. "Yes, that is possible. The outcome is a little shaky, though." Mezula rocked her hand.

"How so? Can it hurt her?"

She smiled. "The initial part of the love is fake. Implanted. It's like an arranged marriage; it binds you to each other, but eventually if things go well, you will fall in love naturally."

He thought about how vehement Cori was about not thinking of him that way. He wondered if she could learn to love him. "And if she doesn't fall in love... naturally?"

"Then it's just like dating. You are together for a while, and things don't click, so you break up. It wears off and what's left is what's left."

He shook his head. That didn't sound like an appealing spell to him; too many variables to go wrong. "Maybe we could just keep her from being with someone else."

"The woman you have in mind, she is in love with someone else?" Mezula asked.

"I don't know. She is seeing someone else. I just think in the end she shouldn't be seeing him, even if she isn't seeing me, either." He knew that sounded barbaric. *If I can't have her, no one can.* But he was genuinely concerned that Vince was only going to break Cori's heart. She had already been at the hands of evil men once in her life. She didn't need to be emotionally raped as well.

"I can't break love. I can block it if the love of another is stronger. But be warned, it's only temporary. Unless something changes in her perception, she will grow her love back. Many a husband and wife have tried to save their marriages via that particular cure. Unfortunately, they all come to realize that love is fragile. Once it's been broken or depleted, there is no going back, no matter what the other person feels for them.”

“So, if she is truly in love with him, it won't work?” he asked.

“Not for long, anyway.” She shook her head sympathetically. If your love is strong enough, it may work long enough for you to woo her properly. Ethan didn't know how strong his love was. Cori was no one to him a few months ago, but now she was his connection to the outside world.

Danato did an admirable job trying to make them feel at home here, but it was really Cori that made him feel grounded. He couldn't imagine how hard it would have been without someone to confide in—someone at least familiar with basic pop culture and movie references.

He knew she didn't see him as a man yet, but he hoped that someday she would. He just wanted that day to be sooner rather than later.

“Bring her to me.” Mezula seemed to sense the debate he was having. “I'll read her and find out if it's worth trying any spells on her.”

“I don't... yes, I'll get her here.” He sprinted away without another word.

“It doesn't have to be now,” Mezula hollered after him, but he didn't answer.

Ethan found Cori in her *now* second-favorite spot in the prison. She was doing a new dance routine with her doppelgangers. She didn't hide her show from him when she saw him coming.

"Check this out, Ethan. I finally found a move the transmorphs can't do." She rolled her body like a wave from top to bottom. The transmorphs moved stiffly, unable to copy her. She laughed at their attempts.

"Yes, they are surprisingly inflexible," he said, slightly out of breath. "Their muscle tissues are devoted to changing size and texture on command. They have no room for other manipulations of that muscle. It's just too much for them."

"Really?" Cori tried out a couple of other moves that proved difficult as well. "Ha!"

"Cori, I need you upstairs," Ethan interrupted.

"I'm cleaning," she said as she arched herself backwards.

"Clearly, but this will only take a second. Come on." He touched her arm gently to urge her with him without inciting her annoyance.

She repositioned and glanced down at his hand, then shrugged. "Okay."

He was impressed by how easy it was to get her into the elevator, but when he stepped onto the seducer's floor, she was reluctant to follow him. He waited for her.

"Danato hasn't cleared me for this floor," she protested, peeking around the corners of the elevator. "I just stick to the lowers. I only—"

"Come on, you're with me." He reached out his hand for her to take. "I'll tell you exactly where to walk and what to do."

"I've heard that before," she grumbled, but stepped out. She didn't take his hand, but as they walked, she stayed right behind him.

When they reached Mezula's cell, she was still standing with her arms looped through the bars. "Hi," she said, blasé, indifferent to any oddity of the situation.

Cori looked at him, concerned. He nodded to Mezula. "This is Mezula. Mezula, Cori." The two women nodded to each other civilly.

"Why am I here?" Cori asked.

"I just need to get a quick reading from you, love." Mezula reached out her hand. "No trouble."

"I've already had my reading done this year," Cori said, backing away.

"Cleos?" she asked with a smirk. "I'd be careful around him. Pretty little thing like you, he might eat you up."

"I thought he wasn't a vampire?" Cori asked.

Mezula bit her lip, hiding the depth of her smile. "Oh, he's a vampire alright, just not the kind that sucks blood."

"And what about you?" Cori stiffened and raised her chin. "What's your monster name?"

Mezula tipped her head and leaned against the bars. "Do I really look like a monster to you?"

Cori looked her over and shrugged. "You kind of look like a pro—"

"Okay!" Ethan gave Cori a hard sideways hug. "Don't mind her Mezula. She isn't very good at making friends with women."

Cori tried to shrug him off, but his grip was too tight.

"Too bad." Mezula retreated from the bars. "I'm very good at making friends with women." She perked her brow and Cori stilled in his grip. She looked at him, concerned at the direction of the conversation.

"She isn't dangerous, Cori. I just want you to let her read you."

"Just read me right." Cori murmured between gritted teeth, trying not to let Mezula hear.

"Yes." Ethan released her, letting his hand drag down her back as far as he could while seeming incidental.

"Why?" Cori asked, searching his eyes.

He struggled to answer under her scrutiny, but Mezula jumped in to save him. "It's part of the job description to be cooped up in this hellhole for years; it's my duty to evaluate the mental competence of every one of Danato's employees. Given the nature of your enlistment, there is concern that you won't be capable of meeting the demands of the job."

Cori scoffed. "And if I can't meet the demands of the job. Do I get to go home?"

"Yes," Mezula answered.

Ethan stared at Mezula, shocked at the lies she was spewing out like second nature. She seemed to know exactly what to say to get Cori's attention.

Cori looked back at him. "Is this for real?"

He didn't want to lie to Cori, but what was one lie compared to a spell bound manipulation? Calling Mezula's bluff would only shed light on his own scheming.

"Yeah, I thought if there was a chance you could go home..."

Cori's eyes brightened, then dimmed. "You would do that for me? I mean, if it meant being left here... alone?"

Ethan felt his heart sink. He was in deeper than he wanted to be. She was giving him the credit of an altruistic hero, when in reality he was the villain cackling against the background of a lightning storm. "I don't want you to leave, but I do want you to be happy."

"Damn it, Ethan, why do you have to be so freaking sweet?" Cori reached around him and hugged him. It was a moment he could have lived in for days, unfortunately it was all a lie.

"I'm not that sweet." He glanced at Mezula. "Not really."

"What do I have to do?" Cori drew away from him and looked at Mezula for the answer.

Mezula came forward and reached her hand through the bars. Cori took her outstretched hand.

"You should know something," Mezula spoke softly. "Cleos has a soft touch. He's in and out of your mind before you ever knew he was there. A very dangerous trait for mind readers, if you ask me. But don't worry, I won't be sneaking around in your mind like a cat burglar. You'll remember having me inside of you." Cori frowned, and Mezula winked at her. "So, just try to relax... and scream as loud as you want."

Cori's eyes widened. "*What*?"

Mezula's eyes flared with sinister intent. Cori's head wrenched back, her eyes clenched shut, and she screamed. She thrashed as if she was being shocked by electricity.

Ethan jumped forward to pry the women apart, but something blocked his effort and he wasn't able to grab onto either of their hands without slipping off. He was about to run for help when the connection broke. Cori catapulted back to the floor. Mezula stumbled away from the bars toward her bed.

"What the hell did you do to her?" Ethan yelled, rushing to Cori's side, where she was unconscious in a folded heap.

"Exactly what I said; come back tomorrow for your answers. I must sleep," Mezula said with drooping eyelids.

"What about her?" he asked.

"She'll wake up soon enough. She's young, she'll recover." Mezula slipped into her bed and fell asleep.

Ethan picked Cori up with strength he wasn't aware he had and took her back to the house, being careful not to be seen by Danato or Belus.

S EVERAL COLD WASHCLOTHS LATER, Cori woke in her bed as Ethan frantically tried to revive her. "Thank God." He wiped his hands down his face.

"What happened?" Her throat cracked.

"You passed out," he admitted the half-truth.

"That bitch knocked me out."

He frowned and kneeled beside her bed. "I'm so sorry, Cori, I had no idea it would be so painful. I just assumed..."

Cori sat up on her elbows, examining him. "What? That you could trust a convict? Did you even read her file?"

"I read about her type. I heard about her from the other guards. I know Danato uses her for—"

"You just met her today, didn't you?" He stared back at her. His mouth slowly dropped open, but nothing came out. "Was she really evaluating my competency?" Cori's eyes flickered over him as if she couldn't identify who she was looking at. "What was she going to tell you?"

"It's complicated. I just wanted to know..." Ethan cleared his throat, unable to admit the lunacy level his crush had taken him. Danato was right, he needed to get a grip on his emotions. Unfortunately, Ethan was a little too late for that epiphany to maintain his dignity.

"Know what? If I could handle electric shock therapy?"

"I'm so sorry. I didn't think it would be like that."

"How could you be so careless? With your head in those books all day, you should have known the risks. I thought we had each other's backs."

He hesitated, understanding the full extent of the damage he had caused. "We do," he stuttered. "Cori." He moved to sit on the bed with her. "We do. I was being stupid." He squeezed her hand tightly, as if he could express regret through the strength of his grip.

"What was so important that you were willing to use a mind reader instead of just asking me yourself?"

Ethan frowned and shook his head. "Nothing. I made a mistake. I won't make it again, I promise you that."

Cori stared at him for a long moment before pulling her hand from his. She rubbed her throat. "I'm thirsty."

"I'll get you some water." He jumped out the door and bounded downstairs, hoping to do anything that might repair the wedge he had put between them. With only slightly less bounce, he brought the water back up the stairs. Her door was closed. He tested the knob, but she had locked it. He knocked. "I have your... water." He sank down against the wall when he realized she had no intention of letting him back in. "I'm just going to sit out here for a while. Just yell if you need anything else, anything at all. I'll take care of it."

He banged his head rhythmically against the wall behind him and wondered if it even mattered if she was in love with the werewolf, since there was no chance any spell could overcome the hatred she now held for him.

Later that night, Cori emerged from her room to start supper. He helped by setting the table, but he didn't have the nerve to speak to her. When he had finally mustered some backbone, Danato came home and interrupted him. "Where were you all day?" he asked Ethan.

"Just some hands-on studying. The pictures don't always do it justice."

Danato grunted in response and finished hanging his coat. He sniffed the air and smiled at Cori. "That smells wonderful."

"Good." Cori smiled over from the stove.

Danato looked back at Ethan suspiciously. He wasn't sure what had prompted the inquisitive look, but Danato continued to look back and forth between them. He was a bloodhound on the scent of trouble.

"I like the pictures in that eighth volume though," Ethan said, trying to break his concentration.

Ignoring his comment, Danato went to the stove and pushed the skillet of food off the flame. He grabbed Cori's shoulders and turned her to face him. He pulled her chin up to look at him as if her eyes would tell him everything he needed to know. She stared at him wide-eyed and wavering, unbalanced by the unexpected analysis.

"What's this? Your eyes are bloodshot." Danato's voice was low and threatening. "Don't tell me you're just tired."

Ethan broke into a cold sweat, wondering what punishment he would receive for defying the rules. He had never gotten the full brunt of Danato's anger. Cori was usually on the receiving end of his ire, but only because he was ultimately concerned for her. This time, it was Ethan who was putting her in danger.

"It was cleaner. I got it in my eyes," she lied.

His panic eased, thankful that Cori could lie comfortably, but the reason she had to lie made him sick with guilt.

"How?" Danato asked, narrowing his eyes on her.

"It fell off the cart. A transmorph sprayed it in my face. I washed out my eyes. I think the water was worse than the cleaner," she quipped.

"You didn't call me," Danato said.

"I asked one of the guards to help. It really wasn't a big deal. A stupid mistake; it's not like I don't have a trophy case of stupid mistakes."

"Stupid or not, I want a call. Understand?" His voice was soft, or as soft as it ever could be. She nodded. Satisfied, he stepped back, ensuring her balance before releasing her. "That smells delicious," he said, pulling the pan back onto the burner.

"Thank you." She glanced at Ethan. He exuded as much thanks as he could without giving away anything.

Danato sat down at the table and poured himself a glass of milk as an appetizer. "I suppose that burn mark on your right hand is from making dinner?"

Ethan's heart went back to super speed and his stomach clenched. Cori looked at her hand. He shifted to get a view of the red mark between her thumb and forefinger. She glanced over at him and he pleaded with his eyes for another lie.

"Yeah, hot pan." Cori nodded at Danato and shuffled the beef in her skillet.

Dinner was tense and quiet. Ethan tried to make eye contact with Cori, but she was denying him all forms of communication. Danato kept a watchful gaze on both of them, no doubt trying to discern the reason behind the obviously awkward meal.

"I'd like to go see Vince tonight," Cori said abruptly, halfway through her plate.

Danato's fork dropped loudly on his plate, and his partially chewed mouth full of food sat immobile for several seconds before being forcibly swallowed without its final mastication. "You're confused," he informed her.

"Tonight," she repeated.

"You know what tonight is." His eyes fixed on her like an attack dog.

When neither of them spoke, Ethan spelled it out for both of them. "It's a full moon, Cori."

She looked over at him with bold defiance. "I know what night it is."

"He isn't Vince anymore," Danato said.

"I know." She pushed her food into a blob on her plate.

Ethan looked at Danato, hoping for the angry reactions that, up to this point, had defined his character. Instead, Danato appeared to be thinking about it. "He's an animal!" Ethan slammed his fist into the table, unable to contain his repulsion at her interest in the werewolf.

"Ethan, enough." Danato raised his hand to shush him. "Cori, this won't do anything to subside your fears. He isn't human, not in *any* way."

"I want to see Vince tonight. I want you to take me there and show me this horrific beast. I want to know exactly what it is I'm supposed to be afraid of, before..." She lowered her eyes for a moment. Her eyes returned to him with pleading in place of the determination. "I need to see for myself."

Danato shook his head, but Ethan could already see the shift in his body. His tense muscles relaxed, and he leaned back in his chair. His upper lip twitched, as it usually did when he felt disgusted. "I will take you there once." Danato jutted his index finger at her for effect. "You will leave when I tell you. Your presence will agitate him. I won't allow your infatuation to endanger my men. Do you understand?"

Ethan's mouth dropped, and he struggled to find an objection comparable to his astonishment.

"I will see him and then I will leave. That's all I want."

Danato growled under his breath as he stood and grabbed his coat. Cori jumped to grab hers. She was ready, complete with scarf and gloves, before he had even finished buttoning up.

Ethan watched them from the back seat of his eyes. "What?" He jumped up, finally finding his voice. "I can't believe you are allowing her in there. *I* haven't even been in there on a full moon!" Danato glanced at him, but he seemed too annoyed to bother with Ethan's petty jealousy.

Ethan went from sick with guilt to hot with rage in an instant. He couldn't stand watching her walk out the door to see Vince again. "I took Cori to see Mezula!" He blurted out without thinking about the consequences. Danato shot him a shocked look.

In for a penny.

"That's why her eyes are bloodshot. The burn is from their connection."

In for a pounding.

Danato took a menacing step toward him. "You did what?" His voice was a whisper of his normal level.

Ethan tensed, prepared for his verbal and possible physical beating.

Cori stepped between them. She placed a firm hand on Danato's bicep. "Danato, he's just saying that to distract you. He's jealous. Look." Cori moved to the skillet on the table and placed her hand high on the handle. The cleft of her hand met up with the metal pan. Danato glanced over.

"See, he's a smart boy. Let's not argue about this now. He just wants to delay this."

Danato glanced between the two of them. He probably didn't know whom to believe at this point. Ethan's seething anger only added to her case.

"Let's go," Cori said, calmly ushering Danato to the door.

"I'm coming too," Ethan protested.

"You stay here!" Danato boomed. "Clean up these dishes and get to bed."

He stormed out behind Cori and slammed the front door. Then Ethan heard the unthinkable: the exterior lock latched.

He couldn't help but see his future before him in that one moment. His future alone in that house.

34

THE ELEVATOR FELT A great deal smaller to Cori with Danato beside her. He hadn't said a word since they left the house, but his expression told her he wasn't happy about doing this for her. Before they reached the part-time floor, he pressed the stop button and turned to her for yet another lecture.

"You must understand that he won't recognize you. He won't feel something deep down inside for you. There is nothing human in him at all. He would kill you just as he would kill a wounded animal: no mercy, no recognition, and no sorrow. He wouldn't even know he had killed you when he returned to human form. The memories don't transfer."

She stared at him, patiently waiting for the end of the sermon. She understood everything he was saying. She didn't even care whether or not Vince recognized her. It was curiosity that had brought her there.

"Why are you really doing this?" Danato asked when she didn't defend her actions.

"I think the best way to get to know someone is to see them at their worst moments. If someone can still love you after they've seen you at your least proud, then there is nothing that can come between you."

Danato took in a deep breath. "I like that reason. I don't like it in this case, but I suppose I can't protect you from this." His gaze lingered on her, begging her to change her mind.

"If you don't take me now, I'll just have to find a way. At least this way you can say it was your decision."

Danato's jaw clenched. "You are stubborn to a fault," he grumbled. "Stay to the red line. Not the yellow. The yellow is for human containment. The red is for the wolf. Don't reach out. Don't speak to him." He yanked the stop button, and the elevator continued to the part-time floor.

"Follow me," Danato said as they stepped out of the elevator. He followed the red line to the cage. She waited by the elevator to prepare herself.

Danato saw her lingering and waved to her to come over. She followed the line carefully and precisely to the other side of Danato. Her peripheral vision detected the great mass to her right. She could smell wet dog. She heard a breathy snort that sounded like a bull preparing to charge.

She swallowed hard and turned to see Vince's other self, head-on. She had expected the furry coat, the wolf's face, and the claws, but what she hadn't been prepared for was his size.

The cages were oversized for his human form, but the beast filled the space. It left him room to stand, but barely enough to turn around. The creature that stood before her was ten feet tall and at least 300 pounds bigger than his former self. His frame was burly at the neck and shoulders, and leaner through the waist. The legs were muscular, but she could see the upper body was where the bulk of his strength was.

His black, bulbous eyes stared her down, like she was delivering his dinner via a not-so-virgin sacrifice. Bright white canine teeth overhung his lower jaw by at least an inch, dripping drool on the cement floor below him. His paws needed only to make contact with her and "decapitation" or "shattered spine" would be on her autopsy report.

Three guards stood watch, poised with electrical shock prods, prepared to stifle any malevolent behavior that was beyond acceptable limits. She could see Danato out of the corner of her eye, watching her. Everything she did or said would be under microscopic analysis. She revealed nothing. The less he construed from her actions now, the better her plan would go later.

"How is this possible?" she whispered. "How can he be bigger?"

"Hyper-hydration of the muscle tissues, the bones become like rubber, they stretch and solidify. The claws are recessed into his hands, the lungs expand..."

"Does it hurt him?"

"Oh, yes, the transformation is very trying on the body," Danato offered with a twinge of sympathy in his voice. "He can smell you now. Watch yourself."

The creature hunched over and looked at her, eye to eye. For a moment, had she not been so vehemently warned, she would have thought he recognized her.

As soon as the moment came, it went. His claws extended in a broad reach and ripped the air just inches from her face. Her hair lifted from the gust it produced. The entire room took a step back. She didn't move and didn't flinch, except to blink from the air wafting in her face.

The guards prodded the beast in retribution for his attack. He reared in anguish, howling more than yelling.

Danato looked between her and the creature, still trying to decipher her emotions. She looked down at her feet, realigning herself perfectly with the life-preserving red line. She turned and followed it to the elevator.

Danato followed her. At the elevator, she stepped in and pushed the button. She looked back at him as he watched her go. Concern etched his face. She kept her expression passive until the doors had closed. She didn't want to reveal anything to Danato.

35

F OR THE FIRST TIME ever, Cori visited Ethan in the gym. His workouts must have been going well, since he had already gained a good deal of muscle size. Soon she wouldn't be able to see his boyish features past his brawn.

A punching bag was taking a good beating when she came in. She sat on the bench and patiently waited for his attention. He looked back at her, sweating and panting from his cardio. She didn't smile or say hello. "You should keep your right arm tucked a little more on the upper cut. You'll get a better hit."

He nodded absently. "You're the expert," he said as he continued to punch. She was sure he had meant it sarcastically, but it came across as an admission. She wasn't really an expert. She had taken a self-defense class her freshman year of college, per her mother's request, but given her current situation, it hadn't really done her any good.

"They should put mirrors up in here. It would help you watch your form."

He punched the bag one last time and leaned against it. "What do you want, Cori?" His voice was hard. It stung a little, but she pushed the feeling aside.

"I want to know what Mezula told you about me." She was sure that Ethan had not been entirely honest about his purpose with Mezula.

"Nothing I don't already know." He ripped off his gloves. "I never went back to see. I'm not going back. It was stupid." He leaned over and snatched up his water bottle for a long swig.

She picked up a random weight at her feet and did some bicep curls. "What was she supposed to tell you?"

He looked at her through hurt and angry eyes. "I got my answer last night. Better a beast than a boy, right?" She looked up from her weight, surprised he had voiced anything resembling his real feelings. When she didn't respond, his jaw clenched, and he shouted. "*Right?*"

She dropped her weight and stood up straight and tall. "What do you want me to say, Ethan? Yes, I choose Vince. I told you I wasn't the girl for you. It doesn't mean I don't care about you."

"You told me you couldn't be anybody's girl. When did that change?"

"Vince is...different."

"What? Because he isn't technically a man." He moved over to her and put his foot up on the bench behind her. "So you went from never being able to love a man again to… loving a werewolf. I didn't know you were into bestiality?"

She knew he was just trying to make her mad, but she couldn't help being baited by the insult. "That's disgusting, Ethan!"

He chuckled. "You're telling me. You know they really are just glorified upright dogs."

"He is not a dog. He is gentle and affectionate—"

"Until the full moon, when he could not so metaphorically rip you in two."

"At least he hasn't hurt me."

"That's bullshit! The first time you met him, you got scratched up in the basement."

"I meant my heart!"

"Yeah, well, the feeling's mutual!" he yelled back at her.

Cori groaned and turned away. "Damn it, Ethan, I didn't come here to end up in a yelling match. I came to give you a chance to apologize."

"Me?"

"Yes, you! You fed me to that damn harpie!"

"Yeah, and I'm gonna be on Danato's hit list for a month because of it."

"I didn't rat you out! You did that to yourself!"

"I was trying to protect you!"

"No, you weren't. You were trying to control me." Ethan opened his mouth to respond, but he couldn't defend himself. "Oh, come on, you're the one with the psychology degree. Is any of this really about werewolves and men? Don't you think this is more about an abandoned boy feeling more abandoned?"

Ethan closed his mouth and shifted his chin a little higher. The ire in his eyes shifted into something Cori had never seen before. His hard stare turned downright cold. She might have made a mistake by trying to use his psychoanalysis against him.

"You're right. This isn't about werewolves and men." His voice was calm, but laced with a condescending threat. "It's about a girl. A broken girl who wants to feel safe. So she seeks out the biggest, scariest monster that she can to keep her safe." Ethan tucked his gloves into his pocket and moved closer to her. "Do you even love him?"

She gritted her teeth against the implied accusation. He wasn't wrong. Although she couldn't deny a natural attraction to him, love was not what was driving her to pursue him. Much as Ethan suspected, she was using Vince. She resented that he could still read her like a billboard.

"Maybe I dodged a bullet," he added.

Cori's stomach clenched at the hurtful remark. He was trying to wound her again. Trying to sabotage their relationship, so he had a reason to hate her—other than her not loving him back.

He looked her over, no doubt seeing the controlled pain in her eyes. Sympathy pushed back into his hard eyes and he shifted away from her. "I wish I hated you enough to tell you why you shouldn't choose him," he muttered before he stormed out.

In the gym's solitude, her true emotions spilled to the surface, and she wept quietly. She had never known Ethan to be so unkind. She shouldn't have even come to see him. She should have just written him a goodbye letter.

36

CORI PULLED HERSELF TOGETHER, dried her eyes, and found her way to the part-time level. The reduced guards took no notice that she brought her janitor's keys with her. No one bothered to follow her in, since she knew the visitor's routine.

Vince was resting on his bed when she unlocked the door. He didn't even look up when the door creaked open. When she touched his arms, he jumped. "Cori." His voice was hoarse. His eyes were bloodshot and yellow. He tried to sit up, but he fell back, panting at the slight effort.

"Cori." He looked panic-stricken by her presence. "It's too early. I could still hurt you."

"You seem weak as a mouse," she said, straddling his hips.

"Yes, but so is my mind. I can't resist my animal instincts in this state."

"You don't have to." She leaned in and kissed him.

"Cori." He protested only once more.

She plied her most natural strengths, knowing that feminine wiles were as dangerous to men as bullets. It should have been beneath her to go to such lengths, but she always pursued her goals with persistence. No matter how outrageous the route or the endpoint.

At first, all she could think about was her last encounters with men: violent and forced. In his debilitated state, however, Vince was more of a spectator than a participant. Wielding her body as a weapon, she found the confidence she needed to carry out her plan. Her own pleasures rapidly doused her fears and ignited her desires.

Her mind slipped into the vacuous world of ecstasy, where there was no shame, no regret, and no schemes. For the time being, they were only lovers.

Cori collapsed onto Vince's chest in a heap. Slightly sweaty and panting, she listened to his heart race beneath her ear. Though it was all part of her plan, she hadn't prepared for how much she enjoyed it. She also hadn't anticipated how much she would relish being enveloped in his arms afterward.

His fingers traced her back along the spine. It was soothing and made her want to confess her love to him. Before that moment, she had never understood love. She didn't know what compelled one to say it to another person—outside of her family.

A smile twitched at her lips as she lay wrapped in her new lover's arms. All it took for her to understand love and its expression was to sleep with a werewolf.

As the sweat dried, and the cool air goose-pimpled her skin, Cori got herself back on track. She may have found a new understanding of love in his arms, but she wouldn't let it stand in her way. What she wanted more than love was freedom.

She spoke somberly against his chest about them being far away from the prison, together, in a home instead of a cell. She traced her finger along his chest, occasionally tangling in his mat of chest hair, which she found surprisingly soft. Intoxicated by her, his mind was unrestrained by human logic. She could see the gears in his mind clicking into place. He suggested they run away together, and she was more than prepared for the idea.

They dressed and waited for the guard to come and release him. She offered to walk him to the dock, and the guard never questioned it. A bit of violence to the dock manager and Vince's ride out of the prison left early, with one extra passenger.

37

T HE NEXT MORNING, THE prison was a melee of alarms and running guards. Ethan found Danato in amongst it all, barking orders. His small assistant, Belus, was no less agitated, also yelling orders.

Ethan came in on the middle of it, dodging guards that were running to their newly appointed tasks. "What's going on?" He joined Danato and Belus in the prison's main floor vestibule. "Can I help?" He was eager to join the fight. Up to this point, nothing truly exciting had happened at the prison, though he had been bombarded by the many stories both Belus and Danato had regaled him with. It was probably something he shouldn't have hoped for, but he valued some kind of change in his schedule.

"Cori's gone AWOL," Belus blurted out, followed by a *'what the hell?'* look from Danato.

"What?" Ethan's eyes widened as he thought of the many treacheries that could have befallen her.

"Belus," Danato muttered as he pulled Ethan away from the chaos and down to his office, which was apparently soundproof, since the noise of the alarms stopped the instant the door shut.

Danato leaned against his desk, which, to its credit, didn't budge against his weight. Ethan didn't sit. He could hardly hold still. He wanted to run around the prison screaming her name. It would have been fruitless with the alarms blaring, but the desire was still gripping.

"Vince left late last night. He usually waits until the morning after his transformation." Danato paused as if Ethan should have gleaned some grand conclusion from this information. "We think he took Cori with him."

Ethan's eyes narrowed and Danato stood, apparently readying himself for an explosion. After a long pause, he asked, "She escaped with him?"

"Yes, but Vince is an impulsive man. I don't know if he took her away for the day or if he actually just took her."

"You mean they might just come back on their own?" Ethan said it aloud, trying on the words. They didn't fit any better on his lips than they did in his mind.

"Vince is obligated to be here, and violation of his contract would generate a retrieval operation. However, I don't know that Cori would agree to return with him."

"Can't you just retrieve her, too?"

"I have no legal right or authority to do that," Danato said.

"You don't have any legal right to hold *me* here. What difference would bringing her back make?"

Danato's face turned sheepish. "Cori is not officially on the books yet, so I can't send hunters after her. I can't send the collectors after her, because she isn't of supernatural origin."

"So, send out some guards," Ethan suggested.

"They can't leave the prison. They are restricted, and besides, where would they go? Vince isn't likely to head to his apartment. We have no way of knowing where they will go, or if she'll even stay with him."

"Then you might as well give up. I mean, you already have, haven't you?"

"No, but it's complicated. You have to understand Ethan, Cori's knowledge of this place makes her a liability. Reporting her now would be like signing her death warrant."

"She could be killed just for knowing about this place?"

"Yes."

"This is all your fault. You should have just left her behind."

Danato's thick finger sprang into Ethan's face. "Don't pretend with me, Ethan. I know how much you care for her and goddammit, if I don't, too. I may not know what it is like to have children, but I can't imagine my distress would be any different if she were my own daughter. I also don't think for one second that within your bitterness you don't know how wrong it is to suggest that I should have left her there with *those*...” Danato’s lip twitched. “...vermin.”

Ethan hadn’t really meant to suggest that he leave Cori in the slave trade, he only meant that he should have taken her elsewhere. He shook his head and removed every ounce of animosity from his expression. “No, Danato, I would never suggest that.”

Danato’s finger sank along with his tensed shoulders.

“I’m sorry,” Ethan said. “I’m bitter about the situation, but I shouldn’t have suggested that you are to blame for it.”

“Of course I’m to blame.” Danato looked away. “This position doesn’t offer many contentions.” He stood and moved around his desk. He looked at his rolling desk chair as if it were a symbol of that position. The gray metal frame and faded green vinyl cushions barely offered a seat to the large man, let alone a representation of the burdens he faced. “I have to make decisions that don’t always please my conscience. You know I wouldn’t have forced you into this life if I had any better solution. As I said, I have no children of my own.”

Ethan could see the veiled pain in his admittance, and wondered if the great man regretted his lonesome bachelor life. “My mother and father died early on,” Ethan said. “If my life had progressed on the path I was going, I would be in prison by now. I find it karmic that on this alternative path I am confined to a prison, anyway.” He smiled, but Danato didn’t share in his amusement of the irony.

He took a step toward Danato, raised his chin, dropped his smile, and spoke firmly. "I don't resent being brought here. I know it sounds ridiculous, but I feel like I was meant to come here. I can do this job and I can make you proud. I don't know what it's like to want the approval of a father, but I don't imagine that it would feel any different from what I feel with you."

They stared at each other, locked in an emotional stalemate. Propriety of male restraint left them silent and observant to the moment. After the pregnant pause, Danato nodded. "I will do what I can to bring Cori back...safe."

Ethan nodded and left.

38

E THAN WANDERED ABOUT HIS day, trying not to think about Cori and how angry he was that she had left. He couldn't imagine living this life here without her. He had made his peace with only being her friend, but to lose her entirely? It was too much.

He made his way to the gym to start his usual routine, but ended up sitting on a bench, gloves in hand, brooding instead. He thought about his last encounter with Cori and a painful enlightenment stabbed his heart. He had tried so hard to wound her, but in retrospect, he realized he had wounded himself.

She found a new talent for revenge served cold, though. He would now have to live with those cruel things he said to her as his last conversation with her. What was worse, she would remember him for those remarks as well.

He cursed and threw his gloves. His cuss echoed in the gym, bouncing off the useless depth. He cussed again, a long loud blasphemy that made his throat hurt. It didn't make him feel better, but it released some pent-up energy.

He wished he could go back in time and rewrite the last two days. Undo his horrible words. Undo his trip to Mezula.

Ethan's head snapped up. Mezula had read her. She would know where Cori would be going. He jumped up and raced away to see her.

Mezula sat in her usual spot on her bed, in her mansion cell. She wore her green dress that made her red hair pop. She looked like she was waiting for her next customer, which just so happened to be a return customer.

Ethan slid to a stop in front of her cell. He found answers to questions he hadn't even asked yet on her face.

She frowned at him, mocking his pain. "You should have come yesterday, like I told you." Despite her grimace, her eyes twinkled with joy. She was enjoying his pain. "You could have stopped her." She stood for her dramatic recitation of his could-a, should-a, would-a. "One outcry and the alarms would have gone off. One whisper of escape and Danato would have locked this place down. You could have held onto her."

"You knew?" He banged the bars. "Of course you knew." He ran his fingers through his messy hair.

"Don't worry too much. I have a feeling even if you had known, you might have let her go, anyway. Your love for her is stronger than even you realize."

Ethan resented her assumption. "It's just a crush. I'll be over it in no time." He paced, trying to convince himself it was true.

She smiled. "Do you want to know where she is?"

He stopped and looked her over, trying to decide if enlisting her help was yet another bad choice in a series of *really* bad choices. "Danato can't go after her unless he knows where she is," he conceded.

"I can tell you that, or at least where she plans to go, but be aware, if Danato brings her back, he will go so far as to chain her to these walls rather than let her go again. There are rules to this prison. The rule is: everyone who enters becomes a prisoner to it in one form or another. Are you sure you want to tell him where she is? Are you sure you want to be the one responsible for taking her freedom? Danato is prepared for that guilt, but are you?"

Ethan wondered how long it would take Cori to forgive him for that indiscretion. "I'm not sure I want to be here without her."

"You won't be. She'll return."

Ethan returned to the bars. "What are you talking about?"

"You know what I'm talking about." She approached the bars and looked him over like she was appraising his value.

He shook his head, still not understanding her. "When is she coming back?"

"You know when. The secret she didn't want to know about. It was a wise secret to keep from her. Without the truth, she can freely love him. She's already starting to now."

"I'm the reason she can love him? Yes, very wise of me." Ethan rolled his eyes at her interpretation of wise.

"Love will break her walls and quiet her anger. The violence of her past will be consumed in the fires of their carnal passions."

"Christ!" He leaned on the bars, lowering his head in case he might need to puke. "Thank you for the heart-wrenching visual honesty."

"When she returns to you..." Mezula reached through the bars and raised his chin with the tips of her fingers. He shifted his feet under him, prepared to pull away. "She will have no resistance to your affections, apart from her grief, which will be great but surmountable."

Despite the risk, Ethan stepped closer to the bars. "It doesn't matter. When she finds out, I knew and didn't tell her, she'll hate me all over again. I'll just have to get over her, somehow."

"You know, I can do that." Mezula drew him in closer with the hefty weight of her gaze and two delicate fingers.

He leaned into the bars and let her kiss him. The softness of her lips persuaded him to participate. He reached around her, cupping her head and pressing her toward him. She responded with a tongue thrust that sent a lightning bolt of desire through him. His knees weakened, and he repositioned to get closer to her, but the bars kept him too far away to access her body.

The world swirled in his mind, and he felt a little part of him let go of Cori as a potential love interest. He pushed back from the bars and out of her reach. "Emotional amnesia?" he asked, trying to slow his heart.

"Mm-hmm." She nodded, reaching out to him. "It only takes once with me, and you'll forget all about her."

"You said I had a chance with her, if I wait."

"You still will, but there is no reason to..." Mezula looked over his body, which was far too approving of her attentions. "...ache, in the meantime. You'll forget her temporarily after each encounter. You will control how often you need to forget. Nothing I do will break your connection to Cori."

The offer was appealing. Damn appealing. He knew she would help him forget. He knew he would enjoy every minute of forgetting. He also knew it was cheating. Not cheating on Cori, but cheating on himself.

He had never loved anyone before Cori. He had never hurt this badly before, and he liked it. He didn't remember his parents well enough to miss them like this. As masochistic as it was, he liked feeling this pain. It meant something to love someone enough to hurt this badly.

It was also against the rules to fraternize with the inmates, and Danato would kick his ass if he got caught with her. "No, thanks. I've heard heartbreak only makes you stronger." He walked away, thankful that his lower extremities had already gotten the message loud and clear.

"Just remember," she called after him, "what doesn't kill you... will eat you alive."

39

After a quick stop in Paris to collect his painting supplies, Vince and Cori were on their way to a small cottage in the south of France, an inherited estate that no one knew about. With unfamiliar familiarity playing the role of hostess, they found the first few days as uncomfortable as a never-ending first date. On the third day of Vince toiling with his paintbrushes and not so much as kissing her, Cori decided not to skirt the issue any longer.

She entered the living room, which, except for the couch and television, was now an artist's studio. Three easels flanked Vince. A long wooden table behind him held all manner of paint. Scattered across the table were tubes of oil paint, half rolled up, missing caps, and bandaged where punctured. Several stacks of watercolor palettes sat at the back of the table. A few large paint cans filled with latex house paint seemed out of place, but appeared frequently used. The smell of turpentine filled the air along with a leather musk that came with the house.

She climbed over the back of the couch that was shoved against the side wall, barricading him in between the table and his easels. A white sheet covered the couch, likely protecting it from paint splatters or hiding its hideous floral pattern. Whatever the purpose, it was an improvement.

Vince was working on his fifth canvas. Along with the three on easels, two more leaned against the shelf of the bay window that looked onto the front drive. Garbled colors and images marred all the canvases. Not one of them looked like artwork to Cori. Luckily, they didn't seem to look like art to Vince either.

His face wrinkled deeper into abhorrence with each new swath of paint. He smacked his palette with his brush and grimaced at the canvas, as if *it* was responsible for the hideous, tangled images it was projecting. Cori hated to interrupt his heated work, but his concentration was fragile.

He froze mid-stroke and looked over at her, seemingly trying to figure out why she was there. She smiled, trying to improve his somber mood. "Hi."

He frowned at her as if she had lost a family member to a deadly illness and he didn't have the right words to express his condolences. "Are you hungry? I can make something," he offered.

Make yourself at home. Can I get you some tea? Feel free to peruse my library if you get bored. The grounds are beautiful; you should take a walk. Please, take the bed. I will be much happier on the couch in case I get the urge to paint in the middle of the night.

That was the extent of their conversation over the last three days. What he was really saying was, *"Could you please get away from me, so I don't have to deal with you and this convoluted as hell situation you've gotten me into?"*

"You're mad at me." She stated it rather than asked. She didn't want him to deny it instinctively, as everyone does when accused of a socially amoral emotion.

He still shook his head. He turned back to the canvas. Looking at it with fresh eyes, he scoffed and crisscrossed it with his paintbrush. Satisfied with his banishment of the offensive image, he set it against the window, adding to his retrograde work.

"Do you want me to go back?" she asked.

He paused on his way back to his easels to look at her. She knew he wanted to say yes. Like the morning after a drunken hookup, he wanted so much to get her out of his house and out of his life. He regretted taking her out of the prison, but he was too much of a gentleman to say so.

He said nothing official to answer her. He just picked up a new white canvas and started afresh.

She stood up and moved to block his arm movement with her shoulder. He paused, but persisted to paint with a smaller stroke. She grabbed the paintbrush and pulled it from his fingertips. He finally looked at her. He wore the same emphatic expression that screamed: *I don't know what to say to make you feel better.*

"I know we don't know each other well yet," she said softly, "so I'll let you in on a little insight into my personality." She snapped the wooden paintbrush between her fingers. His faced hinted at the pain of his beloved tool being mishandled. "I don't do well with being ignored, and this is me controlling my temper."

"Yes, I've sensed that," he said. She kept forgetting that he could smell her emotions, which brought to light even more questions as to why he was treating her this way. He knew she wanted to be near him, with him. Why was he denying her? Did he really not return those feelings?

She dropped the brush to the floor, and all but pushed herself between him and the canvas. "Are you mad at me?" she asked this time.

He shook his head again, and she almost screamed the question back at him to demand he speak to her, but he spoke just before her anger peaked. "Not mad. I just don't know why I took you. I mean, I want to help you, but Danato and I are friends. I've betrayed his trust."

That wasn't the answer she wanted. What she really wanted to know was if he felt anything for her. If he still wanted her. However, that wasn't what she asked. "You agree with his slavery?" she said, addressing the issue that was apparently primary to him.

"You didn't have much of a life to look forward to without his help."

Her mouth gaped a little. She couldn't believe what he was suggesting. "So, if he saves my life, I owe him the rest of it?"

"I think you underestimate the care he has offered you," he said.

"A fancy prison is still a prison."

"He would have given you anything. You just never thought to ask."

"Everything but my freedom," she said.

Vince smirked and shook his head. "You never asked for it. He would have given it, if you explained how important it was. Danato has a weak spot for you. It doesn't take my senses to detect that."

She shook her head. She didn't believe him. "I made you betray your friend. That's why you are mad at me?"

He sighed and dropped his head. He tossed his paint palette on the table behind him. "Not mad," he reiterated. "I'm just disappointed."

"In me?" Her eyes flared.

"No, in myself."

"You're disappointed that you helped me."

He leaned down and picked up his broken brush. He took it back to his table to wash the paint off it and bandage it like the rest of his wounded supplies. "You came to me before my mind was clear. You seduced me with my own lust. I would have done anything for you at that moment. Can you really ask me to believe that this was all just spontaneous?" He glanced back at her, challenging her to say otherwise.

"You think I used you, sex and all?"

He nodded as he attended to his brush.

"Can't you sense what I'm feeling? Can't you sense the truth?" she mocked.

"I sense confusion. I sense you aren't even sure what you're feeling."

He was right. She was questioning her love for him. She had felt it so strongly after they were together, but now, three days without so much as a peck on the cheek, *she* was feeling used. She was resenting him. "Well, you're right," she said.

He looked up and waited to hear more from her. His face revealed nothing beyond his interest.

"I knew that very day an escape attempt was well overdue. I knew you were the key, and I knew you would be blinded by your instincts. I had every intention of seducing you for my gain." She spoke the words with no shame or apology.

His face turned bitter. "You're out now. You don't need me anymore." He nodded to the front door that wasn't visible from where he stood, but he made his point. "I guess I'm just waiting for you to run off."

Cori gulped down the knot in her throat before she spoke, lest it wrench tears from her eyes on its way out. "You are ignoring me, because you don't want to bother getting any closer if I'm going to ditch you, anyway?"

He nodded, losing some of his coldness.

"I think ditching you *was* part of the plan at some point." She could see the pain in his eyes at the honesty of her plot. "I wonder then," she motioned to the nefarious front door, "why I'm still here?" She sat on the arm of the couch. "Why, three days later, I'm pestering you instead of just making an excuse to go to town and never come back?"

"You're waiting to see if they followed us. You want to keep me as protection in case they come for you."

She chuckled. "That would be a logical assumption. Unfortunately, I never really thought about that. My intricate plan tapered off pretty fast after *leave prison*." She dashed out the words with her hand.

"So, why haven't you left yet?" He crossed his arms.

"I haven't been thinking about leaving. At all." She looked him over. "I've been thinking about how that little spot above your nose crinkles when you're concentrating. I've been coming to terms with a werewolf who paints." She looked over his messy studio living room and snickered. "A slew of things have been running through my head, but none more so than your hands and your lips..." Her voice tweaked a little on the subject matter, but she fought through the words. "...and why they haven't touched me once since we arrived."

He looked at her with the same sadness he had before. "I want to, very much," he said softly.

"But...?"

"I want to trust you." He shook his head, adding the nonverbal, *but I don't* to the end of his sentence.

She nodded, wiping the maiden tears from her cheeks. "I'll wait," she said resolutely, with a false contralto to avoid the emotional squeak in her voice. "I'm not known for my patience," she chuckled, removing a few more tears, "but I'll wait. I owe you that." She cleared her throat, trying to purge the raw emotions that were threatening to overwhelm her.

She could see Vince averting his gaze, either to spare her embarrassment or spare his guilt for letting her weep openly with no offer to console her. After a few deep labored, trembling breaths, her determination caught up with her sentiments and she was back to herself.

She slipped between the table and couch rather than crawl back over. She looked back at him, wanting to say about a thousand things. Most of all she wanted to say, "I love you," but at this point he wouldn't believe her, and she was much too unsettled with her own emotions to be spouting out proclamations of love.

"I am hungry, though," she said when she couldn't find anything else worthy of saying. It was the only thing she was certain about at that point.

He smiled. "Well, I may be an ass, but I can't have my reputation as host sullied."

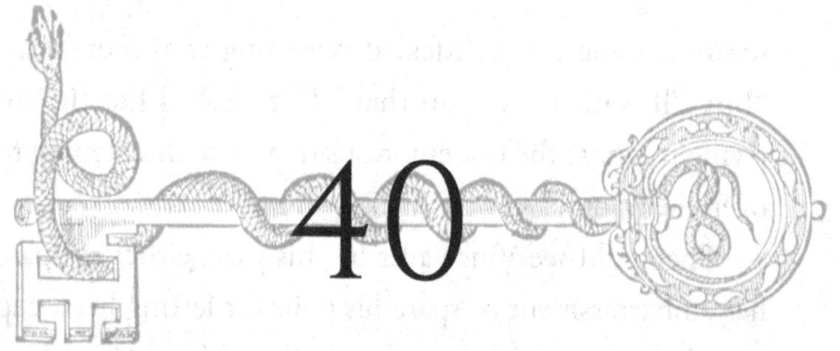

40

S EVERAL WEEKS INTO HIS loneliness, Ethan found some camaraderie amongst the guards. Apparently, heartbreak was an excellent conversation starter. One of the guards, who called himself "Duke" even though his nametag said Dwayne, introduced him to the "prop room."

On the main floor, several doors down from the cafeteria, was an unmarked door. It had one lock that was meant for a bathroom. The right-sized screwdriver was all Duke needed to pick it. "Bathroom stalls have better locks than this," Ethan commented as Duke swung open the wide metal door.

"It's hidden in plain sight. It's one of Danato's tricks," Duke said. Ethan noticed his Texan accent got stronger when they were doing something they weren't supposed to. Everything about him screamed cowboy: His blond curls begged to be clustered under a cowboy hat. His bowed legs hinted at a childhood of excessive horseback riding. His thick nose either meant those horses had bucked him off a lot, or he just got into too many bar fights in his youth. "It works pretty well," Duke said, "until a couple of lonely guards start looking for a love shack." Ethan eyed him, a little uncomfortable with the discussion, since he had never seen a female guard on the premises. "Not me, Bud." Duke winked and flicked the light switch just inside the door.

Three dangling fluorescent bulbs hummed to life, lining their way through the room. The room was at least twenty feet deep and ten feet wide, and filled to the brim with crap: beautiful, abnormal, expensive, ancient crap. The sum total of the world's worst garage sale was hiding in this room.

"What is all this?" Ethan grazed his finger across an old wooden desk. His finger turned black from the thick layer of dust.

"Fetishes."

"Pardon?" Ethan sputtered, wiping his finger on his jeans.

"Fetishes, idols, religious paraphernalia; this stuff is confiscated from the prisoners when they get collected. Some of it is supposedly magical, so we can't let the prisoners get hold of it. Like this." Duke held up what appeared to be a stick.

Upon closer inspection, Ethan determined that it was in fact... "A stick?"

"Yeah, to you and me, but to the Sorcerer Ogana, this is the very instrument that could free him from his prison."

"You've seen the sorcerers?" Ethan asked.

"Once, for a second or two."

"Danato still hasn't let me in there. What's it like?"

"Dangerous."

Ethan rolled his eyes. "Everything around here is dangerous."

Duke gave him a smirk before picking up a horse statue. He poked around its belly, as if he expected little Trojan men to pop out of it. "There's no way to contain a sorcerer, so they roam freely inside the time bubble. It's constantly monitored to stabilize it. It isn't the type of place you just visit."

"I see. I think. What about the Elementals? Have you seen them?"

"Yeah, they're a pain in the ass. They are no more imprisoned here than the sorcerers are."

"Have you been stationed on the top floor?"

"No one has. Only military personnel are allowed to guard them."

"Military?" Ethan had never been told this. "I didn't even know we had military."

"Yeah, they are an exclusive contract. No one but the military can handle the elementals. We don't even see them unless something goes wrong."

"What about the rest of the guards? Are you contracted?"

Duke laughed. "Oh, you're serious." His smile faded. "Boy howdy, he's keeping you at arm's length, isn't he? No bud, we're all cons."

"Cons?"

"Armed robbery, twenty-seven counts." Duke patted his chest, recounting the number of crimes like home runs. "We're prisoners from other facilities. Most of us have life sentences, but the right candidates can get reduced sentences—or delayed execution in the case of death row inmates—if we cooperate and obey the rules. It's hard work, but you're either doing something in prison, or you're doing nothing. Either way, better here than in a nine-by-nine cell."

Ethan stared at Duke, trying to match him with the new description.

"Man, you really didn't know. I'm sorry if that's a kill-joy."

"I guess I thought you guys were allowed to leave on vacations or something."

"Our vacations are going back to our original prisons to visit with family and justify taxpayer dollars."

Ethan nodded. "I guess that should make me feel better. I'm not the only one stuck here."

"Yeah." Duke wrapped his arm around his neck and ruffled his hair. "This place isn't so bad. It would be downright pleasant if it weren't for the lack of television."

"Thank you!" Ethan threw up his hands. "I thought I was the only one being tortured by that. Not even a bloody radio."

"I definitely hear that." Duke pulled a mask from a pile of equally ugly masks. "Hey, check this out. You ever see *The Mask* with Jim Carrey?"

"Sure." Ethan reached for the mask.

Duke pulled it away and waggled it in his face like an index finger to a disobedient dog. "Don't put anything in this pile on your face." He threw the mask back in the pile. "Oh, and don't put any rings on, or rub any oil lamps."

"Seriously?" Ethan smirked. "Are there really genies in them?"

"Oh yeah, I rubbed one lamp, thinking that a genie would pop out and grant me three wishes. Instead, I got a skin rash, the runs, and hair loss. Apparently I wasn't worthy."

"Why? Because you're a criminal?"

"No, because I wanted three wishes; it's a conundrum for the ages. What's really messed up is even though Danato explained the "desires clause" very clearly, I still went back and did it two more times. I was bald for like a whole year. So, trust a very slow learner: don't... rub... the lamp." Duke pointed at him vehemently.

Ethan laughed for the first time in ages. "Damn, is everything cursed? I was really hoping to bring something back with me."

"Like what?" Duke started looking around for something safe. "You pick. I'll tell you if it's cursed or not."

Ethan surveyed the room and saw a set of mirrors leaning against the walls. He remembered Cori's comment about watching his workout for good form. "How about a mirror for the gym?"

"Let me check." Duke climbed over a set of table and chairs to get to them. "As long as there aren't any people living in it, you can have it."

"People live in the mirrors?" He wondered why he even bothered to question anything anymore. He had pole-vaulted down the rabbit hole the minute Danato rescued him from a village that jumped continents at will. It was a waste of energy trying to stay on top of this new reality.

"Sure. Mirror people. It happens. I don't really know how, but... let's see." Duke pulled a small mirror from the stack and reflected it back on the first mirror. The image of a little girl came up on the small mirror that didn't reflect into the larger mirror. "Oh, hell no." Duke put it aside and checked another one, and when that one reflected nothing but white, he grimaced and shook his head and put it aside. The third showed no reflection in either mirror. "That's your mirror. It's a little big."

"That's fine. I need it for my workouts."

"That'll do it, then. I'll help you get it to the gym." They lifted the mirror and headed out. "Needless to say, this isn't the type of excursion you should share with Danato."

"Against the rules?" Ethan asked.

"No, just frowned upon. Dangerous stuff is against the rules. Mischief is *frowned upon*. I'm just not particularly fond of Danato's frowns."

"Understood," Ethan said.

41

THREE WEEKS AFTER ARRIVING in the south of France, Vince was already packing to leave again. Cori looked on with concern from the bed while he rummaged through his dresser drawers. Although their relationship had remained at the level of platonic roommates, she kept her word to wait for him to trust her.

"I can't believe you're going back there," she said, leaning over her crossed legs to play with the frayed ties on the quilt. The bedspread looked like something Vince had gotten from his grandmother. She liked it, though. It had kept her warm, which was good since she had spent every night alone in the queen bed.

Vince looked up as he packed his extra clothes. "You know I have to."

"I know. I just thought you could go somewhere else."

"If I don't go back, Danato will send the collectors out for me."

She shrugged. "So? We'll hide out here. Put on disguises when we go out."

He shook his head with a serious smirk on his face. "Still think you're tough, don't you?" Her eyes narrowed.

"If I'm worried about the collectors, you should be worried too."

"I'm not afraid of bounty hunters." She pushed back on the bed and leaned against the headboard.

He smiled full-on. She enjoyed seeing it, even if it was at her expense. "They aren't so much bounty hunters as beasts from hell, trapped in semi-human form. As much as I'd like to show you one, I'm not willing to endure their capture again."

"They captured *you*?" she mocked his ego.

"I missed my curfew once." He threw his bag near the door and dug his coat from the closet. The long black trench, although still overkill for a werewolf, reminded Cori of how attracted she was to him. She looked over his familiar features that were so close to her, yet so off limits.

"What will Danato do when you get back?" she said, pulling her gaze back to his eyes.

He shrugged into his coat. "Yell... a lot."

"Will he keep you locked up?"

"No, in my human form, he has no right to detain me." With his coat on, Vince pulled his duffel bag over his shoulder and left the room.

Cori sat on the bed, waiting for him to come back, but she heard the front door open and shut. She ran out after him. She jumped onto the front porch, which wasn't much more than a wooden pole supporting an awning over a short stone patio. Vince was already walking down the drive toward town, where he planned to catch a ride to the nearest train station.

"Hey!" she yelled at his back.

He turned around and waited for an explanation.

Cori stood with her mouth agape, waiting for *his* explanation. She hadn't expected a tearful heart-felt goodbye with kisses and hugs, but a grunted "see ya" would have sufficed.

She lifted her arms to the sky in a silent w*hat the hell?*

He said nothing.

Tears were her only response to his silence. She couldn't withhold them. Not after this insult. She lowered her hands and backed up to the cottage door.

Her voice trembled and cracked as she snarled, "Bye."

Vince didn't wave or offer any words of apology. His stony face turned from her view. He walked on with long strides until he was around the bend in the drive and out of sight.

Cori stumbled into the small cottage and slipped to the floor just inside the door. She sobbed long and hard over the slight and wondered how much longer she could endure this humiliation.

42

THE ELEVATOR DOORS TO the part-time level opened and Vince walked out, this time handcuffed and flanked by guards. Danato waited for him at his cell. He signaled the guards to stand down and Vince walked the remaining fifty feet on his own.

In his human form, Vince was nearly four inches shorter than Danato and *looked* eighty pounds lighter, but Danato never made assumptions about size with Vince. They had never come to a physical altercation in human form, and hopefully never would, no matter what foolishness Vince had undertaken.

For a moment, neither spoke. He saw Vince sniff the air, trying to determine his mood.

Danato had always been fond of a good, long silence before an argument. It offered just a moment to reflect on each other before introducing semantics. It also unnerved the crap out of people.

"She's safe," Vince opened.

Danato's face broke character for a moment, revealing his relief that Cori was still with him. "She damn well better be."

"I think we both know what happened here." Vince glanced at the floor; his guilt was apparent. "That is, I think you know how determined Cori is."

"I should have seen it coming. That was my fault," Danato said.

"I should have brought her back," Vince contributed his own fault.

Danato nodded and broke their face-off positions to meander along the cells. "Why didn't you? Bring her back?"

"I..." Vince paused. Danato looked back and saw him, too pained to form the right words.

"You love her," Danato said it for him.

Vince exhaled a breath he must have been holding onto. "If I brought her back, she would hate me, and we would be done. I guess I just wanted to be with her for more than a few hours before and after the full moon. Besides, I don't even know if she loves me back. I might have just been part of her plan, and she even said I was, but..." He shook his head and broke the handcuffs from his wrists with little more effort than breaking a rubber band. They clanked on the glossy concrete floor, now useless.

"I'm being stupid," he said, absorbed in his thoughts. "I see that now. I should just bring her back. I know the trouble you could get into. That she could get into."

"You're only saying that because she isn't here. Once you return to her, you will change your mind again," Danato said.

Vince shook his head, but when he looked at Danato, he nodded. "You're right. I've avoided this for so long, and now I can't resist it."

"Are you sure you want to do that to her?"

"Is it selfish?" Vince looked forlorn. His eyes pleaded with Danato to give him the answer he wanted.

"Not if you both choose it."

Vince's face fell. Danato knew that wasn't what he wanted to hear. "I can't tell her. She'll pull away. I know it. She'll protect herself from me. I don't want that. I want normal, two normal people in love." Vince stepped into his human cell and closed the door. "I will bring her back... when it is all said and done. I promise. I will make her promise me."

Danato moved to the cell door and locked it. He reached his hand between the bars and gripped Vince's shoulder. "I won't look forward to that day."

With a nod of agreement, they left their feud behind.

43

CORI WAITED FOUR DAYS. She expected Vince home by supper, but he never showed. The dining room table, previously the paint table, had been cleared off to make room for a bouquet of fresh-cut flowers she picked from the gardens outside.

Floral china from the cabinet in the hallway sat on white linen place mats. A pitcher of crisp lemonade in a metal pitcher waited to be poured into the crystal glasses by the plates. The smell of turkey with roasted potatoes permeated the house from the kitchen oven where it was drying out. Two big hunks of meat had already been removed when Vince didn't show.

The tall candles on the table were down to nubs, leaving very little light for the room. The sun was already gone, and so was Cori's anticipation. She had curled up on the couch to sleep. She expected to wake up in the morning alone, or to find Vince asleep in his own bed without her. Either way, she was done. He had walked on her enough. She had no more room left in her ego to bolster his trust.

She was content enough with that scenario that she didn't even hear the door open and shut. By the time she realized she wasn't alone, her company was standing over her at the foot of the couch, watching her.

As awareness kicked in, she jumped and pushed back on the couch. Her heart was in her throat and a shiver of adrenaline coursed through her. She blinked at the shadow before her. "Vince?"

He said nothing. He looked over to the table where two place settings invited a romantic dinner.

Cori rubbed her face and caught a glimpse of something pink on her hand. Her lipstick had become a casualty of the evening as well. She wiped the remainder of her lipstick off and wiped it on her jeans.

Vince looked back at her. "You're still here," he said in a low voice.

Cori scoffed. "Don't worry, not for long. I'm going in the morning. Dinner's in the oven if you're hungry. Do me a favor and stick it in the fridge when you're done. I'll take the couch tonight. You can have your bed." She scooted back down on the couch to return to her slumber.

"I saw the lights out when I came around the drive," he whispered, almost to himself. "I thought you had gone."

"I should have," she mumbled through her hands tucked under her cheek.

"Yes, you should have."

Anger filled her heart beyond the pain of the statement and she pushed back up to her knees to face him. "I said I will leave tomorrow. Do you expect me to wander the streets at night?"

The room was dark, but she was close enough to see him now. His eyes were red and the skin below them moist. She leaned back, not prepared for this emotion from him. She looked him over and saw something in his hands.

He followed her gaze and lifted the small bouquet of baby roses adorned with baby's breath. He looked them over as if he forgot he had them. "I treated you so horribly. Why did you stay?"

"I don't know. You wanted proof that I wanted to be with you. If you can behave like that much of a jackass and have me still stay, then I must really love you."

Vince's eyes widened. She felt her cheeks flush. She hadn't meant to say that aloud. She had thought about saying it so many times, but controlled the urge. Now she had just blurted it out right into his ears, where she could never recover it.

"Love?"

She shrugged, unable to talk herself out of the admission. "Yeah, well, I thought so." She sat back on her heels. "Just as well I didn't say it sooner; you might have kicked me out sooner."

Vince shook his head. "Cori, I'm glad that you're here. I'm relieved you're here. I never wanted you to go. I have never *not* wanted you."

"You were just testing me to see how much I would take?"

"No, I was giving you the opportunity to leave. I didn't want you to stay with me out of obligation or convenience."

She could see the pain in his eyes. She had not expected that. "I'm sorry I made you betray Danato." She paused, rolling the ring on her thumb. "How is he?"

"He's angry about the situation, but he's coping. We can discuss that later." Vince's tears had dried up, and he was looking at her hard, like he was angry. "I'm sorry for... the last month."

She nodded and looked away. She wasn't entirely ready to say it was all forgiven.

"I will make it up to you. I promise." He tossed his flowers on the table and slipped out of his trench, which he folded neatly on the back of the couch. "Starting with tonight."

Vince crawled onto the couch, easing her supine on the way. He rested his body against her and stopped there. Her heart was back to racing and images good and bad flashed through her mind. She wasn't in control of this encounter, and it was making her tremble and sweat.

He drew his finger along her cheek. "I won't hurt you," he said, apparently sensing her apprehension. She nodded and tried to kiss him. He pulled back. "I can wait until you're ready."

It was another minute before she felt the heat of his body more than the fear in hers. He kissed her softly. Waited. Kissed her again.

The slow motion foreplay eased her mind and riled her spirit. She soon found herself leading. She pulled off her clothes and helped with his. She drew him in and wielded him. He did everything she asked, and some things she only thought.

As if trying to make up for the last three weeks in one night, he exhausted her anxiety, her cynicism, her boundaries, and finally, her stamina. She collapsed in a ball on the couch mumbling, "I love you" into the sofa cushion. He curled up around her, pulling the drop sheet from the sofa back over them.

He whispered into her ear, "I love you too," before squeezing her and falling asleep.

44

E THAN LOOKED DOWN AT the "protein drink" Danato had poured for him. The same lime-colored smoothie sat on the desk, just as it had every morning for the last three months. The thick slimy beverage tasted slightly sweet and grassy.

He had obediently downed the beverage every day, but his not-so-gradual muscle gain had left him concerned about the contents of it. He wasn't entirely sure he wasn't being drugged.

Danato was deep in his paperwork, unaware that Ethan was having second thoughts about his nutritional supplements. Belus was watching him from the open office door. He was waiting for him to drink so they could be on their way.

"Come on, kid," Belus urged.

He picked up the glass and examined its contents. He couldn't deny that his strength had improved. Nor could he deny his increase in speed. And one would be blind not to notice his change in muscle size. But at what expense was he to achieve all of this? What would the side effects be? He had a right to know what he was putting in his body.

"Drink it," Danato said, eyeing him over his glasses.

"What's in it?" he said, lifting the glass to examine it up close.

"The same as yesterday," Danato said flatly, still watching him. "The same as the day before that."

He looked back at Belus, who bowed his head at the beverage. "I just don't want to be taking steroids. I think this is too much."

Danato shook his head. "It's not steroids."

"What is it?" he asked again. Belus groaned and came all the way into the office. He closed the door, giving up on an early start. Danato shook his head. "What?" Ethan pleaded. "Shouldn't I be allowed to know what goes in my body?"

"Yes." Danato rested his cheek on one of his hands.

"Well?" He motioned to the glass.

"It's just..." Danato looked to Belus. His second threw his hands up, imparting no assistance on the matter. "It has an ingredient that sort of..."

Danato's apprehension only disturbed Ethan more. "Is it dangerous?"

"No, it's perfectly safe. I've taken it for years." Danato posed a bicep. "Still do, occasionally."

"Then what is it? God help me, I couldn't drink it now for fear of it, anyway."

"It has a biological element mixed with wheat grass and citrus." Danato stopped there, but Ethan wasn't that easily satisfied.

"What the hell *is* it?"

Danato glanced once more at Belus before his face turned somber and he mumbled the missing ingredient. "Dragon semen."

The lime-green smoothie slipped from Ethan's hand and dropped back to the desk. Shards of glass, and the biological element it held, splattered the room and its occupants.

"*What?*" Ethan shrieked.

Belus dropped his face into his hands and laughed. Danato and Ethan, wearing the majority of the beverage, didn't share his jovial outlook.

"Now you know why I didn't tell you," Danato grumbled as he scraped green gook from his face.

"That's disgusting!" Ethan spat the beverage from his lips.

"Of course it's disgusting!" Danato pulled tissues from his desk drawer and cleaned up more thoroughly. "I drank the stuff for years."

"I can't drink that now." Ethan motioned vaguely to the splayed contents.

"Bullshit, you can't. You wanted to know; now you know." Danato jabbed a finger at him. "Instead of having a protein shake potentially laced with steroids, you will now drink dragon sperm laced with wheat grass."

"No way," he said resolutely.

Danato's face hardened. "Let's not pretend that you have a choice here."

"It's dragon..." Ethan's mouth formed the words, but he gagged.

"Yes, it is." Danato threw a cluster of tissues in the trashcan. They hit the bottom with a sickening splotch. "More importantly, it is the safest, most effective natural steroid *not* known to man. You will drink it, just as you have every morning for the last three months."

"I'll puke it up! Look at me!" He held his mouth, feeling himself heave again.

"I have an endless supply of it."

Ethan was about to object again, but he saw the determination in Danato. There was no more arguing this point. He forcefully swallowed as he looked down at the mess of green on him.

"There's a lesson for you, kid," Belus said as he opened the door. "Never ask a question you don't want the answer to." His uproarious laughter continued until the door shut behind him.

45

THE HANGAR DOOR LOOMED before Ethan. He stared at it curiously. He tilted his head one way, then the other. Belus stood beside him, looking from the door to him. "What are you looking at?"

"It must be huge," Ethan said.

"It is."

"How does it live in there?" He shifted the sword holstered on his hip.

"They are surprisingly docile creatures. They prefer cool, dark places. I suppose it stems back to the days when they sheltered in caves."

"I could see that." He nodded absent-mindedly.

"You ready for this, kid?"

He shook his head. "I don't suppose we can postpone it?"

"Nope, gotta stick to the schedule."

Ethan took a deep breath. "Just one more thing: is this the one you guys get the stuff from?"

Belus thought about what he meant and shook his head. "No, this one's a girl," he said and ran back to the front of the gym as fast as his legs would carry him. He pulled a large red lever by the light switch. The massive garage door on the opposite side of the gym shuddered and lifted with a groan. "Good luck!" Belus hollered over the noise.

Ethan looked back at him. A long red line separated the gym into the safe half and the not-so-safe half. Until now, he had paid little attention to it. He took a deep breath and pulled his sword.

The rising door revealed curved yellowing claws, dull blue-green scales, and flaring nostrils with just a tinge of mucus. Just as Ethan suspected, she was the size of a private jet—give or take some variations in girth. There was one thing he hadn't expected, though.

As he stood at attention, prepared to fight, the massive dragon sprawled before him was fast asleep.

"She's sleeping," he whispered and glanced back at Belus.

"Yeah, they're like cats," Belus said, leaning against the door with his arms crossed. "They sleep most of their life. Which is good, because she's a pain in the ass to walk."

Ethan gave Belus a questioning look about this statement, but movement drew his eye back to the dragon.

"Oh, she's waking up now," Belus said. "We ought to have a good battle in twenty minutes or so."

Ethan looked back at him to verify the time and dropped his sword with a scoff.

Thirty minutes later, Belus still leaned against the door to the gym, while Ethan resorted to lying on the floor. He brandished his sword at the ceiling. "So, she really doesn't spit fire?" he asked.

"No, the answer hasn't changed. She is a big, fat, lazy mammalian lizard. She isn't magic, and we don't call her Puff."

"But she flies, right?" Ethan asked.

"When she feels like it." Belus looked up with interest at the hangar. "You know that… stuff you drink?"

"Yes."

"You're about to find out why we make you take it."

He raised his head to look at the hangar. The dragon was awake. Bowed down low, she twitched her tail furiously. Her wings shuffled as she eyed a certain someone within her perimeter. Her low grumble vibrated his eardrums.

Game on.

She darted at him with surprising speed. Ethan jumped upright and blocked her bite with a clumsy sword parry. Her sheer strength of mass pushed him back. He regained his balance, only to be knocked down with her tail.

Her head darted in again for a bite. He blocked. The sword bounced off the hard scales around her mouth. It made a satisfying clank, but did nothing to hurt her.

He retreated into the curl of her body where he could see her tail and her face, a mistake he would never repeat. He shrieked as her rear claws ripped into his back.

Her massive paw pushed him face down onto the cold cement floor. He could feel the weight pressing on his lungs. He couldn't inhale. He could only exhale.

Over the sound of his own wheezing and the dragon's congested snorts, he heard Belus yelling, "Toss away the sword!" His right arm was outstretched in front of him. He was no longer holding the weapon, but it was within his reach. He pulled it back to him and slid it out again.

As the blade gained distance from him, the weight of the dragon lifted. He inhaled deeply, feeling the first of many cracked ribs that would come from these exercises.

He saw Belus rushing to his aid, and then nothing.

46

WITHOUT CONCERN OF BEING caught, Cori and Vince were free to return to his apartment in Paris, where they flourished. Vince spared no expense in romancing Cori with dinners, clothes, and jewelry. They took every opportunity to enjoy the nightlife the city offered.

On the way back from one such evening, Cori's high heel got stuck in a grate. "Oh, wait," she said as their linked hands threatened to break. "I did it again." She groaned.

Vince laughed and returned to rescue her. They were both dressed in their finest clothes, having just come from dinner. She was wearing a flirty red dress that lifted when she spun and, of course, stilettos that she didn't have an operating license for. He was in gray slacks with a light blue shirt that felt like a sweater, but was as thin as a t-shirt.

He pulled up his sleeves, revealing two wide leather bangles that decorating his wrists. He kneeled down to remove the shoe's heel from the hole it had lodged in.

"Maybe stilettos are not the best shoe for me," she said, leaning on him for support.

"I don't think high heels, in general, are good for you." Vince released her shoe and looked around the sidewalk behind them. Cori could see him sniffing the air. He did it more at night when he was concerned about muggers. Not that he felt threatened by human attacks, but his concern was for guns. She was still vulnerable to gunshots, even if he wasn't.

"See someone?" she asked. His eyes shot up to her, and he shook his head. Even if he had sensed something, he probably wouldn't tell her. He got her shoe out and ushered her to move along.

"What's the hurry?" she asked, feeling the strain in her shins from the quick pace.

"We should get home."

"No, I want to go dancing."

He looked at her pleading eyes and smiled. He sniffed the air again. "Yes, we can dance, but not too late. I need to be at the gallery tomorrow."

They walked on toward their destination, without concern for anyone or anything that might lurk in the dark behind them.

"Don't you think I should start looking for a job?" Cori asked.

"I would prefer if you didn't."

"Why? Don't you like money?" She scoffed.

"Sure, but I would rather you stay out of the public eye while you're dating me."

"So, when I break up with you I can get a job?" she asked cheerily.

"Precisely," he smirked. "Do you, by chance, know when that will be? I have a few girls lined up and they won't wait forever."

She punched his shoulder, and he pretended it hurt. "You slime, now I'm never going to break up with you." She shoved him against the brick building they were walking along, which took a great deal of effort on her part. "You'll just have to suffer with me forever."

He pulled her body against his. "It will be an arduous task, but I will have to endure it." He gave her a lascivious grin and let out a low rumble in his throat that could only be described as a growl.

She could feel the heat of his body as he leaned in for a kiss. She pulled herself out of his arms. His hands dragged along her body but didn't hold onto her. He was always very careful never to force her or subdue her. His face showed his confusion at her retreat.

"We should save this for after dancing." She waited for his response. She expected either a complaint about her rejection or a begrudged surrender, but he just smirked and crossed his arms.

"Come on." She tugged at his arm.

He shook his head and let his eyes traverse her curves.

"No, we're in the middle of Paris. Someone will come by any moment."

He said nothing, but raised his index finger to point at her. He turned his hand and motioned with that powerful finger for her to come hither.

She bit her lip and came over to him slowly. He laughed at her reluctance. He pulled her close and gave her a long, sultry kiss, but she no longer felt the heat in his body.

"You are such a tease." He swatted her butt before taking her by the hand to walk on.

"We're right on the street," she explained.

"Yes, yes, but refusing me even one kiss is just cruel."

"Crueler to give you *only* one kiss, don't you think?" She looked away, hiding her red face.

"I suppose, but..." He stopped her mid-step and dipped her back for a long, sensual kiss that sent shivers down her body. He parted from her and brought her back up swiftly. Her head spun from it and the kiss. She leaned her head against his shoulder. "The one kiss is for your benefit, my love," he whispered in her ear. "Think of it as priming."

She lifted her head from his shoulder and looked into his twinkling brown eyes. She loved the power he had over her. She was defenseless against his charms, and she savored the defeat. She lifted herself up to his lips for another kiss, but he pulled away. "No, no, we're in the middle of the street." He clicked his tongue.

"What about priming?" she said, licking her top lip.

He smiled and laughed a little. "You'd better be careful, love." He kept a smile on his face, but his words were heavy with warning. "Unlike you, I have no reservations about ripping off your panties and putting you against that wall."

She pulled back and stood away from him for a moment. As hot as it sounded to have sex in a public place, the reality was embarrassing and illegal. She smiled and put her hands behind her back. They walked for a few blocks without touching or talking to cool themselves off.

"How about there?" She pointed to a club two blocks up where a steady stream of people kept the volume of the music adjusting with the opening and shutting of the door.

"Sure," he said, taking her hand again.

Vince pushed through crowds of people huddling by the front door. A few annoyed patrons tried to keep him back to maintain their position in the immobile herd, but trying to stop Vince was like blocking an elephant: possible, but never successful.

Cori tucked in tight behind him, slipping through the parted sea of people before it closed behind him. He kept his hand to his back so she could keep in contact with him. If her fingers slipped from his hand, he would stop and go back to retrieve her.

Waves of tobacco smoke, pot smoke, and maybe a few more Cori hadn't jaded herself with, billowed through the air. The booming music would have been an instant headache to anyone over the age of forty. Truthfully, it made her head hurt too, but somehow the youthful desire to party overruled the brain shaking-volume.

They found a spot on the dance floor where they could hide inside the crowd. Cori did better on the dance floor with stilettos than she did walking. A few heavy songs got her moving. She hadn't really considered herself a good dancer, but she liked to move to the music. She closed her eyes and moved in whatever way felt right. The memory of dancing with her doppelgangers made her smile.

Several songs later, they played something slower for the romantics in the club. Mostly, it was an excuse for everyone to grind. Cori hung onto Vince in spite of being hot and sweaty. She laid her head on his shoulder, an opportunity she rarely had without stilettos. As she looked around the room at the couples grinding to the love song, she caught a few couples outright dry humping each other. Cori chuckled at this. At least they weren't out in the street.

As her survey moved up to the balcony section, she saw eyes staring back at her. A woman, typically French: tall, slender, with short black hair and a cigarette between her fingers like a natural extension of her hand. She was staring right at her. Cori averted her eyes for a while and looked back, but the woman was still openly staring at her, and wouldn't stop.

"Vince." Cori spoke without moving her lips.

"Yes."

"There is a woman staring at me up in the balcony. Do you know her?"

He looked up and immediately looked back down.

"Well, who is she? A nut-job ex-girlfriend?"

"I've never met her before," he said.

"Why did you look away so fast, then?" Cori leaned back to look at his face. He looked flustered, to say the least.

He pulled away from her. "I have to go talk to her."

"Why? If you never met her…"

He grabbed her shoulders. "I'll explain when I get back. Please wait for me at the bar." Without further explanation, he disappeared into the crowd. The wake of people closed too rapidly for her to follow.

She went to the bar as he had asked and bought herself a drink, so someone else did not offer her one. She sat on a stray bar stool that was only free because a cluster of people were blocking it from view. She kept her eyes fixed upstairs, dodging between heads to get the best shot.

Vince approached the woman, angrily shaking his finger and pointing vaguely in Cori's direction. The woman remained calm. As the one-sided argument went on, the woman kept her calm, but Vince lost his ire.

He pulled his fingers through his hair and shuffled before her, frustrated as she took her turn to speak. At one point in her dialogue, she touched his arm, which he sloughed off, but she grabbed him with a tighter grip, and he didn't resist. He glanced down toward the bar, probably looking for Cori, but her people cluster hid her.

Even with a full drink still in her hand, a man came to Cori and offered to buy her one. She glanced at him, held up her drink, and shook her head. When her attention returned to the balcony, she saw the woman kissing Vince. Open-mouthed and full tongue, by the looks of it. Vince wasn't pulling away.

Cori's eyes locked onto the scene like a car crash. A head in her way left her craning to see around. She had no thoughts or emotions yet. She was in shock that the event was even taking place.

As soon as the embrace was done, the woman disappeared out of view. Vince looked over the balcony again, searching for her. He looked tired and distraught. He pushed off the railing and headed back downstairs to find her.

Upstairs, the French woman returned to the balcony. She looked directly at Cori, having no trouble finding her. She smiled down at her. The bitch was pleased as punch that Cori had seen the encounter. Before she could decide if it would be childish to flip her off, Vince reached through her protective people cluster and grabbed her by the arm.

He pulled her off the stool and dragged her away, much to the concern of the cluster, who, until then, didn't know she was there. Her full drink was upset by the abrupt movement and wound up on the shirt of the gentleman previously offering her one. She mouthed "sorry" to him as she backpedaled through the crowd in tow behind Vince.

Vince stomped down the sidewalk away from the club, still holding Cori's wrist in his concrete grip. She knew better than to try to escape his clutches. It was hopeless.

With him in such an irate state, she didn't dare confront him on the kiss, nor did she mention that the pace they were moving at was causing her to blister in her shoes.

After six unbearable blocks, an uncontainable squeak escaped her lips. It was quiet, but it made him stop. He looked back at her for the meaning behind her yelp. She said nothing. He examined her, trying to see what harm had come to her. She stood silent, not willing to admit to any pain. His eyes settled on her shoes. Her heels were bleeding. The stilettos' tight fit had rubbed her raw.

Vince shook his head and released his grip on her. He leaned down, gently removed her shoes, and handed them to her. Rather than make her walk the mucky sidewalks barefoot, he swept her into his arms and carried her the remaining five blocks to their apartment.

Once there, she still didn't broach the topic of the woman. Vince seemed aggravated enough as it was. He focused his attention on her heels. He sat her on the couch and carefully disinfected her cuts, placed salve on them, and bandaged them.

When he was done, he crawled onto the couch with her and made love to her with a certain sadness, as if the next morning he would be gone.

47

To her relief, the next morning he wasn't gone. She found him in the kitchenette making her breakfast—French toast, her favorite. He usually refused to make it because he said it was like eating cake for breakfast. He always preferred eggs and toast, which she argued was exactly what French toast was, just without the syrup.

He turned from the griddle with his spatula in hand and smiled at her.

She couldn't muster a smile. Too much of last night was still fresh in her mind. "Are you leaving me?" she asked, trying for mature honesty.

"No," he said, with no hesitation or confusion about her abrupt question. "I am concerned how long you will be staying with me after I tell you who that woman was."

She sighed and tried to remain levelheaded, which essentially meant she had to wall off her emotions for the time being. "That bad?"

"I think you'll think so." He put down the spatula and turned off the griddle, letting the remaining heat finish the batch of golden slices.

"So, who is she?" Cori sat on the step stool to hear his story.

"To clarify, I have not met her before last night. She is, however, a kindred spirit, in the sense that she's a werewolf."

"A female werewolf?"

"Yes, there are a good number in Paris, most of which I have met. Most of which I have mated with. They rarely choose the same male twice." Cori said nothing. She realized all at once that werewolves were not sired like vampires, if that was even true, but birthed like all mammals. "A female chooses her partner for mating once a year."

"Just once?"

"Once a year for the purpose of procreation. Beyond that, they often seek out human males. During their annual fertile time, they won't touch a human male. They'd likely kill them if they did, anyway."

"She's chosen you as her mate?"

"Yes."

"You've done this before, I take it."

"Yes."

"But not with her?" she verified.

"No."

"I assume you told her *no*."

Vince shook his head. "It's not that simple."

She raised an eyebrow. "It usually is. No means no."

"Not for a female werewolf. She has chosen me, just as all the others did; I had no choice in it."

Cori laughed. "Fine, she wants you, but that doesn't automatically mean she can have you. Tell her to find someone else. She can't just force you to do it."

Vince's head lowered to hide a certain shame on his face.

"What? She will make you mate with her? You can't tell me she is stronger than you."

Vince nodded.

Cori shook her head.

Vince nodded again.

"This woman will force you to have sex with her, and you aren't strong enough to fight her off," she said, losing a few bricks from her emotional wall.

"Strength in female werewolves fluctuates, but they are generally stronger than males. If she is looking to mate, the hormones running through her will make her even stronger. I tried to fight off a female once. She nearly killed me, and in the end, I still ended up doing her bidding."

Cori stood and took a few steps away from Vince before proceeding. "This sounds insane. It sounds made up. It sounds like an excuse for you to just sleep with some other woman. How would I begin to verify this? This could be a load of bullshit and I wouldn't know, because I'm just a stupid human!" Down went the wall.

"Cori, I love you. I could have met up with this woman on the sly and never told you. It might have spared your feelings, but I need you to know that this is the downside of dating a werewolf, at least one of them, and if you don't want to deal with this, then you shouldn't stay with me."

Cori's mouth dropped. "You're just begging me to break up with you."

"No!" Vince reached out before she could move away. He wrapped his arm around her waist and pulled her to him. She fought, but his arms wrapped around her, holding her captive in his embrace. For the first time in a long time, he showed his dominance. "Please understand what I am seeking from you. I want to know if I should simply deal with her and go back to life as usual, or do you want me to fight her off?"

"You just said you nearly died last time." Despite his clutches, she continued to struggle, a marker of the warrior within her... and the fool.

"What will make you more comfortable: a half-dead raped man or an unfaithful one?" He released her and she nearly fell back.

She recovered somewhat ungracefully and shot him a scowl. Her face softened when she looked at him. He looked miserable with worry. He wanted to do the right thing, but he honestly didn't know what that was. She shook her head. "I don't know what you should do."

"Neither do I."

For the first time since they were together, Vince didn't have the answers. He wasn't leading her. He wasn't giving her the solution. He wasn't strong enough to fix this problem. And if Vince wasn't strong enough, then all hope was lost.

Vince grabbed his spatula and tossed the remaining French toast onto his platter, each scrape on the pan a little more aggressive than the last. She moved behind him and touched his arm. He tensed, but didn't turn to look at her.

She tugged on his bicep. He stopped moving, but he still didn't turn around. She gave up and wrapped her arms around his stomach. "Vince." She stood on tiptoes to whisper into his ear.

"I'm sorry," he said before she could continue.

"I'm not leaving you, Vince," she said. "Not ever. I love you. That doesn't just go away when things get tough. We'll figure this out, together."

He turned to face her. His eyes were red and skirted with moisture. It was the second time she had seen him this upset, and she got the distinct impression that it was a rare spectacle.

Despite the grief in his eyes, a slight smile crossed his face. He brought his arm around her waist, slower this time, in case she wanted to pull away. He lifted her up onto the counter beside the plate of French toast.

He tossed the spatula away and pulled her face down to kiss him. His hands gripped her waist and pulled her just to the edge of the counter against him. She knew he wanted to have her right there; his apology for the events to come, and his celebration of her devotion to him. But she couldn't.

She pulled back and smiled. "That French toast smells really good," she said, glancing at the plate of warm, soft, buttery bread, soon to be sticky sweet with syrup.

He glanced over at them, not understanding what she was talking about. With visible disappointment, he backed away from her. "I made them just for you." He smiled and gathered the remaining ingredients for breakfast.

He glanced over at her a few more times, and she smiled at him. She pretended it was just the French toast that had put the damper on their intimacy, and so did he.

48

CORI THOUGHT ABOUT THE choices Vince had given her. It wasn't even a choice, really. Sleep with the woman, or be beaten to death by her. Hmm, which one would *she* choose?

She also thought about how he could simply justify sleeping with another woman because she was a werewolf. *Oh, sorry honey, I ran into another werewolf at the store today. Had to mate with her.* How many "werewolves" could he sleep with and still be the innocent victim?

She trusted Vince, but her insecurities kept telling her she was being used. She tried to rationalize that if he told her about it; it was proof of his honesty. But in the back of her mind, she knew that it just made her culpable in the affair. She could hardly deny him the second werewolf if she had told him to sleep with the first, and so on and so forth.

On top of all the questions brought on by mistrust, self-esteem issues, and general paranoia, she found one question that couldn't be pushed away by rational thought. Could she forgive or forget once it was all said and done? If she knew anything about herself, she knew she was selfish. Vince wasn't the only one with territorial instincts.

Sitting around with this final question in mind, she knew she only had one choice.

In Vince's black trench coat and hat, Cori fled from the apartment. She waited until he had laid down for a nap. He hadn't let her leave the apartment without him for two days. She was feeling overburdened with the stress of this decision, and being cooped up wasn't helping matters.

Strained conversation and a dead sex life were taking their toll. Since Vince had not left the apartment alone either, she assumed that the nefarious werewolf was casing the place in case an impromptu opportunity arose to molest Vince on his way to work or the store.

She got the impression a hotel wouldn't be required for the type of meeting the woman had in mind. With that thought, Cori dodged through people and traffic, making her way to a small park only a few blocks from the apartment.

If the werewolf fell for her bait, she would assume that Vince had given in and was sneaking off for a tete-ta-tete.

She turned into the park and waited by a big metal statue of some man that must have done something important to earn him a big metal statue. A brief thought crossed her mind as she looked up at him: He probably never had to deal with werewolves in heat.

"I wasn't going to follow you," a woman with a thick French accent said behind her. Cori turned in time to see her approach. The lanky French woman looked like she had just stepped out of a business meeting with her dark gray skirt-suit and black heels. "I'm Leona." She grimaced as she looked Cori up and down. "You're a good deal shorter than him, and your smell is distinctly human, undoubtedly female... and you're blond." She brandished her hateful appraisal of Cori's efforts, despite them being adequate enough to lure her out.

"Why *did* you follow me?" she asked.

Leona shrugged apathetically. "You seemed to want my attention. I hope this wasn't a lame attempt to help Vince escape. He isn't that stupid, is he?"

"No, I wanted to talk to you alone."

Leona laughed. "Please." She turned to walk away.

"Wait." Cori jumped in front of her, removing her hat. "I need to speak with you."

Leona blinked as if she couldn't comprehend what her eyes were showing her. "You have no say in this." She pushed past her with a firm shove that Cori sensed was restrained.

"He is mine!" Cori yelled after her. Leona turned back. Cori suspected her ego was just as contentious as Vince's.

"*That* is what makes it oh, so sweet." Her melodic tone draped her words with a pinch of conceit and a handful of ardor. "We females feel it is our duty to choose werewolves that are content in their lives. We like to disrupt that."

"You just enjoy being a bitch?" Cori regretted the insult the minute she said it, but Leona didn't flinch at it.

"It's hard to explain, since I doubt you know the entire truth about werewolves." Leona moved to an open bench and sat. She crossed her finely chiseled legs that had no need for panty hose. Cori hated leggy women; pure jealousy, of course. She wasn't particularly short, but she certainly fell on the side of chicken legs. "We feel it is our obligation as women to break up the relationships between human females and male werewolves."

"Obligation? You're telling me you're doing me a favor?"

"How long have you been with Vince?"

"About six months." Cori wasn't sure if she should be honest, but she got the feeling Leona might smell a lie... literally.

"Then yes, I am doing you a favor." Leona patted the bench for her to sit. "You should break up with him before the one-year mark."

"Why? Because you want him?" she asked.

Leona guffawed, losing her enigmatic facade. "God, no, I only want his fertility. Truth be told, female and male werewolves can't stand each other. We are the fracture of the same creature. That doesn't mesh well. One always has to be submissive in a relationship, or it doesn't work. Our males rarely appreciate that privilege like human men do. Human men rather enjoy it."

Cori sat with her to force the camaraderie even further. She could smell the pungent perfume on Leona. It was a wonder she could smell anything beyond herself. "He says he can't stop you. Is that true?"

"You doubt his honesty?"

"No, I just doubt myself. I don't mind being the submissive one, but I don't want to be the naïve one."

Leona smiled at her and nodded. "As I said, we are not male and female like other animals. We are the same animal. Our procreation is as vital and irresistible as water is to you. He told you that once I have chosen a mate, I can't change my mind?"

"Sort of," she said, doubting it still.

"Well, I can't. For whatever reasons, hormones, whatever, I can't pick another. His scent is all I crave. I won't even eat again until I've had him."

Cori looked away from her. The suggestion of this woman having Vince made her ill. "There is no way that you would be able to leave him alone?"

"Short of you putting a silver bullet in my chest." Cori jerked back to face her. Leona laughed. "I was certainly not suggesting you try. I would likely kill you before you got it near me, but even so, werewolves have few penetrable areas. Besides, silver is more of an irritant than a guaranteed killer." Leona tipped her brow. "The best you could do is make me severely ill."

"Would that allow you to leave Vince alone?" Cori asked it sarcastically, but she was actually considering this as an option over planned cheating.

Leona lost her levity. "You really think you have a chance against me, don't you?"

Cori sighed and leaned back on the bench. There was something easy about speaking to a woman that she knew could kick her ass with her pinky. There was no tension, no question of what to do or say. She was powerless against her, so she might as well just be honest. "I don't mean to insult you, but I need you to understand how important Vince is to me."

"I can see that six months is already too long for you." Leona stood up, dusting off any particles the park bench may have left on her designer skirt. "You know, if you went to jail for murder, or *attempted* murder, Vince wouldn't be here waiting for you."

"Of course he would."

"No, I promise you, even a few years in jail and you would be without the very man you were defending. You can certainly ask him why, but I doubt he would tell you."

"You're just saying this to put distrust in our relationship." Cori stood.

Leona returned to her and leaned in close, nearly rubbing cheeks with her. Cori got another whiff of her perfume and the underlying musk that it was masking. "There is already distrust there, or you wouldn't have come to see me." As she leaned back, she raised her hand to cradle Cori's chin. Once again, knowing the woman's strength, she didn't resist. "As a werewolf, I find kindred spirits far more often in women than men. So, let me say with candor that you will only be hurt by staying in this relationship, but if you do stay with him, I wish you the best of love.... and strength."

Leona's voice seemed to hypnotize Cori. The femwolf leaned in and pressed her lips against hers for a tender kiss, a gentle gesture that was as confusing and cryptic as the rest of their conversation. Leona was gone long before Cori truly felt her absence.

Disappointed by their meeting, but satisfied that Vince was without options, she shook off her daze and returned to the apartment.

WHEN SHE ARRIVED HOME, Vince was still asleep, so she put his coat back and went into the kitchen to make something to eat. She decided on dessert instead of an actual meal and started making cookies. It was a nice benign task that took her mind off... everything. Plus, any benign task that emptied your mind *and* resulted in sweet, chewy goodness was a good thing.

After the first tray went into the oven, she stuck her finger in the batter to take a taste. She raised her finger to her mouth, but before she could eat it, a firm grip simultaneously grabbed her waist and her wrist. She squealed and fought for her delicious bite.

She was no match, of course, and her finger found its way into a different mouth. She giggled as he took the opportunity to not just eat the dough, but suck her finger. She couldn't help but blush at his suggestive play.

She turned around and smiled at him. He smiled and drew himself close to her, letting his face tower over her. "How thoughtful of you to make me cookies."

"These aren't for you. They're all for me."

"Are they? I bet I could convince you to share." He kissed her forehead. "That's one of your attractive qualities." He kissed her nose. "You always offer so much of yourself to me." He kissed her lips, a rich, deep kiss that made her instantly forget everything that was keeping her away from him.

His lips ripped away prematurely. He took a half step back and looked at her with panic in his eyes. He sniffed her neck and face.

"What is it?" she said, surprised that he would break away from a kiss, especially such a heated one.

"You met with her today?" He looked at her, deadly serious. His eyes flashed with anger and concern.

Cori's heart skipped a beat, and she felt instantly hot in the face. She licked her lips, no longer confused by the sweet gesture. "Calm down."

"You did!" He turned and punched an innocent wall. The drywall was no match and cracked.

"Deposit, hello!" she reminded him.

He turned back to her and frantically searched her body for cuts, bruises, and bites.

"It was a civil meeting. She wasn't violent, and neither was I."

"What did you discuss? Me?"

"What else would we speak of? Without you in the mix, we would never have crossed paths." Cori defended against her manhandling with the back of a wooden spoon. One pop was enough to bring him out of his search.

"I don't want you speaking to her." Vince put up a hand, now smudged with chocolate, his parental finger wagging in her face.

"Vince, I already did."

"Why did you speak to her?" He put his hands on her shoulders and shook her, apparently to make the stupidity fall out of her.

"To verify your story and make sure there was nothing I could do to stop her."

"Verify!" His hands were up, his hands were out; eventually he folded them in prayer before his face to keep them still. "You didn't believe me?" His eyes were angry, but his voice faltered at the accusation.

"I trust you with my life, Vince. I am still practicing on trusting you with my heart. As strange as it sounds, I came closer to that conviction today. Speaking with her helped me understand what you are up against. She is a mean and spiteful creature, and she won't do either of us any favors."

"I..." He seemed to struggle not to yell. "I could have told you that."

"You did tell me that, but seeing it in person has helped. I'm sorry if you're disappointed, but I must be as honest with you about my concerns as you have been with yours. You asked me to make this decision. I had to get firsthand knowledge."

Vince nodded at that, but his mouth tightened. "I don't want you to see her again. I don't trust her not to hurt you just to spite me. Male and female werewolves don't mesh well socially."

Cori nodded, so he knew she wasn't ignoring him. "I understand that concern, but I think it's unwarranted, at least for the moment."

"For the moment? What does that mean?" Vince rubbed his face, barely containing his angst. With their deposit at stake, he tucked his hands under his arms.

"I just mean our meeting was civil. Thus far, I have nothing to fear from her, and clearly I have nothing for her to fear. Though I very much wish I did."

"So you've met her. You understand. You... believe me." Vince backed away from her and took a few calming breaths. "Cori, what do you want me to do?"

"I've thought about that." Her eyes glazed over, and she licked the back of the wooden spoon.

Vince paused. "And...?"

She looked at him in mid-lick. She couldn't avoid saying it out loud any longer. "I would prefer for you to give in to her. Just let it be over with, and after a lot of hot showers, I'm sure I will turn the other cheek, and we will go on as before."

Vince looked disappointed, but his body relaxed. It may not have been the answer he expected from her, but it was an answer, and that must have been a relief to him. He moved a little farther from her, as far as the tiny kitchenette would allow without simply leaving the room. He pulled his hands out of his pockets and leaned on the upper cupboards.

"This is why I've led a mostly one-night-stand lifestyle. I never wanted to put anyone through this. I shouldn't be putting *you* through this! I should have left you! It would have been for your own good. You would have hated me and moved on."

Her chest ached with the words he was saying. She shook her head. "No, I would have been so bitter I never would have spoken to a man again. I'm happy to be with you, Vince, happier than I ever thought possible. I understand dating a werewolf is difficult, but I will take on that burden, and you must release it. I have chosen this just as much as you."

Vince moved to her and kneeled before her, hugging her body. "I promise I will make our life together as wonderful as possible, outside of these horrible moments."

"I know." She pet his head all the while staring off into nothingness, thinking about her conversation with Leona, and wondering how many more horrible moments there would be.

50

L ONG LEGS ENTERED THE café. Leona had adorned her lean figure with another power suit, this time a solid black skirt-suit. The skirt was several inches shorter than any respectable employer would allow, and the white satin shirt she wore under her blazer offered a clear view of her small but perky cleavage. Cori couldn't help but feel self-conscious in the woman's presence.

She looked down at her jeans that were stained with Vince's paint. Her chicken legs were a sad consolation prize. No matter how much Vince said otherwise, there was no way he couldn't enjoy being with Leona.

She raised her hand to wave, but Leona spotted her the instant she walked in, and she didn't look happy.

She walked over and sat across from Cori at the counter high table. "What the hell is this?" She looked to Vince, who was already squirming in his seat between them: the third wheel and the object of desire. "I won't be in heat for much longer. Soon, civility will be off the table."

"Tonight," Cori said, to ease her anger. Saying it made her stomach sick. Thinking about it made her heartsick.

Leona paused. "Tonight?" She glanced at Vince to see if this was indeed the agreement.

Cori grabbed Vince's hand and he nodded. He couldn't seem to manage looking either of them in the eye.

The waiter came to the table to offer Leona a coffee. She kept her eyes on Cori as she flipped her mug over to accept the offer. He left without offering a refill to anyone else.

"Where?" Leona said, sipping her coffee. She grimaced at the strength of the brew, but went back for another sip.

"Our apartment." Cori pushed the cream over, and Leona diluted her coffee with it.

"When precisely?"

"Seven o'clock." Cori looked at Vince for approval, but he was no longer a factor in this negotiation. "We prefer to think of this as if it never happened."

"Of course. I can be in and out in an hour, or at least, he can." She smiled at her own joke.

Cori ignored the baited humor. "What I mean is, I will leave at 6:45. I will come back after."

"You know, maybe you're going about this the wrong way. Maybe you should stay and participate. Perhaps that wouldn't make it feel so underhanded. It could just be the one crazy night you had a threesome." Leona's eyelids perked for effect.

Cori had no doubt she was serious about the invitation, but Leona only said it to incite her anger. Anger that was useless to her, since she had no recourse. "I won't have to see you ever again after tonight."

"Paris is not that big."

"No." Cori tapped her coffee cup. "But you know my scent. You could certainly avoid me."

"Yes." Leona sat back and sipped her coffee demurely. "Why would I make such an effort?"

"Because I'm asking you to."

She lifted an eyebrow. "We are not friends."

"No, for all intents and purposes, we are enemies, but since I am not a threat to you, I concede. I surrender." Something sparkled in Leona's eyes, no doubt a tinge of that werewolf ego. "I think you know how hard that is for someone like me. I hate to lose. I hate even more to never put up a fight."

Leona cleared her throat. "I still don't see how that makes me owe you anything."

"You don't, but that's the point. I am the loser in this scenario. The least the winner could do is to be gracious and not rub my face in it. So, I ask you one simple solace: let this afternoon be the last time I see you."

Leona laughed and coughed. She sipped her coffee to settle her throat. "You are a stubborn woman."

"So I've been told. I hope you can respect that in me, because as much as I hate the situation we are in together, I think I respect you for yours." For a moment, their eyes locked. Leona nodded and sipped more coffee. "May I have your word, Leona? When I leave this coffee shop, I will never see you again?"

"Yes," she said rather hoarsely. "I promise. Excuse me." She cleared her throat again, more ardently this time. "I don't know what's wrong with me today. The air is so dry."

Cori frowned at her. "I hope you're right about the silver. It won't actually kill you, right?" Both Vince and Leona looked at her, baffled and horrified. "You said it would just make you sick." She raised her brow, hoping to verify her interpretation.

"You poisoned me?" Leona asked as she grabbed at her stomach.

"Colloidal silver and a very well-paid waiter."

"Cori." Vince stood, looking between her and Leona. He looked worried for Leona, who was now looking dreadfully ill. He was probably more concerned about what punishment would arise from this act. "I can't believe you did this."

"I had to try, Leona. I couldn't just let it happen. Not without a fight," she explained with a certain pleading in her voice, an imploring for Leona to respect her actions rather than take revenge on them. "Trickery was my only option. I imagine you will be sick long enough for you to go out of heat, but if you are not, I hope that you will respect your promise to me. I meant what I said to you. I do respect you, but I've made my choice to be with Vince, and I can't let anything stand in the way of our happiness."

Cori grabbed Vince by the sleeve of his trench and pulled him along. Dumbfounded and shocked, he followed her lead. Leona doubled over with stomach cramps as they moved past her.

"Cori!" Leona called to her when she reached the door. She looked back. Leona looked up from her bent position. "Well played," she said through gritted teeth.

She nodded and pulled Vince out the door behind her.

She ran from the café with Vince in tow. They dodged cars to get as many streets as they could between them and the woman who could rip her open with her bare hands. As they distanced the scene, Vince slowed to a stop, becoming dead weight to Cori.

She looked back at him. His compliant shame had worn off, and he was looking at her with anger. She let go of him and backed away. "I didn't kill her. She said it wouldn't kill. I'm sure she'll be fine."

"What if she comes after you?"

"She won't."

"Why? Because she gave her word?"

"Yes. Tell me werewolves don't have honor."

"You shouldn't have risked yourself," he said firmly.

"I did it for us." She stepped toward him to take his hand.

"Bullshit!" His voice boomed, and she backed away again. A few passersby took notice and gave them a wide berth. "You did it to prove that you're smarter than her.

You wanted to prove that even though she is stronger than both of us physically, you can still beat her mentally."

She bit back her lips, but she had no defense. Her ego was far more to blame for this than her claim to Vince. When she put aside her insecurities about herself, the only issue she had with the affair was that she couldn't let another woman have her man. It was a territorial instinct.

"And you did it. You beat her." Vince's face softened as that realization finally sank in.

She nodded.

"She will be sick for days. She will be out of heat before she is well enough to mate. She will probably keep her word and avoid you." Vince looked at the ground.

Cori shrugged. "Isn't that a good thing?" She questioned whether he really hated the idea of being with Leona.

He looked up and smiled at her. "It's a great thing." He jumped forward and picked her up in a bear hug.

"So, you're not mad?"

"No, I'm fucking furious." He kissed her. "I'm just too happy to care right now." He put her down.

She looked behind him. "We should probably stay in a hotel for a while, just in case."

He looked around. "Yeah, good idea."

51

D ANATO REACHED FOR THE phone. His hand touched the receiver, and he pulled away. He picked up his newspaper and read it. He soon peeked from behind it to check the clock.

Belus sat on the short file cabinet with one foot propped up while the other swung freely on the side. He watched Danato's every move.

Danato sighed, put down his paper, and rubbed his hands together. He checked the clock on the wall and checked his wristwatch. When neither said what he wanted, he compared them to an old pocket watch he pulled from his desk drawer.

Belus twisted his red beard, eyeballing his boss.

Danato took a deep breath and picked up the phone. He set it down again. "What does your watch say?"

"You know what it says." Belus nodded to the phone.

"He would never miss his curfew."

"The truck came in an hour ago. Are you going to call, or am I?" Belus pried.

He glared at the suggestion. "I am the warden here."

"Yes, you are." Belus crossed his arms and nodded to the phone.

"He would have no way of contacting me if something had gone wrong."

"*Something* is not a valid excuse to change protocol, even if he did contact you about it."

"Why are you telling me things I already know?" Danato barked.

"Why are you stalling?" Belus barked right back.

"Because he's my friend."

"Make the call!" Belus ordered.

"Stop telling me what to do!" Danato fumed.

"I'm just your right hand, guiding your left hand!"

"If I call, it goes on permanent record. I'll have to report it to the board."

"Yes, you will," Belus agreed.

"You can see why I would want to avoid that paperwork."

Belus hopped off his cabinet and leaned over the desk; all of his 56 inches loomed *over* Danato. "He's a good guy, Danato, but he's also a werewolf. We can't let him miss check-in. We are minutes from being to the point of no retrieval." Belus picked up the receiver and offered it to him. "You have to make this call, or people will be in danger, including Cori."

That thought alone was enough to persuade him. He took the phone and dialed one number. The line picked up. "I have a werewolf late for check-in. Prisoner is non-combative in human form. Also, he has a human female companion with him." Danato glanced at Belus to see if he would object to the misuse of his authority, but any objections he had about retrieving the girl were ultimately secondary to the prison's security protocols. "I need both of them. Send out the collectors."

52

CORI RAN DOWN THE crowded sidewalks, dodging umbrellas left and right. The rain was coming down heavily, but that wasn't the only contribution to her wet cheeks. She wiped tears and rain from her eyes as she paused for traffic on the cross streets.

She continued on her panicked flight to a hospital. She lurched through the emergency room doors and yelled for a doctor in hobbled French. A nurse at the check-in intercepted her. "Are you hurt?" She asked first in French, and then reluctantly switched to English when Cori didn't understand.

"No, my fiancé needs help."

"Where is he?" the nurse asked, looking behind her for an accompanying man.

"He is only six blocks away at our apartment."

"You should have called an ambulance."

"No phone. We hate phones," Cori explained.

"They have their uses," she mumbled as she went back to her station to radio the ambulance.

Within minutes, she was barking directions to the paramedics from the back of an ambulance. Between the cold rain and her adrenaline, she couldn't keep from shaking. The vehicle pulled to a stop and Cori shouted the apartment number three times. The driving paramedic grabbed her shaking hands and repeated the number to her so she would know they understood. He asked her to wait while he and his partner went in to get Vince.

She nodded. Part of her wanted to go up with them to help, but another part couldn't bear to see Vince again. She settled on doing what she was told and slipped into the shotgun seat of the ambulance cab.

The paramedics grabbed their supplies and went up.

Five minutes passed.

Ten minutes passed, and she began to think of horrible scenarios. She didn't know what was wrong with Vince, but she knew he was in terrible pain.

Fifteen minutes passed, and she knew something was wrong. She slipped out of the cab and shut the door gently behind her. Reluctant to enter a horrific scene of resuscitation, she buzzed her apartment, hoping the paramedics would answer on the intercom and tell her everything was fine.

No one answered.

She entered her apartment building. Climbing up two flights of stairs, she found the hall light outside her apartment broken, its shards strewn in front of her open door. She crunched through them and went in.

It was silent. When she left, Vince was wailing in agony.

It was dark. When she left, nearly every light was on. They had been in the middle of packing his bags for his return to the prison when he started to feel ill. It wasn't until he coughed up blood that she realized something more than food poisoning was happening.

The living room was empty. Vince was there when she left, lying on the couch, going in and out of conscious seizures. He begged her not to get a doctor. She insisted. When he finally agreed, he begged her not to come back. She asked him why, but he wouldn't say.

She walked through her living room, past her kitchen and bathroom. She felt a breeze on her back. She whipped around, but no one was there.

Convinced he had crawled to the bedroom, she continued her search. She knew there was a chance he had changed forms prematurely, and she would walk in on a ten-foot werewolf, but she couldn't stay away.

Peeking around the doorframe to her bedroom, she saw the two paramedics lying face down on the floor. Unconscious or dead, she didn't know which. She covered her mouth to hold in any audible reaction.

She felt the hairs on the back of her neck stand on end. A shiver crept up her back as hot breath nipped at her neck. Her eyes watered, a visceral reaction to her fear. She turned to see her fate.

She caught a glimpse of a pallid bald man wearing dark sunglasses. He growled at her, showing his yellow stained sharp teeth. Something hit her from behind. She landed against the soft carpeted floor and then she was out.

53

T HE FREEZING COLD AIR revived Cori. The faint smell of tar and hay registered. She was on a rocking metal floor. A rhythmic thump sounded beneath her. She was on a train, in a cargo car.

She lifted her head, blinking out the stars from her eyes. She saw Vince beside her. Her heart leaped, and she scurried to him. He was unconscious, but alive.

At the farthest end of the car, her captors sat back-to-back on wooden crates, eating. They bit into fists full of fur and tail with their jagged teeth. The fresh blood from the rodent snacks dripped off their hands and chins. Their bald heads were rutted and their fingers tipped with thick yellow nails. She could smell their body odor from across the boxcar.

"Who are you?" she demanded.

They each looked at her and growled before continuing their feast.

"They don't speak," Vince said. He sat up, still groggy.

"Thank God you're alright." She hugged him, but he groaned, so she let go. "What's going on?"

"I didn't check-in. They sent the collectors."

"Those are the collectors?" she asked, appalled. "You made them sound so dangerous. They're just gross."

"They are more dog than human. They're pack hunters. You never see less than three in a group."

"Then why are there just two in here?" she asked.

"Because the other two are guarding us from over there," he pointed.

She looked to the other side of the car and saw two pairs of eyes staring out from behind stacks of crates. "Geez, I didn't even see them. What are they doing?"

"They're waiting for us to try to escape."

"If we..." she started.

"We wouldn't make it to our feet, let alone the door."

She nodded. "We're headed back to the prison, aren't we?"

"Yes. It's protocol."

"Can Danato help you?" She looked everywhere but at him.

"Danato has always helped me."

"Can he make you better?" she clarified.

"He will take my pain away."

She nodded, but didn't look at him.

After a few moments, he said, "You may not be able to leave the prison again."

"What?" She finally looked at him.

"I may stay at the prison if they find something wrong with me. I need you to understand the obligation Danato is under to keep all knowledge of the prison a secret."

"Who would I tell?" She pulled her hair from its usual ponytail to let it down over her cold ears.

"I just don't want you to blame Danato. He is a fair man, but the seedy underbelly of the board of directors makes the line between employees and slaves a little thin to begin with."

"Why does he do it then?"

"He doesn't know anything else. It's a family legacy that has unfortunately been sullied by certain necessities and moral compromises." Vince raised his arm to touch her hair, but he seethed in pain.

"Is the pain back?"

"It never left, but they must have given me something, because it's manageable now." Vince took in a few quick breaths.

"What hurts?" She looked him over.

"Everything," he grimaced.

"Your arms, legs, head?"

Vince paused as if he didn't want to answer. "Every bone, every muscle, and every inch of skin," he explained.

She looked at him in a dazed shock. She hugged her knees and rocked slightly. She wanted to hold him, but she knew it would be too painful. She buried her face in her knees to warm her cheeks and hide yet another round of tears she didn't want him to see. She wanted to be strong for him.

He lay back down, trying to meditate through his pain. "I love you, Cori."

"I love you too, Vince." She didn't look at him. She kept her face buried in her knees.

54

THE ALARM SOUNDED AFTER sundown. Danato was still in his office, trying to keep his mind off the situation. He looked up at the clock on the wall. It was before midnight. He shook his head and rose from his desk to join the others trampling through the building.

The hall leading to the loading docks echoed with Cori's irate screams, shouting guards, and the snarling of an animal.

He arrived on the scene to join twelve other men. Two men held Cori back as she struggled to get closer to the truck trailer. The other ten had their attention on Vince, now in full wolf form.

Several darts hung from the beast's chest and legs. Still, he roared, beating the sides of the semi-trailer he had arrived in. Ethan and three others plied ten-foot electric prods to him. The beast reared and bucked with each electrocution.

"Now," Ethan yelled, thrusting the prod at Vince when he reared. In unison, the men attacked and withdrew on his command.

Danato gaped at the events unfolding, far more intrigued by the man than the beast. With his short-cropped hair, tight black t-shirt and army-issue black cargo pants, Ethan blended in with his fellow guards; his leadership was his only defining characteristic.

Somewhere in the last few months, Ethan had come into his confidence. His camaraderie with the guards had paved the way for their respect and devotion. He noticed far fewer problems were coming to his door. Ethan was making necessary changes and repairs that prevented such matters from arising.

"How many more tranquilizers do we have left?" Ethan hollered at the men behind him.

"None, but we have more upstairs," answered one of the guards.

"Never mind." Ethan nodded to the back wall. "Rip that breaker box off the wall."

Two men ran to the circuit breaker and grabbed the sides of the metal box. They pulled. Nothing. They pried with their gun barrels. No luck.

Danato reached past them, gripped the top of the frame, and pulled. The box broke free with a screech, a snap, and a poof of cement dust. The lights in the room went out, but returned with the help of the backup generator lights.

The men looked back at Danato with wide eyes. "Thanks, boss," they each mumbled.

"Anytime, gentlemen." He stepped back and let them finish yanking the sparking wire clusters from its base.

They pulled on the slack cables, but they only gained enough to reach the edge of the platform. "This is all she'll give!" one yelled.

"It'll do." Ethan stepped back to meet his cattle prod with the wire. He nodded at the men surrounding the truck. "Let him out!"

The guards distanced themselves, giving the beast slack. The werewolf emerged from the truck. He stood tall, pushed his chest out, and roared at Ethan.

Danato resisted the urge to jump between them. Ethan was past the point of needing a defender. He, like every mentor, had to step back. Ethan had to fight his own battles, even if that meant getting his ass kicked by an incensed werewolf.

"Don't hurt him!" Cori shrieked.

Ethan glanced at her with a cold glare. The beast lunged. Ethan drove his prod into his neck. The added cable shot a new level of voltage through the beast. He convulsed and dropped.

"No!" Cori struggled with newfound vigor.

Ethan stood over his triumph, kicking his paws. "We'll need a forklift." He looked at the mound of a beast before him. "Maybe two."

Danato approached the guards, holding back Cori. "I'll take her from here, boys."

They released their grip, and she bolted forward toward Vince's alter ego. He latched onto her waist with his arm and pulled her away. She pulled against him, beating his shoulder until she saw it was hopeless. Changing tactics, she tried to reason with him.

He walked her back to his office, ignoring her pleas, negotiations, and curses.

In his office, she collapsed into a chair. When he was sure she was resigned to staying, he poured her a pointed paper cup of water from the water cooler. "Drink this. You'll feel better."

She backhanded the proffered water into the wall.

He sat down in his chair and waited. Far too many emotions were inundating her for him to interject any comfort.

She stared at him. Her sniffles lessened and her cheeks dried.

He waited still.

She took in a stuttered breath. "What's happening to him?" she eventually asked.

Danato leaned forward on his desk and laced his fingers together. "Vince is a werewolf. He has changed from being human to a wolf creature over a hundred times. The outward physical changes are obvious, but he also changes internally. The stress on his body..."

"What is *happening* to him?" she yelled.

Danato leaned back again. "He's dying." Her face distorted. Her cheeks filled with rivers of tears with no audible sob. "He, like all werewolves, has a short lifespan. Thirty-four is rather old for a werewolf."

"I want to see him." She strained to get the words out.

"My reservations are the same as when you first asked to see him in this state," he said.

"My determination is just as high as it was then," she said resolutely.

Danato nodded. He didn't want to put her through this again, but he knew she had to do it. If he refused her this right, she would hate him forever, and that was something he couldn't endure.

C ORI AND DANATO ENTERED the werewolf complex. She followed the backs of a long line of guards. They parted for her and Danato, allowing them an audience to the spectacle they were intently guarding.

The beast lurched and bellowed in his confinement. He alternated between slamming the iron bars with his shoulder and biting at them. The structure remained secure, designed especially for him.

She had hoped against hope that there would be something of Vince in the beast, but there wasn't. Just as before, the beast seemed agitated by her presence. There was no unspoken connection. He wasn't the man she loved. He was just a beast.

Danato had taken his position beside her, but slightly in front. She knew he did it to give himself a half-second response time, in case she got the bright idea of throwing herself at the cage. "Are you sure you want to be here?" He eyed her over his shoulder.

"Is he in pain?" she asked.

"Yes," Danato said without hesitation, "tremendous pain." His honesty didn't surprise her, but in this particular case, she wished he had underemphasized the truth.

Her tears had dried up. The salty flesh under her eyes burned, just as irritated by the cumulative emotional assaults as her mind was. "What's happening to him?"

"His muscle tissues are liquefying." Her mouth gaped. She stared expectantly at Danato. "The transformations require absorption of water to allow the muscles to expand to that size. Until then, the muscle is compact and short. When the muscles swell, they expand and lengthen, making him bigger and stronger."

Danato must have realized her brain was far too foggy to understand what he was saying, because he seemed to stop mid-thought and backpedal for her. "I could go on for days about their anatomy, but the bottom line is, his muscles won't be able to retract anymore. They will just swell." He paused, looking back at the beast. "And swell. Until..." He never finished the sentence. He looked down at his feet. She saw him close his eyes and tense his jaw. She hadn't known Danato to be anything but reserved in his sentiments, but she thought perhaps he was fighting back his own tears at that moment.

Her mind being so thick with grief at the prospect of Vince dying, it took her a moment to register Danato's last words. She shook her head as if her ears were culpable for her lagging comprehension. "They won't retract?" She said it out loud, but it was still just her brain trying to interpret the words. "They won't go back to normal? He won't go back?" Her eyes shot up to Danato, begging and pleading for that not to be the right words.

Danato's face melted at her obvious pain. She started shaking her head even before he answered. "No, sweetheart, he will die as a wolf." She started hyperventilating. Her lower lip trembled. "We will bury him as a wolf. We will remember him as a man."

She gaped at the monster before her. He wasn't even a shell of the man she knew, but that was all that she had left of her lover. She would never see, hear, or touch Vince ever again.

She wasn't aware of taking any steps back from Danato. The ache in her chest was as far away from her as her racing heart. The room spun, and she shifted her stance to accommodate, but her legs gave out.

A muscular arm caught her around the back. One of the guards lifted her back to her feet. He supported her a moment before she nodded, giving her approval to let go.

She looked at the floor, consciously slowing her breathing and decelerating her heart. She looked at Danato, who had since closed the breach between them. "There's no reason to be here," she said. "There's nothing here for me."

He nodded and looped her arm around his before walking her out.

56

CORI STEPPED INTO THE house, flooded with memories, good and bad. It was less than a year ago that she had slept, ate, and bathed in this house. It seemed like a lifetime ago. She had expected it to feel like home, but nothing felt like home without Vince.

Danato removed his long coat and slipped the borrowed cloak off her shoulders. Without a chance to pack before being collected, she was back to being without a decent wardrobe.

She paused in the entryway to look over everything, while Danato proceeded to the kitchen to make tea. She wandered around the large open living and dining space, touching things, pretending to be interested in them.

The decorations were the same as they had always been, the consummate hunter's lodge. One would never have guessed antlers could be used for so much. She was certain, however, that a fireplace without a bearskin rug was simply sinful, no matter what your motif was.

When she had nothing left to touch, she sat at the table with Danato and waited for the teapot to whistle. She stared into nothingness, trying to grasp onto some sense of now. Coming into the house, she felt like she had been gone a hundred years. Now, sitting at the table next to Danato, she had to remind herself that Vince and her time away wasn't just a dream she had.

"I suppose I'm your slave again," she posed when no other topic seemed pressing.

"Don't worry about that now. We'll figure that out later," Danato said, reaching across the corner of the table to squeeze her hand.

She looked down at his hand. She was vaguely aware of the pressure and the genuine sympathy, possibly even empathy, radiating from his grasp. She knew she needed to be comforted, but everything seemed so distorted. Her mind kept going back to the same thought. *He's dead.*

She tried to cycle through an inventory of events that may transpire now that she was back at the prison, but her mind kept going back. *He's dead.*

More than a thought, it was a whisper in the back of her mind that only spoke to interrupt her effort at concentration, like when someone says your name in a crowded room. You don't actually hear it, but it gets your attention, anyway. *He's dead.*

Cori shivered at the creepy repetition and decided that thinking about the future would have to wait for now. She would have to rely on the present to get her through this. She looked around, suddenly aware that something, or rather someone, was missing. "Where's Ethan? I'm surprised he's not studying by the fire." She rubbed her face, wiping away what felt like a layer of salt built up on her cheeks.

Danato's brow deepened into bewilderment. "What do you mean? You saw him in there."

She shook her head. "No, I must have missed him."

"You didn't recognize him." Danato's mouth tipped up with a hint of a proud smile. "He's moved past studying. He's one of my guards now. Rather a fine leader, if you can believe that. He was the one who took down Vin... the werewolf."

Her eyes shifted from his; she obviously wasn't as proud of that moment as Danato was. "It's kind of a blur."

"He also kept you on your feet when you nearly collapsed in there."

Her eyes flickered as she tried to match her memory of Ethan to the man who helped her. All she remembered was the strength in his arms as he caught her. She had the tangible memory of his body pressed on hers as he kept her upright. His emergent muscles were now taut and robust. "He's changed... a lot."

"Yes." The teapot whistled and Danato moved to the stove. He grabbed two mugs from the cupboard and poured them each a cup of water. He brought the mugs over in one hand and carried his tea box with the other. She opened the wooden box and selected a fruity herbal tea. Danato took an Earl Grey.

She dipped the bag and waited for the color to change before releasing the bag to float on its own. "I haven't changed much, have I?" she asked.

Danato set his cup to one side to steep. "I don't know yet. I imagine any change I might have observed yesterday would be irrelevant today."

She nodded. She stood, taking her tea in hand. "My room is still available, right?"

"Of course." He stood with her.

"If you'll excuse me, I'll have my tea up there." She knew he would have preferred to sit with her, to console her as needed, but her social strength was steadily draining dry. She could feel her tears replenish, and she preferred to wallow in her misery alone.

"If you need anything, I'm here. Anything," he said.

She tried to smile, but her cheeks wouldn't hold it. "There will likely be a knock or a phone call later tonight," she said. "I don't need to know about it."

He nodded, understanding. "I know it doesn't mean much right now, but I am sorry."

"Thank you." She headed upstairs for some much needed solitude.

57

ETHAN ARRIVED HOME LATE that night. Danato had *waited up* for him. With his head tipped back on his chair and his glasses askew, his newspaper now provided the big man with a blanket instead of reading material. The snore rumbling through the house sounded like a growling bear instead of a sleeping man.

Ethan slipped the paper off him and folded it neatly before placing it on the coffee table. He removed Danato's glasses and set them on the side table.

He looked up at the open loft to Cori's closed bedroom door. He trudged upstairs and stood outside her door. He raised his hand to knock, but paused. He wanted more than anything to be there for her, to comfort her.

As much as he hated Vince for taking her away, he didn't wish death on him. Especially the death Ethan had just witnessed.

After another moment's thought, he lowered his fist and retreated to his own bedroom. As appealing as it was to his selfish ego to hold her while she mourned, he didn't want her to permanently ingrain himself in her memory as the man who delivered the news of her lover's death.

58

ETHAN STARED AT HIS breakfast of overdone eggs. The over-greased pan had made the edges positively black with crisp and the insides were no longer a creamy orange-yellow, but a powdery pale yellow. Danato was about to dig into his, but he saw the expression on Ethan's face. "What?"

"You burned them again," he said, unable to hide the disfavor in his voice.

"I thought you liked them hard." Danato's brow creased.

"No, *you* like them hard. I like them soft."

"Oh, right. Well, you can make them soft tomorrow and I'll eat them without complaint." Danato took a big bite.

Ethan glanced up at the loft. He kept hoping she would come out and join them, but she hadn't yet.

Danato lowered his fork to his plate and swallowed. "I knew this wasn't about eggs."

"What?" Ethan pushed his plate away but didn't meet Danato's eyes.

"I can't believe you still get in a tizzy over her after this long."

"What are you talking about? The eggs are hard. They are always hard. I hate hard eggs. If I wanted hard eggs, I would hard-boil them."

Danato took a bite and wiped his mouth with his napkin. He leaned back in his chair as he finished chewing, all the while reading Ethan like a book. "You never mentioned the eggs until today, though. The eggs never bothered you enough to complain until today. What's bugging you?"

Ethan shook his head and bit his lip. "She's been in there for three days."

"She just lost the man she loves," Danato said.

"Yes, but she hasn't eaten."

"I leave her a tray. She takes what she wants."

"What about her duties? Is there a freeloader program I don't know about?" Ethan flinched, hearing the words come out of his mouth.

Danato's eyes narrowed on him. "What's gotten into you? It's been three days, not three weeks, not three months. When she feels like peeling herself out of bed, we'll give her some duties to keep her busy. Have some sympathy."

"I have sympathy," he said calmly, trying to smooth out the ruffles in Danato's feathers. "I just don't think locking herself in her room for days on end is a healthy grieving process."

To his surprise, Danato's expression got even colder. "Oh, really? And you've mourned a dead lover, have you?"

Ethan debated whether to stay quiet or risk sticking his foot deeper into his mouth. "There are a lot of questions that we need answered." *This little piggy went to market.*

"We or you?"

"Both." *This little piggy stayed home.*

"Like what?" Danato sat back to listen to his queries.

"Is she back? Is she staying? Are we going to pretend the last nine months didn't happen?" Ethan paused, once again rethinking the size of his foot. "I just don't really want her to stay here if you're going to let her run off with another boyfriend, without consequence." *This little piggy ate crow.*

Danato frowned and pushed out his chest. "I will deal with Cori when the time is right." His voice was low, only threatening to be loud. "The key word there: *I*. You are not to concern yourself with her. When you're the warden, you can deal with people as you see fit. Until then, eat your damn eggs!"

Ethan knew he was poking the bear, but he couldn't help but be bitter about the situation. Cori was supposed to stay at the prison just like him. Losing her was too hard the first time. He didn't want her to come back in and get comfortable just so she could take off again.

He pulled a charred egg off his plate and stuffed it into his mouth. He chewed it forcefully. He paused in mid-chew. "Wait." He sputtered food as he spoke. "What do you mean when I'm the warden? Why would I be the warden?"

Danato's face hinted at a surprise party he had just given away, but he composed himself enough to sound aloof. "What do you think you're training for?"

"I get to run this place?" Ethan hadn't really considered running the prison. He had long since accepted his lot in life as slave labor, but the prospect of running the prison felt like the burden of servitude was being lifted.

"Not until I retire, and only if you pass the final test."

"When will that be?" Ethan asked.

"Whenever you're ready, I suppose, or whenever I am."

59

THE ELEVATOR DOORS OPENED and Cori stared out at the ostensibly infinite line of cells before her. She pulled her maintenance cart out onto the floor. She rummaged through her cleaners until she found the one with the masking tape label that read "transmorphs" in blue indelible ink. She pulled out a cleaning cloth and sprayed some of the liquid on it.

"Hello, my love," Vince's voice purred from beside her. She turned to the cell, dropping her jaw and her bottle at the same time. "How are you?" Vince's doppelganger asked in perfect pitch. His voice was deep, yet soothing to the ear.

For a moment, she basked in the view. His sturdy muscular V-frame that barely hinted at the strength he possessed. His upper lip always threatening a hint of five o'clock shadow before the rest of his face. Loose wavy brown locks, not quite long, but not quite short. He even smelled like Vince, that antique musk that suggested he used the same aftershave as his father before him.

He's dead.

The insistence in that thought was violating to her composure. Her eyes watered as she tried to get back to that first moment. The moment she heard his voice. That split second where it was all a dream, and he wasn't really gone.

He's dead.

"I know he's dead!" she screamed out loud at her mind. She leaned down to pick up her bottle, determined to get on with her work despite this machination to unnerve her.

"Hello, my love," said the same deep voice from a different cell. She looked down the line of cells and, one by one, Vince duplicates stepped forward to thread their arms through the bars. They all in turn said, "Hello, my love."

Cori's hands shook, and her eyes blurred, refusing to blink. The infinite line of Vinces was just too much. One Vince could shock her into letting her guard down, thereby leaving room for an escape attempt. However, multiple Vinces was torment. Her pain was one big joke to them.

She leaned on her cart and tried to compose herself. Not wanting any more of her grief on display for them, she latched onto her favorite tried-and-true emotion—anger. She fumbled through her cleaning supplies and pulled out an orange bottle. The bright bottle displayed several faded hazard stickers.

Cori had trained to exhaustion on Material Safety Data Sheets before she could do her janitorial work, so she was familiar with the coding on the bottle. Class E substances erode metal and...

She ripped the top off her bottle and threw its contents on the first Vince doppelganger. She almost looked away when he began to scream and thrash.

...destroy animal tissues. Acid, and a nasty one at that.

Vince's facial features rippled and jumbled to disfiguring Picasso proportions. The transmorph fell to the floor, lamenting his agony as he crawled to the far corner of his cell. He cowered there, cradling his blistering face.

She turned to the remaining replicas, some visible, some just hands through bars. "Anyone else?" she asked with menace in her voice.

One by one they retreated from view, first the faces, then the hands.

An hour later, Cori sat in Danato's office alone. She had been called up after a guard discovered the wounded transmorph on a walk-through. A quick inventory of her supplies, and he carted her off to face her judge and jury. She wasn't really concerned about being yelled at. She didn't even care what her punishment would be. What she did care about was that she had been waiting in the office for twenty minutes.

During those twenty minutes, the clock on the wall insisted on ticking loudly. The chair she sat in was determined to make farting sounds every time she shifted her weight. The water cooler had plenty of opportunity to make a "glug" sound, but for whatever reason, it was silent today.

Danato entered, slamming the door behind him. She marveled at the strength of the glass window in that door. Danato sat down in his desk chair. The old metal springs groaned and squeaked as he maneuvered himself closer to the desk. The chair had to be from the 1970s. Upgrading apparently wasn't in the budget.

Danato set several file folders down on the desk and tented his hands over them. He looked across the desk at Cori with his mouth parted, and prepared to speak.

She waited... again.

If she didn't know it was impossible, she would have sworn the clock was ticking even louder now. If he didn't say something soon, she was going to rip it off the wall and perform an apen-tick-tomy on it.

"You amaze me, sometimes," Danato finally said without the expected rage in his voice. "It must just be pure luck on your part. The things you stumble onto." He slid the top file across the desk to her.

She picked up the manila folder and opened it. The first page showed a list of stats, medical requirements, and food requirements. Paper clipped on the top right was a photo of the transmorph she had burned with acid.

The acid had blistered the right side of his face, starting at his temple and finishing below the neckline. His right eyelid was sunken and sealed shut.

She closed the file and put it back on the desk. "I'm sorry." She hadn't thought she would be, but seeing that photo, she realized she had tortured that poor creature out of revenge for a cruel but otherwise harmless mockery. "I let them get to me. They appeared to me as Vince. I just couldn't handle them wearing his face. I let my anger take over."

Danato nodded. "You did lose your temper. It was an understandable reaction given the last two weeks, but excessive and certainly not condoned."

She took a deep breath. "I don't need you to baby me just because Vince is gone." *He's dead.* "I'm ready for my punishment."

"Oh, it will be a big punishment." Danato paused. "Which I'll think of later." He pushed the file back to her. "Did you notice anything different about that file?"

She looked down at the folder. "Compared to what?"

He shoved the other files across the desk, which pushed the first one off to the floor. She picked it up and opened it again. She flipped through the others, leaving them open for comparison. One of these is not like the others. "There are no photos in the other files?" she said, questioning whether that was the correct answer.

"Correct." Danato rubbed his hands together. "These are the files of transmorphs. They have never had photos, because we don't know what they really look like."

"So now that I've scarred him for life, you'll always know he's a transmorph," she surmised.

"No, his tissue will repair. The eye may take a bit longer, but... no, no, don't worry about him. The damn creatures never age, they certainly won't scar. What we are seeing in this picture..." Danato stood and moved around the desk to point out the picture to her. "This is his original form. His core shape."

Cori stared at him blankly.

Danato poked the picture again as if that would make it all clear.

She nodded.

He laughed and shook his head. He kneeled down in front of her. "What you did was very bad. Bad, bad, bad." He shook his finger at her. "However, because you did it, we can utilize a similar, albeit more humane, technique to induce the creatures to show their true face. Once we can identify them, we can keep track of them better."

"Why would that help? Just because you know what they are supposed to look like doesn't mean they will look like that," she said.

He laughed again and raised his hands just short of cupping her face. "There is a catch in the creature's defense. If it sees its own image, it has to form into that image."

"Really?" she said, furrowing her brow.

"Yes. Something about the reflection and stimulating the mind and muscle reaction to what it thinks it should be... anyway, the point is, I can now make an entire floor safer."

"Because of bad, bad me?"

"Because of your reactive temper."

She thought for a moment. "So, it never occurred to you to just dump acid all over your prisoners?"

"No, oddly enough, we just figured food and water were sufficient." Danato said, smiling ear to ear.

She shook her head. "I don't know how you survived without me."

Danato patted her arm tenderly. "Well." He stood rather abruptly and opened the office door. "Come with me. I have your punishment picked out."

She put the folder back and followed him out.

OUTSIDE THE PRISON, THE wind whipped around Cori, chilling her to the bone. The snow flurries it carried stung her face. From what she understood, the so-called summer temperatures could reach sixty degrees Fahrenheit, but naturally she had returned to her internment at the beginning of a new winter.

They trekked away from the mostly barren acreage that surrounded the western part of the prison and toward the cluttered outbuildings that occupied the eastern edge of the courtyard. Even during her first tenancy there, she hadn't bothered to explore the countless outbuildings. Aside from most of them being locked, she found that the arctic climate sapped most of her curiosity.

"How much further?" Cori tucked closer to Danato, but so far he had been useless as a windbreak.

"Not far." His booming voice turned to a murmur through the wind.

Cori kept her head down and trotted on until she butted into Danato's back. He had stopped at one of the buildings. The outside wall looked like a grass hut, but the structure itself was as big as the house they lived in. He unlatched the door and ushered her in before him.

She charged into the warm entryway, shaking off the layer of ice that had developed in her hair. Danato pulled the door shut and latched it. He removed his coat and hung it up on a peg by the door.

"Take your coat off," he instructed and reached to take it from her.

She shook her head, not willing to give up the warmth.

"You'll be too warm with it on, I promise." He fluttered his fingers, demanding the coat. She gave it to him and he hung it up by his.

Opaque plastic walled in the entryway. The room beyond glowed with artificial light. A distant, constant hum hinted at electrical equipment. She wondered, though, why she could smell fresh-cut grass and manure. "Oh, crap, this is a sewage plant, isn't it? Oh please, I don't want to know what happens to *my* business, let alone everyone else's."

Danato said nothing, but an amused smirk perched on his lips. He didn't often wear a smile, but this particular smirk was even rarer. She couldn't pinpoint if it was the grin of an evil madman plotting his revenge or him just being coy.

Danato pushed through the plastic straps to the next room. She felt the wave of heat and humidity that he had promised. A familiar fragrance accented the manure smell.

Dirt. She followed with only the slightest suspicion of what lay beyond the curtain.

On the other side, the electrical hum was louder. It was coming from fans that lined the upper walls of the structure. The ceiling was gridded glass. The remaining space aside from its contents was relatively open. As for the contents, from floor to ceiling, plants crawled, climbed, towered, and overflowed into the space.

"Welcome to the greenhouse," Danato said.

Cori breathed in the sweet smell of floral beauty: part dirt, part grassy green, with just a hint of manure. She was very familiar with these smells. She had spent a good part of her life in a greenhouse and, until right now, she hadn't thought she ever would again.

An uncontainable smile spread across her face. If Danato had thought slaving away amidst this beautiful flora would be a punishment, he was mistaken.

61

ETHAN ARRIVED AFTER DINNER for the fourth time that week. So late that the dinner dishes were done and Cori had retreated to her room. Danato was still up, sitting at the table, looking through endless amounts of red-tape paperwork.

Ethan hung up his coat and gave him a nod before heading to the fridge. He grabbed the milk carton from the top shelf and started chugging straight from the cardboard opening.

"You better be finishing that?" Danato muttered, not looking up from his papers.

Ethan tucked the carton under his arm and pulled out a bowl of now lukewarm leftovers. "What is it?" he asked, staring at the aluminum foil top.

"Chili," Danato answered.

"Again," he mumbled, shaking his head. He grabbed a spoon from the dish rack and headed to the living room.

"I don't think so," Danato said as he neared the couch.

"You're doing paperwork. I don't want to spill on it."

"Better my papers than my sofa."

Danato's anal attitude towards furniture always surprised Ethan. He understood the ramifications of a messy home, thanks to Cori. And yet, he was still treated like a ten-year-old trying to sneak grape juice onto the white carpet.

He sat down at the table and shoveled in his chili, guzzling milk between bites. The sweet taste was always a surprise to him. Danato wasn't the best cook, but he had a few dishes he did well. His chili was the perfect combination of hot and sweet.

His only objection to the chili was its frequency. With only the two of them cooking the last nine months, dinners had been bland, repetitive, and occasionally havoc to his digestion. Since Cori was back, he was expecting some change in the rotation. Unfortunately, she had only made a few meals since she was back, and he wasn't about to broach the topic with Danato.

He looked up from his chili and saw Danato staring at him. "You've been avoiding her."

His mouth hung open with his spoon waiting on the sidelines until it was called back into the game. "What?"

Danato scooped up his papers, shuffled them into a neat pile, and set them aside. "You seemed so concerned before that she wasn't joining us. Now you seem to be the one not joining us. Why is that?"

He shrugged his shoulders and continued eating. "You're playing psychiatrist, you tell me?" He took his awaited bite.

Danato tipped his head. "I have no desire to play your childish games."

"What's this paperwork for?" he said, tapping his spoon on the pile.

"Don't change the subject," Danato growled.

"I'm not. What is it?" he snapped.

Danato shook his head.

Ethan dropped his spoon and swallowed. "It's the report about the incident with Vince, isn't it?" he said, shoving his food away from him. He fisted his chest and released a burp. Danato narrowed his eyes at his ill manners. "Is her name even in it?"

Danato's scowl faded, and he looked away.

"It isn't, is it? Belus told me you still haven't reported her. Have you offered to let her go yet? A quick memory wipe and replacement and she's right where she left off." He couldn't keep the bitterness out of his voice. He hated sounding like a spoiled child, but he was sick of not having any say in his life while Cori was treated like a princess.

Danato opened his mouth to explain, but Ethan shoved his chair back. "Forget it." He walked away. After a short distance, he rethought his exit. Danato wanted to know why he was avoiding her, and maybe he should know.

He returned to the table armed with an accusing finger. "You made it so clear to us that this was for life; that we were stuck here. I am your successor. I understand that. I accept that. I think I've made great strides here. I think I've earned your trust and respect. Whether you've earned that from me, you have always demanded it. So this is me demanding respect from you. I'm not a galley boy, a stowaway, or a powder monkey. I'm your goddamn first mate. I shouldn't have to ask what's in those papers. I should be part of the discussion leading to those papers."

Danato sat up straight, taking his tongue-lashing with the respect that Ethan had demanded.

"You asked why I'm avoiding her?" he said, losing some of the control over his anger. "Because I don't want to get attached to her and watch her leave again!"

After a quick breath to compose himself so he didn't look like a child having a tantrum, he retreated to his bedroom. If Danato had any defense for any of the accusations laid at his door, he didn't interject them at the time. Ethan was grateful for that. He had no energy to hash things out tonight.

He opened his bedroom door and headed in. As he closed his door, he saw the light around Cori's disappear as the knob clicked shut. "Shit," he whispered, wondering if she had overheard his rant. He clicked his own door shut, not willing to mash that out tonight either.

62

DANATO ARRIVED AT THE greenhouse and found Cori toiling away, repotting some of the sorrier specimens. She was crouched in an aisle, sopping wet, with smears of mud on her face. He laughed at her dedication to the work.

She peeked over the tables at him and waved. "Come on in!" she hollered at him, as if he had just entered her home. He went over to speak with her. She continued to transplant her herbs. "What brings you by?" She wiped a fresh line of mud across her forehead.

Danato shook his head. "I brought the greenhouse instructions." He waggled a three-ring binder over his head.

"Instructions?" She pursed her lips and shook her head. "There isn't anything dangerous here."

"Actually, several plants here are poisonous," he corrected. "At least to humans."

Cori scoffed and started scanning the room. "Well... elephant ear causes intense irritation of mouth and tongue, which can result in blockage of air to the throat. Rosary pea seeds and castor bean seeds are lethal to humans. Oleander leaves are poisonous." She started counting them off on her fingers. Danato took in the moment with silent awe. "Laurels, jasmine, and yew are all fatal. Rhubarb leaves, of course, and mistletoe. Most people know that. There's nightshade and 'poison hemlock' is kind of a dead give-away."

"Okay, okay." Danato held up his hands in surrender. "Clearly you are far more qualified for this than I would have guessed."

"Plant care is a lot about instinct. The basics are simple: water, sun, nutrients, but the balance and amounts of them are the key. When you bake a cake, you weigh your ingredients, throw them together, and bake. A plant's ingredients change subtly as it grows. What is right today may be too little next month."

"How on earth do you know about all this?"

"In my former life I was studying horticulture," she said, eyeballing her newly split sage plant.

"Really?" Danato said, intrigued by this new aspect of her personality.

"Oh." Cori wiped the dirt off her hands and onto her jeans before moving to an ill-looking tomato plant. "The tomatoes are rotting on the vine. I can fix it, but I need a nutrient spray. What I really should do is transplant them into new soil, but that might stunt tomato production altogether, which means I should start a backup now and spray until I get some decent growth, but no matter what, we may be out of fresh tomatoes for at least three months." Cori looked back at him, waiting for a response.

Danato raised his eyebrows. "Was that a question?"

She grimaced. "I guess not. I just need to find out how to requisition the spray, and who to tell in the cafeteria."

Danato nodded. "I'll get you a form, and I'll... ask Belus. I don't get to the cafeteria much. Perk of the job, I guess. They deliver my lunch to my office." He raised the three-ring binder he still held in his hand. "I guess I'll just put this manual back in my drawer."

"You can leave it. I'll need to know how to adjust the timer of the sprayers and drip hoses." He set the book down on the nearest table, scratched his nose, and fumbled with a file folder he had had tucked under the binder. Cori noticed the folder. "Yes?" she asked, sensing his desire to discuss something.

He looked up and shook his head. "I didn't say anything."

"No, but what you *aren't* saying is being said very loudly."

He took in a deep breath and strolled through the concrete paths of the greenhouse. He didn't want to have this discussion, but, truthfully, it shouldn't have been up for discussion. "I have obligations," he said loud enough to be heard over the fans. "I have to report your existence. I essentially have to put you on the books as an employee.

She watched him as he wandered. "I'm surprised you haven't done that already. Do you need my social security card?"

"It was on my to-do list just before you ran off," he said, ignoring her quip.

"It's still on your to-do list, I gather." She paralleled him down an adjacent path.

"The papers are in here." He held up the file folder and brought it down with a smack against an innocently bystanding ceramic pot. "I wasn't going to put your name in, and then I was, and then I wasn't, and then Ethan..." He stopped mid-sentence, realizing he was about to blame his renewed devotion to his duties on Ethan. "*I* realized that it was unfair. We had a deal: employment for life."

Cori cut over to his path and walked beside him. "You want to give me my freedom, but you can't give Ethan his, so you feel like you're favoring me. Which Ethan no doubt resents?"

Danato stopped. "That's the emotional argument. The logical one is: I'd be risking my job to let you go. The location of this place is so top secret. I'm not even sure I wouldn't be risking your life. It was different when you were with Vince. You certainly couldn't reveal this place without revealing him."

She nodded, taking in his words. A glimmer of pain entered her face before she forcibly shook it away. "I came here with a chip on my shoulder. Do you know where I was heading when I got abducted?"

"Where?" he asked.

"To my aunt's funeral." The statement seemed laced with bitterness.

"I'm sorry."

"She lived in Belgium. I was in London going to school for horticulture, as I said. Third year in, almost made it. She was actually supporting my schooling, since my mother had already passed away the year before that, to cancer." Danato's mouth opened for a pending question, but she shrugged and answered it before he could ask. "The usual: chemo, radiation, blah, blah, blah. 'There's nothing more we can do. Just make her comfortable.' Ya-da, ya-da." Cori pushed aside a stray tear.

"What about your father?" Danato asked.

"In the US somewhere, I haven't seen him since I was seventeen. That's when they divorced and mom moved back to England with me in tow."

"You could find him."

"I'm way past caring about his presence. If he really wanted to stay in contact, he would have. I've seen people fight harder for lesser causes than their own blood." Danato nodded. Having Ethan and Cori around was as close as he would ever get to having children. Even though he was sure it wasn't the same, he couldn't imagine not fighting for her.

"When I ran away with Vince," Cori continued, "there wasn't anyone to call. There wasn't anyone to visit. It was just him and me. Now, it's just me. I don't imagine life outside of here would be easier with just me. As much as your overbearing rules and regulations irritate me, I really have no desire to leave. At least I know people here. At least you noticed when I was gone."

"You were very much missed." He resisted the urge to reach out to her. "Are you sure this isn't just your grief talking?"

"I've been grieving for a long time, Danato. I'm not sure I know how to think when I'm not sad about something."

"There is something else to consider before you agree to this. I won't always be the one being overbearing. What happens to your opinion of this place when you're taking orders from Ethan?"

Her face scrunched up for a second before she chuckled. "Why would that be necessary?"

"He will be my successor. That's why he was brought here. I chose him to replace me when I retire."

She looked away. She bit her lip in contemplation. "I can handle that. Ethan and I were friendly once. I'm sure we can be again. If... Yeah, that's going to be hard."

Danato laughed. "There's something else you should know." He walked away. She followed, but he turned back abruptly. "I had a wife." He threw the sentence out of his mouth like a hot coal that was burning his tongue. The memory of her had long since burned his heart.

Cori flinched at the sudden admission. "Okay."

Danato's eyes glazed as he lost himself in memories. "She was brought here against her will. She was a fugitive, but hardly one worthy of this place. We fell in love. We married. We had a wonderful life together, short-lived as it was. She died well before her prime."

Danato's eyes refocused on Cori, and he moved close to her. He could feel the moisture building in his eyes, but he didn't hide it. "I loved her so much, and would have done anything for her. Including free her from this place, even though that meant losing her." This was the real reason he had so much trouble sending in Cori's documentation. He felt guilty about trapping yet another woman in this arctic prison.

Cori's eyes flickered over his for a moment. "Why didn't you?"

"I did, but she wouldn't leave me. Instead, she remained caged with me."

"She apparently loved you enough to stay in this wretched place. Hardly a death sentence when you're surrounded by people who care about you." She gave him a discreet smile, and he once again resisted the urge to hug her. "Sounds like she made her choice," she continued. "And so have I."

"I'm flattered that our companionship has impressed you enough to want to be surrounded by it indefinitely. However, I just want to be sure that you understand what you are committing to. You say your grief isn't clouding your judgment, but maybe your fear is."

Cori seemed to contemplate the question before deciding on an answer. "Well, now, I'm starting to think you want to get rid of me."

Danato chuckled. "No, sweetheart, I assure you, having you around, as troublesome as you are sometimes, is a welcome change."

"Then I'll stay."

Danato nodded. He couldn't understand why she wasn't trying harder to leave. Aside from loneliness, what did she see here now that she didn't see earlier?

"You surprise me." He looked at the file in his hand. He had been gripping it so tight it had bent in the middle. "I'll adjust my report and send it in." He was glad she was staying, even if she was doing it for the wrong reasons.

"You do that."

Danato headed to the door. He stopped and turned around. "Cori," he said in a soft voice.

"Yes?" she said as she returned to her plants.

He searched his mind for a sentiment to express everything that he felt. This was probably their longest conversation outside of work-related business. "Nice to finally meet you."

Cori looked up at him through the foliage. She smiled. "You too."

63

"**S**HE DID *WHAT*?" ETHAN stood before his mirror in the gym, admiring his muscles.

Belus sat on the bench behind him, playing with a stretch band. "I don't know what she thought would happen. She just turned it in like she had seen a job posting."

"I can't believe she could be so underhanded." He stepped closer to the mirror and leaned his hands against it. He stared into his own eyes. "Who am I kidding? She's always been like this: conniving and selfish."

"She described it as self-motivated and determined in her resume."

He whipped around and glared at Belus. "I was taken from my miserable life, put into slavery, and then rescued into servitude. Just when I think to myself that being warden of this prison could be the highlight of my existence, she puts in an application for my job!" He panted and gritted his teeth, unable to conceal the growing rage inside him.

"Whoa, kid. Seriously, calm down. I didn't tell you so I could watch you go through 'roid' rage. I told you because I haven't told Danato yet. I wanted to get your take on it."

"My take is she is a conniving—"

"Yes, yes, I know that part, but..." Ethan turned back to his mirror. "Listen to me! Danato will assume that she put in the application as a distraction from her sorrows. He might agree to let her compete with you."

"How do you know that?"

"I know him. Look at me!" Belus threw his band at him. It hit him in the back, and he turned around. "There has never been a female warden in this prison. The board is very likely to never approve one. If she is thinking of taking the position, she will have to go through the same trials you did. Then there's the final test. The likelihood of her passing that is slim to none. The dragon... the protein shake won't work on females, so she isn't going to be strong enough to pass the test."

"No, she's clever," Ethan said, eyes narrowed in contemplation.

"So is the opponent. Quick wits will keep her alive, but luck won't..." Belus seemed to pause as if recalculating her chances of winning. "...no way."

"What are you telling me? Am I supposed to congratulate her on reaching for the stars?" He clenched his fist, feeling hot from the anger that was screaming to be released. He knew he was overreacting, but he couldn't shake the emotion. He already imagined every scenario in confronting Cori.

"I'm telling you, don't be surprised if she follows in your footsteps, reading the same books, and working out in the gym. I'm also telling you that you are his apprentice, not her, no matter what happens."

Ethan nodded and turned back to his reflection. He was feeling like he couldn't trust anyone but himself. Cori was trying to take his job. Danato was probably going to gift-wrap it in pink ribbons for her. Belus, so far, was the only one on his side, but who knew how long that would last? "It's so nice to have someone I can trust near me."

Belus said something in response, but Ethan wasn't really talking to him. It was the man in the mirror that he trusted. Only he truly understood what he was going through.

64

After hearing about Cori's application, Danato called a meeting with Belus, Ethan, and Cori. He rocked on his chair behind his desk, arms crossed and his lips actively pursed in distaste. The chair creaked with the subtle movements of his deliberation. "I don't like it," he said for the third time, with no other argument behind it.

Cori sat before him, running her fingers through her hair like a nervous tick. "What is the big deal? 90% of the job is the details, the knowledge; since when is a woman not good with details?"

Belus sat on his file cabinet, swinging his feet like a child. "We don't mean to be prejudiced to your sex, but 10% of the job is physical, and a warden with strength is a better asset for emergency situations."

Ethan leaned on the wall behind the door, glaring at the back of Cori's head. He had yet to offer his opinion, but based on his expression, Danato could guess what it was.

"I'm not without some skill in self-defense." Cori proffered her hand to Danato. "You've seen what I can do when I'm pressed."

Danato thought about the first time he had seen Cori and her incidents here in the prison. He couldn't deny she had a knack for defending herself when necessary. He rocked faster and pinched his lips tighter. "I don't like it." Everyone groaned. "The issue is not just self-defense." He leaned forward. "I am a captain to these men. I must command respect, even when it is not readily offered."

"A woman can't do that?" Her brow lifted, challenging him to be a chauvinist.

He looked away for a moment, resisting the urge to laugh. He knew very well that convicts would have difficulty taking orders from a woman, but he didn't want to get into that argument today. "I'm not referencing your ability to do it as a woman." He leaned back and glanced at Ethan and Belus before continuing in a softer tone. "We did converse about your social graces at one point, did we not?"

As the statement set in, Cori blushed. She pushed her chin up, not willing to acknowledge anything of the kind.

Belus exchanged looks with Ethan.

"I could train," Cori continued. "Maybe I could be a secondary. Someone to take over if Ethan is sick."

"Wardens don't get sick," Ethan chided from the corner.

She didn't look back at him. "Whatever. I just thought I could focus my attention on a higher goal. If Ethan is the *man* for the job, so be it."

Danato looked at Belus. Belus furrowed his brow and shook his head. Danato often looked at him for the right answer. Belus was even more by-the-books than he was. If he said no, then that was probably the best choice.

However, Danato hadn't taken the position of warden to do things by-the-books, and he certainly didn't take his orders from anyone else.

"I wouldn't mind at least letting her compete for it, but..." He added the "but" when he saw three mouths gape in resentment, excitement, and objection. "I would never open the position unless Ethan approved." He offered his palm to Ethan. He knew it was a low blow, but if anyone should squelch Cori's goal, it should be the person she would take it from.

Cori's face fell. She didn't even bother looking at Ethan, to see what his answer would be.

Ethan smiled, apparently enjoying the opportunity to give voice to his opinion. "Kind of a waste of her time, isn't it?" he said with a shrug. "I mean, she really has no chance of winning."

Cori whipped around to glare at him. "Then you shouldn't mind the competition."

"I don't mind the competition." Ethan lost his smile, and his voice turned somber. "I mind your arrogance."

"And what are you bringing to the table now?" she asked, swirling her finger over an imaginary table. "Certainly not humility."

"My pride is earned. Yours is seeded by your acrimony and watered by your bravado." Ethan looked at her without the sneer of a bitter sibling. He looked at her with the severity of an adult to a child.

Danato didn't like where this was going, but Ethan was right. Cori had nothing to recommend herself to the position other than her dumb luck. As clever as she was, she had crossed a line by assuming she could do better than he could with half the time to train. As much as it pained him not to interject, Ethan was justified in his condescension.

Cori held Ethan's gaze.

Danato felt like he was watching a psychic battle. The two stared at each other with nasty sneers. The last one to look away would be crowned with superiority. When they first came to the prison, Ethan was no match for Cori. Now Ethan seemed to have the upper hand. He was no longer weak, physically or emotionally. Their long separation was beneficial in some ways. It gave them both a chance to mature.

"You're an ass-munch!" Cori blurted out when it was clear he wasn't giving in.

At least it gave Ethan a chance to mature.

When Cori finally looked away, Ethan smiled, pleased with his triumph. It wasn't a wholly unexpected response, but what Danato didn't like was how Ethan regarded her even after she had long since broken eye contact with him. Danato looked to Belus. He must have seen it too, because there was concern written on his face as well.

"Let her compete," Ethan said, breaking the moment. He stood upright and moved to Cori's side. "I welcome the competition. It will be good for her to see what real work is." Ethan touched her back. She tensed under his touch, but didn't pull away. Ethan winked at Danato before leaving.

Danato stared at the door a few seconds after he left, just in case he came back in to withdraw his statement. Cori seemed just as surprised by the turn of events. Her face was stuck in befuddlement, as if she was replaying the moment in her head, trying to figure out what made him change his mind.

"Well," Belus interrupted both their consternations, "I guess that confirms it." He jumped off the file cabinet. "You can start training in the gym as soon as you're ready. The library will be available to you." Belus looked at Danato. "Right?"

Danato nodded. "Yes, right. Board approval is still a year away. You'd best hit the books hard. It is a lot of information."

"The gym, also," Belus said. "We aren't equal opportunity employers."

"Yes," Danato agreed. "Physical strength and agility will still play a vital role in the final test."

"So," Cori said, "I need to hit the gym when I'm not studying, and study when I'm not eating or sleeping."

He exchanged looks with Belus. They both seemed to be thinking the same thing. *She has no idea what she is getting into.* He nodded at her.

"Good," she said and left the office.

"What is with Ethan lately?" Danato asked Belus when they were alone.

"I don't know," Belus said. "I've been monitoring his intake. He shouldn't be in testosterone overload."

"Sure seems like it," Danato said.

"Maybe he's just that mad."

Danato rubbed his chin. "I know they've had their issues, but he's never been like that before. I understand his position. He has a right to be mad, but he didn't sound mad. He sounded menacing. You saw the way he was looking at her."

Belus nodded. "I'll keep an eye on him. Hopefully, we can make it to the competition without them killing each other."

65

ETHAN OBSERVED THE DEFINITION in his body. His reflection showed vascular bulges that threaded through his forearms. His hands held taut skin over boney knuckles. His neck was thick and held tension with the slightest twist of his head.

He pulled his shirt off and tensed his chest and abs. His gaunt physique of the year before had given way to distinct muscles. His pride was most definitely earned.

"I have earned this," he said to his reflection.

"Yes, you have." his reflection spoke with obscure lip movement that didn't stem from him. Ethan didn't flinch at his reflection's accolade. He continued to bathe in his own beauty. "She has done nothing to earn this position," the reflection bristled.

"No, she hasn't," Ethan responded, flexing his back muscles.

The reflection sighed and walked away from its source. He sat on the mirrored bench of his world. He sat in view of Ethan, but was no longer his parallel. "She is such a nuisance."

"I agree," Ethan said. "But what can I do about it? Danato loves her too much to say no."

"For such a big man, he is so weak in the heart," the reflection philosophized.

"Aren't we all?" Ethan said. "For all her flaws, I still can't think of anyone but her."

"That's because she is the only one to think of," the reflection explained. "I know a few girls on the upper floors that would have a go at you. You won't be thinking of her, I assure you."

"I wouldn't want to risk the diseases they might be carrying," Ethan said.

"True. Do you really think you love her, though? After everything she's put you through. Couldn't it just be the memory of a crush that has you bound?"

Ethan thought about this. "I suppose you could be right."

"Maybe you don't even like her anymore. Maybe your memories have made you think of her as a friend, when really the only thing between you is a sort of... association."

Ethan had nothing to say to that, but he thought about it. He and Cori had never really interacted privately. They argued. They chatted about prison duties. They hardly ever discussed their personal lives. They never sat together and talked about stupid stuff.

"I don't know about you, but I don't even think she's that attractive," the reflection said.

Ethan shrugged. He thought she was attractive, but for some reason, he didn't want to admit that to his other self. He didn't want to look weak in front of him. "I guess not."

The reflection smiled at Ethan. "I'm not even sure she really has a purpose here. She's kind of a waste of space, don't you think?"

Ethan nodded. He often wondered who would clean the cages if she weren't around. Had she inherited some nameless worker's job? Whoever it was, he was probably rejoicing at the acquisition of a new lackey to take over the arduous duties.

Ethan continued to nod at his reflection's thoughts about Cori and anything else that displeased him.

66

 ORI SAW BELUS SLIP out of the gym door and head toward her. She had been putting in a rather drastic weight lifting rotation. Unfortunately, the dragon beverage that Ethan used to increase his muscle mass had too many side effects for her to take, so it was good old-fashioned muscle recovery for her.

"Are you working out now?" Belus asked as he passed her.

"Just my abs. Everything else is still sore."

Belus looked back at the door to the gym as if he had forgotten something inside. "Okay. Just make it fast. Ethan's in there and he's in a piss-poor mood already."

"Yeah, okay." She nodded before moving on. She hated how everyone was suddenly tip-toeing around Ethan like he was the queen bee. His anger had flared more easily the last few weeks, but she had just attributed that to her recent change of focus. She had no intention of skipping a workout just because Ethan hadn't finished his. Considering how much time he'd been spending there, she was surprised they hadn't crossed paths until today.

She stopped at the door to peek through the window before she entered. Ethan was inside, fixated by his reflection, doing hammer curls. Despite her resistance to tip-toeing around him, she found herself light on her feet as she slipped in. She positioned her back on a floor mat behind him to do some sit-ups.

She gave his reflection a nod. His lips tipped up into a smile while his eyes remained static, concentrating on the movement in his biceps. The length in his arms contracted, bulging into taut, softball-sized masses. She had missed his slow transformation from a lean boy to a sinewy man.

She had always thought of him as a boy, since he was still in the latter years of his teens when they first met, but it was becoming increasingly difficult for her to maintain that image of him. He had chopped off his floppy, blond, curtained hair, leaving him with a dark blond crew cut. Without the hair, he looked older and sterner. The length of his face was more evident and the square lines of his jaw seemed to match his build better.

Not only had his appearance transformed, but his attitude as well. He was strong-willed and commanding. She admired those traits. Given her relationship with Vince, she assumed she was attracted to those traits.

He's dead.

She had observed an attraction to Ethan, one that under normal circumstance might have warranted exploratory flirtation. Unfortunately, their history of ruined expectations and blockaded high grounds left her with complex emotions.

She tried to think of him like a brother, but he had always looked at her in a way that left no room for sibling love. Now that she found herself looking on him with a similar appreciation, she tried to consider him as a coworker: a coworker she ate breakfast and dinner with, and slept across the hall from. The only relationship she seemed to be able to rely on with Ethan was one that guaranteed disappointment, but also guaranteed a tethered devotion that all those disappointments could not break.

And there she had it. She would now have to think of Ethan as her parole officer.

Cori started in on her sit-ups. The movement wasn't as easy as she had hoped. Her flexibility and strength seemed to work against each other.

Ethan looked back at her, apparently seeing her for the first time. "Hello."

Cori paused and looked at him. "Hi." She continued her workout.

"Abs today?" He put down his dumbbells and moved closer to her.

"Yup," she said, straining through her upward motion.

"May I assist you?" he asked, like an automated recording.

She stopped and tightened her ponytail. "No, it's just sit-ups."

"Tsk tsk. I can get you a better workout than those. Let me show you." Without confirmation, he stepped across her, straddling her midsection, facing her feet. He towered above her. "Okay, lift your legs. Keep them straight; bring them up together like you want to kick me in the stomach... or somewhere else." He glanced back and winked at her.

His smile seemed warm and flirtatious. She tried to give him a smile back, but she was already too uncomfortable with his attention to fake any emotion. She lifted her legs. Right as she got through the hardest part of the exercise, he pushed her feet back to the floor. She repeated it, feeling the tension never fully release as he pushed her back down to go again.

"Do you feel that?" he asked.

"Yes," she hissed with another upward movement.

After she completed a set of fifteen, he let her rest. He stepped off her and moved to the water cooler for some water. After drinking a paper cup full, he brought her back one. She drank the water, though she had hardly done anything to warrant a thirst.

After a minute or two, he straddled her again, this time facing her. "I have another for you." Before she could object, he kneeled down, putting his body weight on her upper thighs.

"What are you doing?" she said, instinctively trying to get out from under him.

"Same thing, just the upper body." He squeezed his legs tighter around her. "Come up, support your head, like you're going to head-butt me."

She put her hands behind her neck. She watched him watching her, acutely aware of his body weighing down on her. She contracted her muscles and lifted. She pulled herself toward him. He pushed her down to the mat hard.

"Did you feel that?" he said with the slightest of sparkles in his eyes.

She stared at him, mouth agape. "I think you enjoyed that." She glared.

"Oh, yes, but not in the way you think." His expression of amusement didn't change. Her eyes widened and she could feel her heart race. "Come on, again."

She reminded herself this was Ethan. He was just messing with her, trying to get a rise from her. Rather than bait the argument, she pulled herself up. He pushed her down again just as hard. She stared at him. She waited for something more to be said, but he simply motioned for her to come up again.

She licked her lips and propped herself on her elbows. "I appreciate your help, but I would like to stop now." She sat up to pull herself from under him. He pushed her down again. Without protection for her head, she smacked the mat painfully. "Easy, Ethan!"

"What's the matter? I thought you wanted to get in shape. I thought you wanted to be strong."

She sat up to push him off. He pushed her back and pinned her arms. He leaned in and whispered in her ear. "You seem pretty weak to me. Better get to work."

He released her, and she pulled herself up for another attempt to get out from under him. He backhanded her, sending her flat against the mat again. She tasted blood. She wiped her lip to verify.

"Ethan?" Her voice trembled in fear of what was happening.

He beamed at her grimly. He was enjoying either her pain or her fear, or perhaps both.

She punched him full-on in the cheek. She had hoped the impact would have sent him flying off her so she could escape, but he absorbed the punch with nothing more than a head turn. His lip bled. He leered at her as he licked it away.

She felt her body shake, and her breathing turned to panting. She couldn't understand what had driven him to be this angry. It wasn't like him to lose control.

He punched her back. His fist hit her jaw, sending her head back into the mat for a secondary blow. She tried to roll over, to squirm away. He pushed her back, keeping her flat on the mat.

She stared up at him, unable to contain a whimper of cowardice. He loomed above her, practically salivating at her misery. "You were always against us. You never gave a damn about us. Just ran off with 'Fang.' Left us behind..."

"Who is *us*, Ethan?" She crumpled her brow, trying to make sense of his rant.

"...returned like the prodigal child, and now you want more. More, more, more!" he screamed in her face. "Selfish bitch!"

She turned her head and clenched her eyes, not wanting to see his rage up close.

He moved his hands along her shirt. She felt a familiar fear make her eyes water. She shook her head. "Ethan, please!" She wrapped her hands around his wrists, trying to stop his movement, but she couldn't.

"Get your own prison. This one is ours." He neglected her chest and went straight on to her neck. She opened her eyes and looked back at him.

"Ethan!" she cried one last time before his hands tightened. She felt the pressure buildup in her head. She struggled, prying on his fingers and ripping at his skin, but he was so much stronger.

Her hands grappled out away from her body. She fanned the ground in search of something—anything. There was nothing within reach. Her legs kicked, but his weight incapacitated her. Her hands switched from his wrists to his face, only achieving minor scratches. Without a weapon or vulnerable body part, she was helpless.

She sucked in the last bit of air that could slip through his grip. She felt dizzy. Her hands slipped from his wrists.

Tears streamed from the corners of her eyes. Her face felt tight, like her head would soon pop like a balloon. Ethan's face blurred and she prepared for the blackness that would follow.

67

As soon as Cori felt the black arrive, she felt the light return. She opened her eyes and found herself in the gym with Ethan. She was standing next to him in front of the mirror. He was smiling malevolently at her.

"Ethan, what the hell?" She touched her neck where moments earlier he had been strangling her. "You son of a bitch, you could have killed me!"

"Not yet, but he's working on it," he said, perking a brow.

She backed away from him to get to the door, but when she turned to leave, she realized it was missing. Most of the gym was missing. The room stopped like it was inside of a box. White walls replaced the vacancies, like paper that didn't have the remaining images drawn in.

"Ethan? What's going on?"

"I'm not Ethan. I'm just his reflection."

Cori looked around again. She at least understood the room now. "I'm in the mirror?"

"Yes. Welcome."

"Why? How?" Cori didn't really know what her question should be. She just wanted an answer. Ethan, or

Ethan's reflection, proffered the view of the mirror to her with an open hand. She came back to the mirror, which from this side was nothing more than a window into the real world.

Cori saw the scene with her and Ethan playing out again right in front of her. Him on top of her in the gym, strangling her as she fought uselessly against him. Somehow, seeing it from this perspective was even scarier than having it actually done to her. She couldn't blackout here. "Ethan, no!" She banged on the glass of her mirror window, and the vision replayed from the beginning. "Don't do this! Please!"

"He can't hear you. He can't hear anyone now. All he can hear is that little voice in the back of his mind. Me." Ethan's reflection pointed to himself proudly. "I'm telling him how much he hates you."

"He doesn't hate me!" Cori yelled at the reflection. She wasn't saying it to defend herself; she was defending Ethan. She knew Ethan cared for her, and for this entity to say otherwise was an insult to him. "You don't know anything about him."

"I got in his head, didn't I? Oh, oh, this is my favorite part." The reflection clapped with glee and pushed her closer to the glass. She watched herself give up the fight. Her hands fell away as she blacked out. "Goddamn!" He shook her shoulders with jarring enthusiasm. "That just makes life worth living, doesn't it?" She glared at him. "Oh, sorry, probably not for you."

"Wait, what was that?" Cori asked, just as the image went back to the beginning.

"Oh, don't ruin the moment, Cori." The reflection hugged her tight. "I just really think this experience is going to bring us closer."

"How do you fast forward this thing?" Cori banged on the glass and it jumped forward to the end. "There!" She pointed to Belus's head bob into the window of the gym door. "Show me that."

"Oh Cori, you aren't getting this. You are on the precipice of death. All I need is for your heart to stop beating, and for your pissy little spirit to let go and you will be mine. Forever."

"Show me what happened after I passed out, you jerk." The reflection fast forwarded the image, and she watched the scene play out at super speed.

Belus came back from his break. He saw Ethan strangling her, and he pulled the alarm by the door. He ran at Ethan and dove at him. His intention was certainly to bulldoze him off her, but he went right through him.

"What just happened?" Cori asked.

Belus returned to Ethan and grabbed at him, but his hands separated into disjointed images.

He looked at his hands away from Ethan, and they were fine. As he reached to touch him again, his hands separated into dozens of jagged pieces, like the replications in a broken mirror.

"Ethan has fragmented. His mind, his body, and his energies are shattered—ripped apart by me worming my way in. If he manages to finish you off, he'll return to his former self, with the addition of a hefty broken heart."

Cori's hands slipped on the glass, feeling her hope slip away. Belus whipped around and looked at the mirror with a scowl on his face. For a moment she thought he might see her, so she banged on the glass again. "Belus! I'm here!"

"He can't see you," the reflection enlightened her. "Right now, he is just figuring out how stupid he was for not recognizing the gigantic mirror as a potential problem. Not that he really would have. I exude an innocuous atmosphere wherever I go."

"You son of a bitch." Cori lunged at him. If Belus couldn't save her, she might as well save herself. Her efforts had high expectations, but the outcome was lacking in climax. She fell through his image much the same as Belus did with the real Ethan.

"It's a waste of energy. You're only a reflection."

"I'm the reflection." Cori scooped herself off the floor.

"Yup. Soon after your death, the remainder of your essence will be drawn into the mirror with me. You'll be trapped. Forever."

"Why? Why are you doing this?"

"I'm a mirror demon. It's kind of my thing."

"But why? Are you evil? Or just an asshole?"

"Everything in the universe craves something. Some crave food. Some crave blood. Some crave the fear and self-loathing of others."

"You need pain to live?" she asked.

"No, I just need it to enjoy living." He laughed manically.

68

D ANATO WASN'T ONE FOR believing in precognitive ability, even though a good number of his prisoners were psychic. However, when the alarms went off, he seemed to know that it had something to do with Ethan and Cori.

He raced out of his office to the gym, where the alarm pitch indicated the problem would be. Somewhere in his office was his cane, but he didn't have time to acknowledge his pain. When it really counted, he could block it out, even if he paid for it tenfold after.

When he reached the gym, he did a quick assessment of the scene. Ethan was straddling Cori's unconscious body, his hands on her neck. The guards had already arrived and were facing away from the assault. Belus was frantically pointing. "Shoot the mirror!"

The guards didn't question the order. They were happy to shoot anything that wasn't human. They positioned themselves before the mirror and the lead man gave a grunt more appropriate to hiking a football. The men locked their rifles into their shoulders and prepared to fire at the mirror.

"STOP!" Danato's voice boomed through the gym.

The guards holstered their weapons in unison. Belus looked over at Danato, prepared to object, but then stopped as he realized his error.

"It's too late! It's already got her!" Shooting the mirror would only destroy the portal. If Cori was unconscious, she was already inside of the mirror. She would be stuck there with no hope of extraction. As it was, if they didn't resuscitate her soon, she could get trapped between the mirror and her body. She would be left in a perpetual coma.

Belus let out a growl for his sluggish mind. "Mirror!" he yelled, already running toward Danato at the entrance.

"The kitchen!" Danato shared his epiphany and ran out the door ahead of him.

With long, limping strides, Danato fought through his pain to gain the speed he needed. Just down the hall from the gym, he pushed past the swinging doors of the cafeteria kitchen. His abrupt arrival shocked the stout flour-covered women within. "We need a mirror!" he shouted.

"Anything reflective," Belus amended as he arrived behind him.

The women scrambled about to find something. They started picking up cookie sheets and stainless-steel bowls, but they were all scratched, or greased and floured.

Finally, one woman let out a eureka shout and ran to the cupboard. She pulled out a long rectangular box. "Tin foil!" she yelled and tossed the box to Belus, who in turn tossed it to Danato.

He leaped out the door in a dead sprint, his limp temporarily abated with the help of pure adrenaline. When he got back to the gym, he pulled the foil roll from the box and called a guard to hold the other end. They pulled it out across the length of Ethan's body and set it beside him. In the loose reflection, Ethan's image was strangling Cori, just as in the other reflection.

The guards lined up, blocking the far mirror so all that was reflecting Ethan was the tin foil. As the spell broke, Ethan looked at his true reflection, the reflection that showed him murdering Cori.

"Now!" Danato yelled.

Three guards toppled onto Ethan, pushing him off Cori and pinning him down. Three more began doing CPR on her. Danato stared down at her lifeless body and blue lips, calculating the minutes she had without oxygen. It seemed much too long.

69

F ROM WITHIN THE MIRROR, Cori cheered as she
watched the men save her. She gave Ethan's reflection
an *in your face* look before returning her attention to her
rescue. Belus and Danato stood back, letting the guards
do their CPR. She hadn't realized how well-trained they
all were until then. They must have had their comrades
put in danger often, to be so organized in such complete
chaos. She understood why it was so important for the
men to respect their leader. You would have to be someone
particularly special to lead them.

Her stomach knotted as he heard them say they
couldn't find her pulse. She just assumed they could save
her. Wasn't that how it worked? CPR magically brings
everyone back to life. *Right?*

"Oh, I just hate this part!" Ethan's reflection clenched
his fists. "Will she? Won't she? How long can the brain go
without oxygen?"

Cori watched Ethan struggle against his captors, not
in anger, but with concern. He looked at each of them as
they held him back, begging them to tell him what he had
done. One of the men flanking him repositioned his hand

so he could squeeze his shoulder, but he looked away when Ethan's eyes begged him for answers.

"What's the technical definition of death, anyway?" The reflection asked, knitting his hands excitedly.

Cori could see the guards were getting increasingly more frustrated the longer they worked on her. They searched for a pulse and checked for breathing between rounds.

"Is it when the heart stops or when brain function stops? Oh, I can't take this drama!"

"Shut up, you idiot! If I have to spend eternity with you, I will find a way to kill you!"

Finally, one guard picked up her body and barked for the others to hold the door for him. He carried her out of the gym, taking a bevy of men with him to clear the path. She assumed they were taking her body to the infirmary, where the doctors and nurses could stabilize her with more aggressive methods.

Cori placed her hands on the window as if she might be able to step out of the mirror and chase after her body. Her hands had turned translucent. She looked at Ethan's reflection. He frowned at her, confirming her hopes. She was being called back to her body. "Ha!" she mocked him. "Seeing that look on your face is making *my* life worth living."

While she waited for her exit, she watched the remainder of the scene play out through the mirror. Danato looked sad—even sadder than she would have anticipated. She knew he had a soft spot for her, but she was getting a glimpse of what he really felt.

Belus looked downtrodden, but in an entirely different way. He was looking at the mirror and shaking his head, as if he had just wrecked Dad's car and was waiting for him to arrive and bitch him out. She hadn't had much interaction with him, but she got the impression that whether or not Daddy bitched him out, he was going to be kicking himself for this mistake for a long time.

Danato limped over to Ethan. His leg must have hurt, because he winced with each step. He stopped in front of him and motioned for the guards to release him. Instead of rising, Ethan groveled in front of Danato, as an abject servant to his king.

"Is she..." Ethan looked up, trying to find his answers with Danato. Tears blanketed Ethan's eyes.

If Cori had been surprised by Danato's reaction to her potential death, she was floored by Ethan's. He looked like she imagined she looked after Vince died.

He's dead.

Was that possible? Could he have felt that strongly about her?

"Danato..." Ethan wasn't fully able to voice his questions or remorse, but there were no equivocal sentiments in the room. Danato reached out a hand to Ethan.

Belus took another step forward from the other side of the room, in case he needed to protect him from Danato. Ethan took his hand and stood.

Ethan had shot up nearly two inches since his arrival at the prison, lessening the difference in height with Danato, but today, the shame bending his back and lowering his head left Danato towering over him once again.

"I wouldn't..." Ethan tried to explain. "I love her. You know that." Cori felt her heart clench. It wasn't anything she hadn't suspected, but it was the first time she believed it might have been more than his hormones talking. She didn't know how to deal with that statement.

"I know," Danato said softly. He lifted Ethan's chin to look at him and then embraced him. Ethan held onto him like he was the only thing saving him from falling off a cliff. Danato's monstrous hand patted his back, and he mumbled something that sounded remarkably consoling.

That surprised Cori, too. She had expected no less than a voluminous rage from Danato. She thought he would spout out the errors of his ways, but he wasn't. She should have realized that in the nine months of her absence, Danato would have changed, too. They were less like employer and employee, and more like father and son.

The image faded away, and she realized it was her slipping away, back to her body.

70

DANATO ARRIVED HOME TO a darkened house. The sun was just setting, leaving the house in a pink glow. He had spent the remainder of the day checking into the mirror that was in the gym. Belus had given him continued updates on Cori, mostly because he recognized his concerns, but also he suspected Belus felt guilty about not questioning the mirror earlier.

Danato wasn't sure why he hadn't investigated the addition to Ethan's workout. Mirror demons had the ability to broadcast benign intentions even as they plotted evil deeds in the mind. It wasn't unheard of that the mirror had simply influenced Belus. In any case, he wasn't mad... at anyone. Except perhaps himself.

The mirror had no effect on Danato, since he had never been exposed to it. So what was *his* excuse for not recognizing Ethan's behavioral changes? Cori and Ethan had always had issue with one another. They bickered and bitched like siblings. They chided each other like an old married couple. However, over the last few weeks, his behavior to her had been hostile.

As easy as it would be to blame Belus for the event, it was Danato who had lived with Ethan for over a year. He should know him better than anyone. He should have recognized the danger and dealt with it immediately.

Danato found Ethan in the dark house, sitting with his head down on the dining room table. He looked up at Danato with sallow eyes. He couldn't tell in the dark, but he knew the whites must have been bloodshot.

He stood up, eager to hear the news. Danato had sent him home shortly after the incident. He let him know they had gotten her breathing again, but he hadn't called in any further reports to him. He wasn't intending to be cruel, but he thought it was important that Ethan feel the full ramifications of his deceit.

"Your friend Duke has taken full responsibility for the mirror," Danato said. Ethan's eyes pulled away as he finally realized where the core of the incident started. "He was unaware the mirror had any power. I'm not going to charge—"

"How is she?" he asked impatiently.

Danato took a moment to hang up his coat before answering. "The physical damage is reparable. I imagine we will see her up and about in a day or two. The nurses are insisting we leave her be to rest tonight. Belus and I are planning to visit her in the morning. We will offer her an explanation regarding your actions and express how mortified you are. We decided, however, that you should wait to see her until she is back on her feet. Can you accept that?"

"Yes, if you think that's best."

"We both do." Danato continued to speak for both Belus and himself, as if having the majority vote would make the advisement sting less. Then Danato headed to his room.

"Don't you blame me for this? Aren't you going to punish me?"

Danato turned around, but Ethan didn't face him. "You didn't know what you were doing. The mirror was controlling you by that point."

"I almost killed her!" Ethan yelled out the accusation as if he was chastising someone else for the crime.

"Yes, you did. Isn't that enough punishment for now?" Danato left him alone to ponder that question.

71

T HE NEXT MORNING CORI awoke blurry-eyed and aching, with the worst sore throat known to man. Before she was fully coherent, she felt a plastic straw touch her lips. "Sip," she heard Danato say. She sipped up the cool water and swallowed. It stung, but after two or three more gulps, she felt the moisture soak in.

She blinked away her fog and saw Danato sitting next to her bed on the right and Belus on a chair just off to her left. "Good morning," Danato said, lifting her hand and kissing it.

"Morning." Her voice cracked.

"We brought your work assignments for the day over." Belus grinned.

Danato gave him a harsh glare, but she smiled at him. She knew Belus wasn't the type to offer too much sympathy to anyone. She always got the impression that he started out in life behind the eight ball. Anyone who started with a clean slate didn't deserve to have life any easier than they already had it.

"Thanks, I'll get right on that." His sarcastic grin turned into a warm smile, and she returned it.

"How are you feeling?" Danato asked, still holding her hand.

"Just sore. My chest feels like someone tap-danced on it. My throat..." She paused, considering all the pain in her body. She remembered why her throat hurt so much. She remembered why she was in this bed to begin with. She looked at Danato. She cringed inwardly as she felt the betrayal of the scene she endured and witnessed. Although she met the entity that influenced Ethan, she still didn't understand it. "Why did he do that to me?"

"It wasn't him." Danato pulled his chair even closer. "He was under the control of a mirror. We can explain it more thoroughly when you feel better." Danato cupped her hand in both of his. Her hand virtually disappeared, except for the tips of her fingernails. "I just need you to understand that Ethan would never do that. He..." He paused, looking at Belus as if he held the permission slip to speak. "Ethan cares a great deal for you. I think you know that. He is beside himself with agony over this incident."

"Where is he?" she asked.

Danato once again looked to Belus, who took over. "We asked him not to come. We thought a full recovery would be best."

"Is that... okay?" Danato asked, as if he was trying to anticipate all of her wants and needs.

She shrugged. "I guess so." She paused for a moment, trying to figure out what it was she was feeling. Her near-death experience horrified her. Yet, lying in this bed, she wanted Ethan to be by her side with Danato and Belus. Even if this incident was caused by his hands, she couldn't shake the feeling that his *not* being there was more offensive than him being there. She didn't express this to Danato, since he seemed to have had some debate about the topic as well.

"Since I have you both here," Belus interjected, "I want to apologize for not recognizing the danger of the mirror in the gym. I can't offer any explanation for my lack of concern. Cori, I've put you in danger, and Danato, I've disappointed you. I am sorry to both of you."

Danato shook his head. "No, Belus. You couldn't have been unaffected by the mirror's power. I should have recognized Ethan's change in behavior and investigated."

"Ethan has been under my observation during the day," Belus objected.

"And mine at night. I should have registered his demeanor as unusual," Danato reiterated.

"I'm sorry too," Cori jumped in.

Both men stopped and looked at her.

"What are you to blame for?" Danato asked.

Cori thought a moment. "I don't know. I'm just usually to blame for something when this stuff happens."

Danato and Belus exchanged amused smiles.

"Sweetheart," Danato said, kissing her hand again. "I think there is a shared blame amongst three or four people for this incident, but for once, you are not one of them."

72

TWO DAYS LATER, THEY released Cori from the infirmary. Instead of resting at home, Cori went straight to work, finishing any duties left undone during her absence.

On the fifth level, she attended to a few lighter duties. Prisoner maintenance, as the clipboard described it. "Good morning, Rodan," she said, her voice still hoarse. She smiled broadly at the massive mound of rocks in the cell before her.

A muffled growl emerged from the heap. The rocks shifted, releasing steam and heat as they unfurled into a twelve-foot figure. A body shape became visible as chunks of elongated rocks formed the legs and arms of the beast. Just as a human body had jointed bones, the rock monster had jointed rocks. The beast's structure relied on molten lava instead of tendons and ligaments.

Under a boulder brow, eyes of lava glowered out at her from his head. A puff of steam emitted from the nose of rock. When the creature spoke, she could see the shimmering diamonds that lined his mouth; a temptation which had lured many a man to his death.

"Back again so soon. I thought I scared you off last time." The harsh voice was almost difficult to understand, but she had learned to listen to the high notes in his voice and block out the vibrations the rocks in his throat caused.

"Not so." Cori made a note on her clipboard. "I rather enjoyed our last encounter. Your sudorific personality does wonders for my skin."

"Is that why you brought me a virgin sacrifice?"

Cori snorted with haughty amusement. "I hate to disappoint you, Rodan, but it's been a while since I could fill that position."

The rock creature raised his head, motioning behind her. She looked back and saw Ethan standing two cells down. He stood with a wide stance and his hands overlapped before him. It reminded her of when soldiers were told to stand at ease.

She had not seen him since their violent encounter. The nurses said he had been in the last two nights to sit with her. According to them, he had stayed nearly two hours each time and never spoke nor touched her. He must have taken Danato's advice to stay away seriously, but couldn't resist checking in on her.

Some part of her was happy he had come. They could never find a happy medium with each other. Knowing he wouldn't surrender into oblivion after the incident made her feel better. It meant he preferred to just rip the Band-Aid off the rapidly approaching uncomfortable interaction rather than draw it out.

She could see by the distance he left between them that he was concerned she might be fearful of him. As she looked him over, she saw the reserved observation she had come to appreciate since she had gotten back. Before she left, his quiet reflection made him seem timid, but now his eyes were assertive and vigilant.

He held her gaze as she looked him over. For a long moment, she said nothing. She wondered how long she could look at him before his stare would flinch. She hadn't intended to be the one to break the moment, but Rodan hammered on his bars.

"Easy, block-head," she rebuked the monster.

"Bring me my virgin sacrifice. The innocent ones taste the best," Rodan grumbled.

Cori looked down at her clipboard, trying to hide a smile. In her peripheral vision, she could see Ethan shift his stance. She had never thought of him as a virgin. She had to remind herself that he was only just ending his teen years, and, unless he was an early starter or into dangerous liaisons, he hadn't really had many opportunities to date.

She looked at Ethan again and smiled warmly. His seemingly unwarranted devotion to her made sense all of a sudden. His puppy crush might normally have ended after he found someone closer to his age, but instead it had morphed into a set of compound emotions that probably now mirrored her own.

However, her feelings for him were grounded in a dysfunctional sibling rivalry, and his were still planted in attraction. It was almost as if she had become the baseline to his desire.

Ethan didn't hold her eyes this time. He glanced back at the rock monster and glared. He didn't voice any denial of the accusation. She thought that showed a valor that most men didn't possess.

Cori looked back at the rock man and shook her head. "You don't want him, Rodan. Too much meat. I thought you liked your sacrifices petite and crying like babies."

"Would you like a diamond, boy?" Rodan asked, ignoring her taunt. He opened his mouth wide, showing the diamonds that begged to be pilfered. He laughed, amused by Ethan's lack of amusement, though he probably would have laughed no matter what retort Ethan offered.

Cori pulled the long red lever on the wall opposite the cell, sending gallon after gallon of water over the rock creature. Steam hissed all around him as the water cooled his lava joints, leaving him immobile. She made a check on her sheet and walked away.

"Cori."

"Yes." She continued on her way.

"Can you stop so we can talk?" he asked.

"I'm not trying to get away from you. I'm trying to get away from the steam. It makes my hair kink up."

"Oh." They walked away from the steam cloud and she stopped. He stopped as well, keeping a good distance between them. "I wanted to talk to you about... what happened."

"Don't worry. Danato explained everything. I don't blame you. I know everything you said and did was because of the mirror."

"Cori..."

"You can come closer than that."

Ethan looked at the distance between them and closed it. "Is that better?"

"Danato told you to stay away from me for the last two days." She paused as if she was waiting for confirmation, but then continued before he could speak. "You still came, though. At night, so I wouldn't see you."

"I had to see for myself."

"You should have woken me." She blurted it out even before she knew she wanted to say it. His wide eyes left her regretting it, but she didn't care anymore. "I wanted to see you. I should have told Danato to bring you, but he was so concerned that you might freak me out." He waited for her to speak again. "Honestly... you scared the shit out of me." Her face contorted as she tried to keep the tears at bay.

She saw her pain reflected in him. "I'm so sorry, Cori."

"I know," she said, pushing her emotions back so they could have an honest discussion. "So..." She hugged her clipboard. "I woke up and Danato explained that it wasn't you doing it, and..." She could see Ethan struggling to keep a space between them. "You weren't there," she blurted out again. His brow crinkled. "It doesn't make any sense to me either, but I think as a general rule, if someone tries to kill me, I think you should come and visit me in the hospital even if *you* were the person who tried to kill me."

His mouth tipped, amused by her statement, but his lips were reluctant to show too much amusement.

"You would never hurt me," she said it like she was reading it from a book. When he didn't respond, she stepped closer to him. "Say it," she demanded. "Make me believe you, so I don't have to be afraid of you. You are the only one here who understands. Please don't let me be afraid of you." She wasn't crying, but her hands were shaking, and her already hoarse voice was cracking.

His eyes flickered over hers as she spoke. He finally gave up his resolve for personal space and embraced her. His arms locked around her shoulders, pulling her against his chest. "I would never hurt you, Cori," he said vehemently. "I can't stand to think about what I might have done to you." He leaned down to whisper in her ear. "Nobody is going to hurt you again, including me. Do you understand?"

She nodded against his neck.

"Say yes," he whispered, even softer.

"Yes," she said.

"I will kill whoever tries, including me. Do you believe me?"

She wrapped her arms around him and hugged him back. "Yes."

He pulled her away. She resisted a little, not willing to look him in the eyes. With only inches between their faces, she felt the heat between their bodies rise. "Cori." A sudden panic hit her as she questioned what she had just said. She wondered if he would interpret her honesty as an invitation. His fingers scooped up her chin, and she considered taking a step away from him to reestablish the boundaries she had just ripped to shreds. "I need to tell you something."

She wanted to interrupt him, but his eyes were stern. Whatever he wanted to say wouldn't be stopped by a back step or an ill-placed precursor to a new conversation. Instead, she waited and listened for him to express his long overdue sentiments.

"Everything I did and said was beyond my control, but..." The word hung in the air like a bomb threatening to blow. "Even though the words were wrong, the core belief was still created in my mind."

"What?" Cori blinked. This was not the profession of love she had expected from him. "I don't understand." She took a step back, finding a different reason to make the move.

"Nothing I just said to you has changed. I will do whatever is necessary to make you trust me again, but I came here for a very specific purpose, and I am not leaving until I've said my piece... even if it means pissing you off."

She narrowed her eyes, suspicious of his *purpose*.

"The mirror didn't create my resentment," he continued, taking a few steps back as well. "You did. Your application for the warden's position was brash. Not discussing it with me first was deceitful." He listed off the reasons for his resentment, reprimanding her like an employee. "And not taking into consideration how it would affect me was selfish."

She stared at him, taking in the information, and waiting for something appropriate to say to pop into her mind. So far, only cuss words came to mind.

"The mirror just magnified those irritations and turned them into something worth hating you over."

"Do you hate me?" she asked.

He paused, looking her over. "I think we both know how I feel about you. Whether either of us wants to admit it is the question. Despite that, though, it's important that you understand how important this obligation to Danato has been for me. It has been my focus for over a year. You haven't put in the time I have for this."

"You don't even want me to compete for warden, do you?" She crossed her arms.

He took a deep breath. "No, I don't."

"Are you scared of the competition?" She waggled her head, letting her competitive side come out in the form of a sassy teenager.

With no deference to her ego, he shook his head, keeping her pinned with his eyes. "No Cori, as I've said,

I've been doing this for a year. While you were off enjoying France, I was here, working my ass off."

She furrowed her brow. "You didn't come here to apologize to me, did you?"

"I am apologizing for not being strong enough to defend my thoughts against the mirror. I am remorseful for the pain I have caused you. But I can't take back the anger I expressed at your decision to betray me."

Cori looked away from him. She had not considered his feelings in taking the job. She wanted to make a home for herself in this strange place, regardless of his displacement. However, she was too angry to admit any wrongdoing now. "So, in other words, you came here to say, 'bring it on, bitch.'"

Though she hadn't meant to amuse him, he smiled and laughed. He cleared his throat when she neglected to laugh with him. He couldn't wipe away his smile so easily, though. "I think what I came to say was, you are the dearest, most important person in my life, and I would do absolutely anything to show you that... except let you be warden." He stepped forward and shrugged. "So, yeah, I guess what I came here to say was, *bring it on, bitch.*" His smile faded, and he walked away.

Cori watched him go. After seeing the teamwork involved in saving her life, she had considered letting Ethan have the wardenship. However, that concession was gone now. As far as she was concerned, this was going to be an all-out war and despite what Ethan thought, she was going to win.

FELICIA JEDLICKA

RIVALS

Book 2

THE WARDEN

RIVALS

Sneak Peek

CORI SPRINTED DOWN THE hall of the zoological floor. Her lungs burned, and her side ached, but she was ahead of Ethan, so she ignored the pain. She glanced back at him. Despite the three-foot-long harpoon gun he was carrying, he was closing the distance between them. She had opted for a more civilized weapon. A tranquilizer gun wasn't as effective in these situations, but it was a lot easier to carry.

At the end of the hall, the elevator doors opened unexpectedly. Seeing an opportunity to extend her lead, Cori lengthened her strides to a hamstring-tearing pace.

"Don't you dare," Ethan snarled from behind her, already anticipating her plan.

Reaching the elevator at full speed, she crashed into the back wall less than gracefully. She leaped back to the panel, nearly toppling against it as she pressed the "door close" button.

The doors began to shut.

She heard Ethan roar, and he leaped through the gap in the closing doors. He collided with the back wall before dropping to a heap on the floor. Even with the double impact, he kept his gargantuan harpoon gun in his hand. He glowered at her from the floor, panting his exertion through flaring nostrils.

Cori pinched back her smile and positioned herself in front of the door. He joined her, all but shoving her aside to get equal access to it.

They silently watched the dial over the door that indicated the car's slow ascension. The half clock was virtually useless since most of the numbers had fallen off. All the elevators were in sad order, and she was certain that one day someone might plummet to their death in one. She was just hoping not to be that someone.

While they were waiting, she checked that her tranquilizer gun was still fastened to her belt. Ethan put down the harpoon to tuck his black shirt into his black cargo pants. She wanted to mock him about his monochromatic military style, but the truth was he looked good in it.

She still donned her usual jeans and graphic t-shirt. Today's wardrobe choice depicted a man sitting on a toilet with a big smile and double thumbs-up. It read, "Pooping is Fun!" The shirt had inspired looks of disgust from Danato, which made it her favorite.

There had technically been no formal discussion on the dress code, so she took advantage of it. It was her last vestige of rebellion. That was probably why Danato let her do it. Control of her clothing was the least he could do to appease her need for individuality.

In the closed space of the elevator, Cori became acutely aware of the smell of cologne. She looked up at Ethan, wondering when he had become one of those guys. His jaw clenched as if he were expecting a verbal attack. Instead of taking the opening to tease him, she grazed her eyes along the taut muscles of his neck and down to the sculpted chest that was panting from his exertion.

He's dead.

The reminder snapped Cori away from her appreciative ogling. She shouldn't have been gawking at him like that, anyway. He was too young—not as young as he had been, but of course, neither was she. Perhaps it wasn't so much about him being too young anymore, as her being too old.

He's dead.

Cori shook her head, clearing away the etch-a-sketch. Ethan noted the oddity of the movement and leaned forward to see her face. When nothing revealed itself to him, he went back to staring at the dial. "What are you making for dinner tonight?" he asked.

"Stroganoff," she answered.

"I love stroganoff."

"I know," she answered with a hint of pride for the knowledge.

He looked down at her, eyes fluttering over her with awe. She smirked at his enthusiasm. It was the simple things that struck Ethan's heart. She imagined that his on-again-off-again foster care had left him longing for home-cooked meals.

A slight smile perched on his lips, and his eyes softened. For a moment, she thought he might hug her or kiss her, but he didn't have a chance to do either.

The doors opened with a *ponk* at the seducers' level.

Game on.

Cori lunged forward to take the lead again, but Ethan shoved her to one side before she could even get out of the lift. Her intended momentum redirected her face first into the button console.

"Damn you!" she griped, but he was long gone.

Courtesy of her forehead, several floors were selected, and the doors started to close again. She slipped between them, but her foot got caught up. Fearful that the antiquated device would cut off her foot, she yanked herself free, minus her shoe. "Son of a..." she muttered, ripping off her sock.

She looked down the corridor. Ethan had already made it into the next section. She screamed in frustration and ran after him.

When Cori reached the first airlock, she discovered the broken glass in the door. The result of an escapee with a hard head and no opposable thumbs—or hands.

She tiptoed through the sharp mine field to the door. She considered simply stepping through the vacancy, but the jagged remnants lining the doorframe left it too narrow to pass through without getting cut. Despite the obvious section breach, the system still insisted she close the previous door before opening the next.

When she finally caught up with Ethan and their escape artist, he was already hauling the screeching creature down from the ceiling. Even with the harpoon pierced through the wing of the small pterodactyl-like creature, it was still trying to fly away. It took everything Ethan had to draw the creature down to him.

Though it wasn't inherently violent, it was extremely dangerous. Its knobby head and jet speed designed it to be an airborne battering ram. If it turned on Ethan, he would be the recipient of a skull-crushing head butt.

When it finally flopped to the floor, Ethan used the remainder of his rope to hogtie the beast. It squawked and flailed in objection, but he quickly wove it into a tight bundle, not much larger than a bulldog. Once it was calm, the creature turned to look at Cori. She wasn't sure the elongated beak could project a pout, but it was definitely unhappy to be denied the expanse of the prison as a playground.

Ethan panted over his prey with his hands on his hips. When he noticed her, he frowned. "Where the bloody hell have you been?" he barked.

Her mouth fell open, and she pointed back to the endless sea of glass that had threatened to shred her naked foot. Before she could articulate her explanation, she noticed amusement trickling into his expression.

She glowered at his teasing, and he outright grinned at her. She growled through clenched teeth and stalked past him.

"What happened to your shoe?" he scoffed behind her.

"Shut up!" she yelled back at him as she left the section. She heard the beginnings of his hearty guffaws before she shut the door to the airlock.

Thank you so much for reading. I hope you enjoyed the ride and if you aren't getting off here, I encourage you to sign up for my newsletter so I can return your generosity with new release updates and special offers.

Sign-Up

You can also find me on Facebook or visit my website. Keep reading!

Website

Facebook

AUTHOR

I am a creator and destroyer of worlds; a puppeteer of imaginary people; a manipulator of time, space, and the laws of physics.

I am a murderer and a savior; your best friend and your worst enemy.

I am the jester.
I am the matchmaker.
I am the poet.

I am the curator of secrets and lies; a harbinger of nightmares and a steward of fantasies.

I am a painter, a composer, and a songstress, but to see the beauty of my masterpiece, you must first... open the book.